THANA NIVEAU

Thana Niveau

First Published in 2018 by

Horrific Tales Publishing

http://www.horrifictales.co.uk

Copyright © 2017 Thana Niveau

The moral right of Thana Niveau to be identified as the author of this work has been asserted in accordance with the Copyright, Designs and Patents Act, 1988.

A CIP catalogue record for this book is available from the British Library

ISBN: 1-910283-21-5

ISBN-13: 978-1-910283-21-9

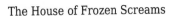

For John, who knows what scares me.

Thana Niveau

PART ONE

IMPLANTATION

CHAPTER 1

Wintergate wore its silence like a shroud.

The stone arches, stained glass and gargoyles lent the house the air of a church, albeit a damaged one. It stood with its back to the cliff wall, as though trying to burrow inside the earth. Dark wet patches dappled the crumbling stone like tears on a grieving face. The windows were dark and inscrutable. They stared blankly, like eyes that had seen too much.

One entire wing had been demolished long ago, amputated from the body of the main building. Remnants of black stone and brickwork jutted up from the weeds in the empty patch of ground like the fingers of a giant skeleton.

The bare trees were just beginning to swell with buds. Spring was on its way, but the cold wasn't ready to release its hold just yet. A raw and bitter wind swept in from the Bristol Channel, chilling the air and rattling the brittle jungle of bushes that surrounded the house. The estate agent's sign swung and creaked like a rocking chair.

Cass Sheehan eyed the imposing façade warily before

shouldering open a pair of heavy oak doors and venturing into the little stone porch. There she stood before a second set of double doors, hesitating with the key in her hand. From high in the sky came the forlorn cry of a seagull. She wasn't superstitious or she might have thought the bird was warning her.

Cass plunged the key into the lock and twisted it until the tumblers clanked into place. The noise frightened something in the bushes outside, which scurried deeper into the withered garden. For a moment Cass stood, listening, wondering what kind of animal it was. Then she realised she was stalling. Once she was inside, she closed the doors behind her and a booming echo reverberated through the empty room.

She stood alone inside an immense hall. Light straggled in through a stained-glass window high above and directly opposite the main doors, spilling blurred colours onto the garish tiled floor. But the splash of colour wasn't enough to lift the smothering gloom.

The house was a testament to faded grandeur. Portraits must have once adorned the walls, judging by the pale oblongs left behind. The thick wallpaper had faded too, and was peeling in places, but its pattern of swirling acanthus leaves had likely once been very elegant. Cass tried to picture how it must have looked

7

in its prime – the wood polished and gleaming, the carpets lush and colourful. But the image faded quickly, to be replaced with the reality of the house's decline. It was sad, really. Like a museum no one visited anymore, filled with exhibits no one bothered to tend. Frozen in time. Or worse – trapped.

Nervously, she unpacked her camera, eager to get to work. The sooner she was done, the sooner she could leave.

A once-grand staircase dominated the hall, branching off to either side at the top, just beneath the stained-glass window. Cass followed the curving stairs with her eyes, then raised the camera to take a picture without bothering to compose the shot. No one would notice or care. She wasn't here to create art, just to do a job. Her talent would be better spent on more worthy subjects.

The digital click of the shutter was swallowed by the cavernous room and yet at the same time the sound was far too loud. It only emphasised how alone she was in here. How *isolated*.

There was something wrong with the silence, something far too deep about it. It was like being in a room where someone was hiding, someone who didn't want you to know they were there. The unwelcome thought sent a chill through her. Even more unwelcome was the notion that the house was somehow muffling any sounds. Cass listened, but she could hear nothing of the world outside. No birds, no wind, no traffic. Not even the creak of the FOR SALE sign. Nothing.

Clouds of dust motes drifted in the air and suddenly Cass found she couldn't breathe. Her lungs refused to expand. She clutched at her chest, her fear escalating rapidly. She could feel the air as she pulled it into her mouth, sucked it into her throat. But there it stopped. The breath couldn't reach her chest. It was as if some terrible weight was pressing down on her. A strangled cry escaped her lips and her vision began to blur. She felt the first stirrings of true panic, followed by the fear that she would never be able to breathe again.

And then, as suddenly and inexplicably as it had come, the strange feeling passed and she found herself gasping, gulping in huge lungfuls of air. For long moments she stood staring around in bewilderment. She could think of no explanation for the sudden attack and she was left wondering what the hell had just happened.

The only thing she knew for certain was that she did not like this house. Did not like it one bit.

Now that she could breathe again, she noticed how foul the air tasted. Stale and pungent, like something rotten. It reminded her of antique shops, crammed so full of clutter you couldn't move around inside. Old things gave her the creeps. She hated dust and decay, couldn't abide the smell of old furniture and old books. Even the thought of wearing someone else's clothes made her feel queasy.

Wintergate wasn't stuffed to the rafters with junk; quite the opposite. And that was even worse. It was profoundly empty. A deep sense of loss pervaded the house. It put Cass in mind of a plundered vault, cold and desolate. But it was more than that. The house didn't just feel empty; it felt *barren*.

Cass didn't want to climb those ugly stairs, but she had to. The estate agent needed photographs of the whole house. As she went she tried to appreciate the sense of ambitious optimism that had gone into the design of such a place. High Victorian gothic wasn't to Cass's tastes, but all the elaborate carving and fussy decoration nonetheless displayed a kind of artistry and pride that just wasn't seen in modern homes. She ran her hand along the banister and forced herself to admire the stained-glass window at the top of the stairs.

It was chipped and cracked in places but the strange scene it portrayed was clear enough. The pipe-playing satyr rather spoiled the churchy effect but Cass supposed you got to choose your own crazy designs when you were a rich Victorian trying to impress and outdo your peers. A few patches of damp marred the wall beneath the window and Cass aimed the camera higher to crop it out. Highlighting damage was the surveyor's job; hers was to make the property look inviting.

She took some shots of the tiled floor from above, but she didn't like the look of the minstrels' gallery that led off to her left beneath the window. The door at the far end couldn't open onto anything but the barren ground some twenty feet below. She hoped it was sealed, for the sake of any children who might find themselves living here with their (obviously loony) parents. The curlicued balusters holding up the banister also looked too widely spaced to be safe. You'd never be allowed to build something like that today. But then, nineteenth century children probably weren't allowed to play anywhere except the nursery. If they were even allowed to play at all. The treatment of children was only one of myriad reasons Cass found Victoriana so off-putting.

The hallway stretched away in both directions and Cass went to the right, away from the sealed door. More windows spilled their weak colours onto the wooden floor of the long corridor. A wide pale streak showed where a carpet runner had once lain and Cass couldn't help but think of the writhing bloodless things you exposed when you lifted a stone in the garden. In fact, there were a few dried husks lying up against the panelled wall, bleached white with age. They looked like silverfish, but they were the size of honeybees. The sight made her shudder, but not as much as the sound she heard next. A soft scratching.

She stood perfectly still, ears straining to hear. Silence. Nothing but cold, dead silence.

Lovely, she thought. *It's got rats too.*

But she knew what rats sounded like. This was different. The scratching had had an unpleasantly soft quality to it, as though the noise was made by fingers rather than claws. *Tiny* fingers. The kind of fingers...

"Stop it," she admonished herself fiercely. She refused to acknowledge the other sound she imagined she'd heard beneath the scratching. No, she hadn't heard that at all.

Cass liked to think of herself as someone who didn't spook easily, someone immune to the wild flights of fancy to which others were so often prone. An empty house was just that: an empty house. Not a tomb, not a morgue, and certainly not a place where the dearly departed walked. When you died, that was it. You didn't get to hang around and drift through old houses in a gauzy white gown, beckoning from high windows or slamming doors to make the new occupants jump. Ghosts were nothing but a romantic delusion. Either the concept reassured you that death wasn't the end or it scared the holy hell out of you for precisely the same reason.

There were no ghosts in Wintergate. It was just another property like hundreds of others she had photographed over the years. Admittedly, this one was a little more unusual, the kind of place they'd advertise as a "character property". The listing would emphasise its period features (kooky old-fashioned design), its charming seclusion (creepy isolation), its lovely view (fair enough, it did have that). Prospective buyers were bound to ask if it was haunted and Cass couldn't help but wonder if such a claim might actually be a selling point. People so desperately wanted to believe in such things.

But no. There was nothing *to* believe. The house was weird but it wasn't haunted. In its peculiar way she supposed it had a kind of sad beauty. Like an ageing film star, its era had passed and its glamour had faded. There was nothing at all threatening about it. So why did Cass feel so unnerved?

You know why.

She shook her head to silence her inner voices. "Just get on with it and get out," she grumbled. She was moody, that was all, and the house wasn't helping. She had never known any place to feel as forsaken as this one. You'd have to be suicidal to spend even a single night here.

The only sound was the noise from the camera as Cass went from room to room, trying to capture images that would make Wintergate look like somewhere people would actually want to live.

She and her husband lived in a modern apartment block, full of modern conveniences. The kind of place that had no secrets and no surprises. And that was just how Cass liked it. She couldn't understand the appeal of ancient historical homes with their never-ending upkeep. They were high maintenance money pits and you were at the mercy of the listed buildings people if you wanted to knock through a wall or put in a skylight. Any home she lived in had to be *her* home. She wasn't interested in being a custodian of history.

But whoever bought this place had better be. They'd have their work cut out for them. She steered her camera's gaze clear of the less photogenic areas – the gouges in the floorboards, the cracked windows, the peeling wallpaper. The house was probably worth a fortune, but only if you were willing to restore and maintain it. No matter how important a building was, surely there came a point where, like with an old, suffering pet, you had to say goodbye. And in Cass's opinion, Wintergate had passed that point. It was just so *grim*. Fancy period details notwithstanding, it would take a hell of a lot more than paint and interior design to bring some cheer to this gloomy old place.

Cass found herself disliking the house even more the further she went inside. Her footsteps sounded like stones thrown into a bottomless well as she made her way to the huge main room, trying to focus on the unique features and selling points. The lavishly carved door, the soaring beams.

"Be a bitch to heat," she said, gazing up at the ceiling some thirty feet above. It was like being in a cathedral. Every bit as cold and every bit as intimidating. But Wintergate did have one truly spectacular thing going for it. The view from the immense bay window was what would sell the place, so she framed her shots to show it off to its best advantage. Even Cass Sheehan, hater of all things old and ostentatious, couldn't deny a twitch of envy at the truly magnificent view.

When she was done she perched on the edge of the window seat to gaze out over the countryside. The Victorians knew how to pick their spots, all right. They could look down on all the humble little peasants below and imagine they were kings and queens in their castle up on the hill.

She tried to imagine how all her modern IKEA furniture would look in this ancient house. The idea of brightly coloured flat-pack furnishings sitting on the antique oak floor made her laugh and it took her a moment to realise that she'd heard another voice then. And it wasn't an echo of her own. There was someone else in the house.

She covered her mouth to stifle a gasp. The hairs on the back of her neck prickled and she got slowly to her feet, debating whether or not to call out. There *couldn't* be anyone else in here. Her own footsteps had been so loud – how could anyone else sneak in without her hearing it? The answer was simple: they couldn't. She was alone. Her eyes crept uneasily to the feature of the room that disturbed her the most. But it, like the house, was quite still.

For several seconds Cass held her breath, listening but hearing nothing. Nothing but the rush of her own blood in her ears, the hammering of her own heart.

And that was when she heard the crying. There was no mistaking it this time. The high, thin keening made her skin feel like ants were crawling over it. It sounded like it was just outside, just on the other side of the north wall. But there was nothing *on* the other side of that wall but rock. The house may as well have been built into the cliff face.

Someone's cat, she thought. *Or a bird.*

She tried to shrug it off but she still felt unsettled. It definitely *hadn't* sounded like a baby, no matter what her instincts told her. It was just the chill and the oppressive stillness. Sometimes silence could be more disconcerting than noise. It made you hear things when there was nothing to hear. She pressed a hand to her swollen belly, as though to calm the tiny life within. As though her own child were the source of the sound she had heard.

Annoyed that she had allowed herself to get so freaked out, Cass shouldered her bag and marched back through the corridor. She hadn't been inside the house more than fifteen minutes but the shadows had deepened considerably in that time. They lay across her path like trenches and she found herself stepping around and over them, not wanting to place her feet in the pools of darkness.

She reached the stairs and started down and suddenly her feet went out from under her. The house swallowed her cry as she fell.

It seemed to last forever, that fall. She could see the whole thing as clearly as if she'd been evicted from her own body for the purpose. The slow pinwheeling of her arms as she flailed at the banister, desperate to grab hold of it. The cartoony scrambling of

17

her feet seeking purchase on the old, worn carpet.

There was time for a single thought to cross her mind: *I'm going to die.* It was immediately replaced by a worse thought. *My baby is going to die.*

She realised that the anguished cry was her own voice just as her fingers made contact with the banister at last. A fingernail broke against the smooth mahogany and the tiny jolt of pain sent her back inside her body. Her knees met the hard, uncarpeted edge of the stair tread as she clung to the banister with both hands, like someone nearly drowned hanging on to the side of a boat for dear life.

Cass didn't believe in God but at that moment she thanked him. Through tears and desperate, panting breaths, she thanked him again and again. It was irrational. Superstitious. In her right mind she'd also have said ignorant. But she didn't care. Tears of relief and gratitude burned in her eyes as she gasped out the words.

"Thank you, oh thank you!"

When she finally dared to stand again she hissed with sudden pain. She had twisted an ankle and she must have also pulled something in her side. It felt as though she'd swallowed a handful of nails. Unless her baby had suddenly grown teeth and claws and was digging its way out of her, digging its way into the house that had tried to kill them both. She was not welcome here.

Disturbed by the sudden thought, she shook her head and made her way cautiously down the stairs, crawling hand over hand along the banister like an invalid. From somewhere up above she heard the soft scratching again, then the sickly mewling.

She gritted her teeth and shut it out. The sounds, the pain, the awful images. She was nearly at the front door. Fifteen feet, ten, five. Her clammy hands slipped on the ornate door handle and for one terrifying moment she was sure she'd been locked inside.

Then the handle turned and the heavy door swung open and she was in the stone porch. She slammed the front door behind her and winced as another splinter of pain pierced her belly. Her fingers trembled as she fished out the key and turned it in the lock. Then she hobbled out onto the gravel drive, clutching her sides. Almost immediately the pain began to fade and by the time she had reached her car, it was completely gone.

She told herself it had nothing to do with the house. Nothing at all. She needed to believe that was true.

Now that she was outside again, she realised just how oppressive the atmosphere inside had been. She took a deep breath, relishing the fresh, clean air. Her job here was done. If the estate agent wanted any more pictures, someone else would have to take them. She would never come back here.

CHAPTER 2

Liz Holland had always hated the rain, but even more so on days like this. The wind seemed to have forged some kind of evil alliance with the water, the one driving the other through a secret crevice in the brickwork. From there the rain soaked into the ceiling, filling the plaster until the inevitable dripping began.

The paper covering the flat's high ceiling dangled in sodden strips in several places, while in others it was strong enough to allow pockets of water to accumulate. These hung precariously overhead like water balloons, swelling until the pressure finally made them burst. Nick and Liz had cleared away the furniture beneath the areas where the leaks were worst, spreading bin liners over the damp carpet and then scattering so many pots and pans around the room there were none left to cook with.

They'd only been there a year and the flat hadn't leaked at all for the first few months. But it had been an unusually wet winter and it was promising to be an equally wet spring. Somewhere along the way, the building had simply surrendered to the onslaught of rain. That or, as Nick suspected, some shoddy repair

21

job had finally met its match and burst like a dam.

Every room in the flat was made smaller by the numerous bookshelves along the walls. These too had been draped with bin liners to protect their contents from splashes. Liz's fantasy-art books and Nick's first editions lived in the bedroom, which so far hadn't leaked, but even the battered second-hand paperbacks whose value was purely sentimental deserved better.

The kitchen and bathroom were dry as a bone, but the second bedroom was almost as bad as the lounge. It was Liz's workshop and the headquarters of Styx & Stones Designs, where she made handcrafted jewellery and accessories. Or at least she tried to. An improvised arrangement of two umbrellas clamped onto tripods shielded her desk from the downpour, but it was impossible to concentrate on such detailed work when it was raining *inside* the studio. Her best friend Gwen had suggested that she change the name to Atlantis Designs.

"Everybody loves mermaids," she'd said with a sympathetic grin.

The landlord had sent workers round on several occasions to find and fix the leaks. They had erected scaffolding and poked around at the ceiling's interior, but they were never able to locate the precise spot where the water actually entered the flat.

Curiously enough, the flat above theirs didn't seem to have any trouble with leaks. Each time the workmen declared the problem solved, another storm would prove them wrong. Finally they threw up their hands and said the whole ceiling would have to come down. It would be weeks of disruption, not only for Nick and Liz but also for the owners of the flat above, who would have to agree to their floor being ripped out at the same time. As the Hollands weren't on good terms with their overhead neighbours, it wasn't a happy prospect.

"Let's just get out of here," Nick had said at last. "Find a place of our own. We can put up with the leaks until then. Then they can demolish the whole building if they want to."

On evenings like this one, Liz wasn't convinced the building needed anyone's help in coming down. It was a wonder the soggy ceiling hadn't already fallen in.

She was balancing precariously with one foot on the windowsill and the other on the arm of the couch when Nick came in. She thought she could just about reach the latest pocket of water with the tip of a screwdriver. With one quick jab she pierced the bubble, lancing it like a boil. Water splashed down on her and she lost her footing, tumbling to the floor in an undignified heap.

Nick was at her side in a flash. "You okay, Hedgehog?"

"You weren't supposed to see that," Liz groaned, wiping her face dry with a sleeve.

"See what?" He grinned and kissed her as he helped her to her feet. "Dare I even ask how your day's been?"

"The fun never ends," she said, gesturing at the new hole she'd made in the ceiling. "And dinner's ruined, I'm afraid. I heard a new drip and came to investigate. Got completely sidetracked and forgot all about the curry until the smoke alarm went off."

"Aww, we'll go to the pub later," Nick said, laughing it off. "I'm parked illegally anyway. Some wanker stole my space and I circled the block three times before giving up."

Liz dabbed at her wet hair with a tea towel. "You know, I'm really beginning to hate Bristol."

"Well, hold that thought because I've got some good news."

"Better than the pub?"

"Before the pub. We've got a viewing."

"What, tonight?"

He nodded. "As soon as we can get there."

"Oh no, I can't go to see a place looking like this!" Her hair hung in wet ropes around her face.

"No one's going to care, Liz. It's pissing it down as it is."

24

"Can't they show us some pictures first? All the other ones we looked at had listings on the website."

He shook his head. "I spoke to someone named Sylvia at the estate agent's and she said there aren't any pictures. They sent someone round to photograph it but the pictures didn't turn out. But the house met all our criteria so she rang me up."

Liz cast a despairing look at the contents of their kitchen, spread out on the floor beneath the dripping ceiling. She sighed heavily. It was likely to be just another disappointment, but at this point they couldn't afford to ignore any possibility. And frankly, they were getting desperate. "All right, let me get my coat. Where is this place?"

"Clevedon. Right by the sea. Sylvia called it a Marmite property: love it or hate it. And so far everyone's hated it."

"Great," said Liz doubtfully. "What's wrong with it?"

"No idea. She just said we had to see it for ourselves, that pictures wouldn't do it justice anyway."

"Okay, I guess I'm as ready as I'm going to be," she said, frowning at her bedraggled reflection.

"You look beautiful," Nick said.

She laughed. "I look like a drowned rat."

"True. But a beautiful drowned rat."

25

That made her smile. She knew he actually meant it.

They'd been saving up to buy a house – their first – and they hadn't even planned to start looking for another year. But having been driven prematurely into the game, they were at a distinct disadvantage. They weren't exactly sure what to look for, or to be wary of. In the first few weeks, they'd seen some fifty places, none of which had *felt* right. The houses were either characterless modern boxes or desecrated Victorian buildings whose charm had been completely eliminated by the breaking up of large airy rooms into multiple tiny cells.

They'd even looked at a couple of flats similar to the rain-soaked one they were in now. Maybe if they couldn't buy an entire period house they could at least buy part of one. But no matter how beautiful and affordable the flats were, they still had the disadvantage of close neighbours.

Liz had grown up in a terraced house with three brothers, so she cherished her personal space and privacy, whilst Nick, an only child, had simply never been without either. They quickly grew to resent the heavy-footed family in the flat above who let their children gallop constantly back and forth on the uncarpeted floor. The Hollands' polite and reasonable suggestion that a rug might help with sound insulation was met with aggressive outrage. The father of the brood had pushed his angry red face right into Nick's and snarled that no one was gonna bloody well tell *them* how their kids should behave. The noise got worse after that.

"Are you *sure* you don't want kids?" they would ask one another in mock-wistful tones as they gazed up at the bouncing light fixture.

"We're going to drive straight into the sea," Liz said, squinting through the rain-streaked windscreen as Nick steered the car up the hillside. "I can't see a thing."

They'd followed the satnav directions from Bristol to the seaside town of Clevedon. The directions had taken them through the town centre and past a beautiful old cinema before losing its signal and abandoning them halfway up an unpromising single-track drive.

"We're almost there," Nick reassured her. "See where the road forks at the top? That must be the hill fort. She said the house was just below it."

The satnav suddenly came back to life, startling them with the announcement that they had reached their destination. And there on a rocky outcropping, crouched in the centre of a round forecourt, was half a Victorian house.

Nick glanced uncertainly at Liz. "Well, she was right about

pictures not doing it justice," he said.

"Where's the rest of it?"

Nick guided the car between two weathered stone pillars. The right-hand one bore a slate plaque that read WINTERGATE.

The imposing structure before them resembled a gatehouse. A large vaulted passage cut through the centre of what remained of the house, but rather than framing the approach to a castle or some great estate, it seemed to lead only to the wall of the hill behind. The arch was flanked by a grand gothic entrance on the left and two ornate bay windows on the right, one above the other. The first floor windows just above the archway were stained glass and above, Liz could make out the figures of gargoyles along the edge of the crenellated roof. It looked as though the architect had been unable to decide which gothic and medieval features to use and so had simply used all of them.

But even more striking than the flamboyant façade was the conspicuously empty patch of ground beside it. There was clearly a large room behind the front door, but to the left of that, the rest of the house had been demolished. Two bricked-up outlines, one on each floor, showed where doors had once led into the missing wing.

The rocky outcropping was just large enough for the whole

eccentric structure, leaving the remaining half jammed with its back against the hill. The left side was where the hill began to slope down, and the missing wing must have offered panoramic views across the whole town and the Channel. Even over the rain, they could hear the splash of waves on the shingle beach on the other side of the hill.

They shared a bemused look at the property and Nick shrugged. "Maybe it got bombed during the war?"

They regarded the house silently for a few moments before braving the downpour. Crowding together under Nick's umbrella, they hurried across the forecourt to the entrance, which had presumably been the centre of the house when it was whole. It actually projected a little way above the clifftop, but it was the only part that did.

A short flight of stone steps took them up to an impressive set of double doors with scrolled iron hinges. It looked like the entrance to a church. Nick tried the doors and they opened with a protesting screech as the wood scraped along the stone floor. Creeping inside, they found themselves in a porch with a small window to their left. Several panes were cracked and warped.

Nick shook the water from the umbrella and rested it against the wall. Even the gentle touch of the plastic handle was enough to dislodge a small chunk of stonework. "That can't be a good sign," he said.

The porch extended out a few feet from the house, so the left-hand window overlooked the empty lot. Liz peered through but she couldn't see anything much in the rain.

Soon they heard the crunch of gravel and a pink VW beetle dazzled them with its headlights as it pulled into the forecourt. They stayed in the dry porch while a matronly woman dodged from the car, sheltering under a copy of *Hello!* magazine. Her pale yellow blouse was an unfortunate choice; the lacy push-up bra she wore beneath it was glaringly visible through the wet fabric.

"I'm Sylvia," she enthused in a broad West Country accent. "You must be Nick and Liz Holland." She pumped each of their hands vigorously as she turned her megawatt smile on them. "Quite a place, eh?"

The couple smiled politely in return but said nothing. The house clearly wasn't going to work out. Still, they might as well take the tour since they were here. Liz was certainly curious to see it, and if nothing else, they could at least take advantage of the temporary shelter from the rain. Maybe it would stop by the time they were ready to leave.

Sylvia dug a bundle of keys from her enormous handbag and

tried several of them before at last finding the right fit. "Now you just wait till you see inside. It's certainly not for everyone, but it's like I always say–" she assaulted them with her smile again "–it only has to be right for *you*."

She threw open the door and invited them in with a grand gesture.

Liz froze, overwhelmed. "Oh my god."

They stood within an extravagant panelled hall with a mosaic tiled floor. The mahogany staircase was an exquisite showpiece. Ornate brass lamps topped the newel posts, which were carved with dragons. A wine-dark runner fixed with iron rods followed the sweeping staircase to the top, where the landing formed an impressive minstrels' gallery with a stained-glass window behind it. A hallway on the right led into the rest of the house, but on the left the landing went nowhere, dead-ending at one of the bricked-up doorways they'd seen from outside.

Sylvia followed their gaze. "We call it a 'detached flat' for lack of a better term."

"What happened to the rest of the house?" Nick asked.

"There was a fire back in 1880-something. Very tragic it was." She made a little moue of regret, as though she'd personally known the nineteenth-century occupants. "It's actually quite a romantic story. But the best romances always *are* tragic, aren't they?"

"I hope not in our case," Liz said with a laugh.

Sylvia flushed bright red. "Oh, of course not, dear."

"So what happened?" Nick asked.

Sylvia beamed, clearly relishing the chance to show off her knowledge of the historical gossip as she led them upstairs. "It was built by a man named Carson Menrath in the 1870s. He was the youngest son of a rich London family and they used to spend their summers here by the sea. The Victorians were very keen on the sea air. Good for the constitution, they said. Personally, I don't know *what* they were on about. It's a real nuisance, what with the damp and that salty wind blowin' in off the Channel. Not good for the paintwork on your car either, I can tell you–" She caught herself. "'Course, I shouldn't imagine that would be a problem here. Oh no, not in a lovely spot like this, protected by all them trees..."

Nick cleared his throat. "The house?"

"Oh yes! Sorry, dear, I do prattle on, don't I? Anyway, I was sayin' as how this gentleman built the house. Built it for his new bride, he did. Her family had come over from America one summer and the young lovers met on the pier, which had just opened. You've seen it, I trust? No?"

Liz shook her head.

"You must do! It's absolutely charming. Anyway, it was love at first sight. Vanora – that was her name – her health wasn't very good, poor thing, so Carson decided they would settle here in Clevedon, for the sea air and that. They had one of those long courtships, I expect, and he took her for walks on these hills, trying to find the perfect spot for their little love-nest. The area is known as Poets' Walk."

She paused at the top of the stairs to allow them to admire the large window there. Standing on tiptoe, Liz thought she could just make out the top of the hill sloping down to the left. But the window clearly wasn't there to offer a view of what was outside; it was a feature all its own. Instead of religious imagery the scene featured highly stylised mythical beasts and a stone circle. Pan himself was there as well, dancing in their midst.

Liz smiled, wholly approving. "Much nicer than solemn old saints and martyrs."

"You could pinch some of those images," Nick said. At Sylvia's puzzled expression he added, "My wife designs jewellery."

Liz dug her pendant out from inside her coat and held it out for the woman to see. It was an elaborate Celtic knot that

33

appeared to be unravelling at the bottom, where a tiny pair of hands poked through. Whether they were the culprit or belonged to someone trying to repair the knot, Liz could never decide. It was one of her favourite pieces, one Nick had insisted she keep for herself rather than sell. She'd been wearing it the day they met. Ever since, she had considered it her good luck charm.

"That's lovely," Sylvia said, not sounding entirely convinced.

They moved along the landing to the hallway, where two stone mullion windows on the left faced directly into the cliff wall just outside. There was just enough space to allow a bit of light in, but it would be a very tight squeeze if a person wanted to walk behind the house.

"That's a pretty eccentric view," Nick said.

"Isn't it just? That's Wain's Hill. There's an old hill fort at the top. Iron Age or Bronze Age or some such. Anyway, Carson wanted to build the house up there but some preservation society or other wouldn't let him. Quite right too, I should say! By the way, that's the original oak parquet flooring," she said, having noticed Liz peering at it. "Missing the odd bit here and there but nothing a good joiner can't sort out for you."

"It's beautiful," Liz said dreamily. She was wholly enchanted by the house and every quirky detail. And while she expected that

Sylvia's Mills and Boon version of events was highly embellished, she nonetheless found herself caught up in it. She came to a door and opened it to find a large bathroom.

"Now, I know you'll like this," Sylvia said, pushing ahead in her zeal to show Liz the room. She swept past the toilet and basin into a little alcove with yet another stained-glass window. "Wouldn't this be just the most delightful spot for a bathtub? Of course there's plenty of room for a shower if you prefer. Or both. There's enough space for whatever you like!"

Liz immediately saw the possibilities. "We can get one of those rolltop bathtubs with clawed feet," she told Nick excitedly. "I've always wanted one like that."

"Decadent," Nick agreed.

Liz pictured herself luxuriating there as the evening light streamed in through the stained-glass window. She could smell the scented candles and taste the wine, anticipating the warm sex that would follow in a massive four-poster bed hung with lacy curtains...

"Why isn't there a bathtub already?" Nick asked, breaking the mood.

"No one's lived here since the fire. It started in the west wing, where the Menraths had their private apartments. They both

35

perished, the poor dears." She shook her head sadly.

Nick looked astonished. "Hang on. No one's lived here in over a hundred years? Why isn't the place a total ruin?"

"Now, now," Sylvia chided. "Just because it hasn't been lived in don't mean it hasn't been *used*. This wing was originally the library, you see, so it's done museum duty over the years. The archaeologists used it to display artefacts they dug up from the hill fort and other ancient sites round here. It certainly hasn't gone to waste."

"I see. Who owns it now?"

"A family up in Edinburgh. They bought it a few years ago with an eye toward doing it up as a holiday home, but they fell on hard times and it just sat here empty. Now the gentleman's got a job in Australia so they have to sell the place quickly."

"So why hasn't anyone liked it so far?"

"Oh, I think it's just not for everyone. Some find it too secluded and – well, it is rather unconventional."

"It's certainly that."

"So as I was saying," Sylvia continued, "he couldn't build the house on top of the hill, but when they came down here they found the remains of this old stone gate half buried in the snow. Well, Vanora, she thought it was just beautiful, and Carson said –

Right, that's where we'll put our house, then. And seeing as how it was winter and all, he called the place Wintergate. That big archway under where we're standing? That's where the gate was." She folded her hands as though concluding a children's story hour. "Now isn't that a lovely story."

Liz wasn't usually a sucker for romantic guff but still, the tale had affected her. She could easily imagine the wide-eyed and lonely little wife, a girl far from home, falling in love with a kind gentleman with surprisingly poetic sensibilities for his time. She smiled as she stroked the mahogany panelling in the hallway. "It's very sweet."

Nick was smiling too, but it was a cynical expression Liz didn't like. "So this bloke took his poorly wife for a walk along the cliffs in the dead of winter?"

Liz exchanged a puzzled look with Sylvia.

"Perhaps it was a nice day," Liz said sharply, feeling defensive even as she recognised the flaw in the tale. "They do happen once in a while."

Nick looked taken aback. "Sorry. I just thought it sounded a little unlikely. You know how these stories develop a life of their own down the years."

Sylvia laughed to show there were no hard feelings. "I'm sure

37

you're right," she said good-naturedly, "although I wouldn't put anything past them loony Victorians. Them in their corsets and top hats and coverin' up the legs of furniture." She tutted and moved along the hallway.

When Sylvia was out of earshot Liz whispered to Nick, "Don't you like the house?"

"Well, you have to admit it's not exactly practical." Liz made a face at that and he frowned suddenly, clasping her hand with a reassuring squeeze. "Come on, there's no way we can afford it anyway. We're just along for the ride."

Liz felt her excitement deflate. In her mind the house was theirs already and she'd already been visualising how it would look when they moved in.

"Are you coming, my dears? I've saved the best for last!"

Liz made herself smile and kissed Nick lightly. "Along for the ride," she murmured. "Okay, off we go, then."

Sylvia was standing at the end of the hallway, where a heavy gothic door stood ready to admit them. They barely had time to glance at it before Sylvia pushed it open and led them inside what felt like a cavernous space. She flicked a switch and the room sprang into view. They gaped at their surroundings, speechless.

"The master bedroom," Sylvia said proudly.

The room was nearly the size of their entire flat in Bristol, with a ceiling so high Liz imagined that she could stand on Nick's shoulders and still not be able to reach it. A large cut-glass chandelier hung from the centre of the room, illuminating the red and gold flocked wallpaper and the parquet floor. But it was the window that really got her attention. Heavy red velvet curtains parted beneath a carved arch to reveal an enormous bay window like a stage in a theatre. And even more impressive was the view that it framed.

Through the slashing rain, the lights of the town far below shone like tiny beacons. A curving ribbon of yellow marked the path of the M5 in the distance. The outline of the Mendip and Quantock hills rose and fell beyond it.

"My God, you can see the whole county from here," Nick said.

Liz smiled to herself. At last he sounded impressed.

"You're facing southwest," Sylvia explained, "so you can see as far as Cornwall. And Wales across the Channel on a clear day."

"A window seat!" Liz cried. "I've always wanted one of these. I could lose whole days just sitting here reading or staring out over the countryside."

She sank down into the cushions to admire the tempestuous view. It was an almost ridiculous luxury to see water streaming down the *outside* of the windows instead of dripping in through the ceiling.

Nick had moved away, exploring the massive room. After a little while, Liz got up and followed him, silently urging him to love it as much as she did. She wanted this house. They *had* to have it.

"What on earth...?" Nick was looking up at the cornice, at a large plaster head that stared out into the room. It was a Victorian man's whiskered face, striking and sombre, its expression inscrutable. "Carson Menrath, I presume?"

"Ah yes," Sylvia said. "Vanora was just opposite, but as you can see..."

The remains of a plaster neck were all that was left of the tragic bride's likeness. Liz felt a sudden and intense wave of sadness. "What happened to it?" she asked.

"No one knows for sure, although naturally there's a story about it. The couple desperately wanted a family, you see, but it just wasn't to be. Vanora's poor health and all. She was bedridden by the end and Carson became something of a recluse, taking care of her. They say the poor girl wasted away pining for the children she could never have, and that sculpture wasted away right along with her." She sighed, then brightened as she turned back to Liz.

40

"Are you planning to start a family?"

Liz bristled, resenting the question. "No," she said with forced politeness. "I, er, can't have children."

Sylvia's face fell and she looked positively wretched over her faux pas. "Oh. Oh, I'm *so* sorry."

Beyond her Liz saw Nick stifling a laugh. He shook his finger at her and mouthed *Bad girl!*

Sylvia recovered quickly. "It's not really suitable for a family anyway, mind," she said, as though the news would comfort any barren woman.

"Just as well," Liz said cheerily, returning to her husband's side.

They admired the marble fireplace that occupied the wall opposite the door, surrounded by an elaborately carved wooden mantelpiece. Along the back wall was a row of fitted bookcases that climbed to the ceiling.

"Is there another room beneath this one?" Nick asked.

"There is indeed, and just as big! There's a door leading down to it from the corridor. I'll show you."

She led them back and opened the door into an enclosed stairwell that took them to the ground floor via a series of turns. An identical bay window displayed the same spectacular view from a slightly lower perspective. The room had been partitioned along the west wall to conceal a kitchen.

"This used to be a café when the house was a museum, so the kitchen's a bit basic, I'm afraid."

"Is that the only way in here?" Nick asked, nodding back at the stairs.

Sylvia nodded, biting her lip as though she'd been hoping he wouldn't ask. "But you could probably get planning permission to add another door that leads directly in from outside."

"Expensive."

Liz dug her nails into her palms. It didn't matter what it cost; this house was meant to be *theirs*. It was perfect. Couldn't Nick see that? She almost felt as if the house *wanted* her there.

"Well, I love it," she said. Her voice wavered as she screwed up the courage to say, "What's the asking price?"

Sylvia rifled through her paperwork, as though she didn't know it already. "Let's see... It's gone down quite a bit since it came on the market. Like I said, there hasn't been much interest and the owners really need to shift it. Ah yes, here it is." She named a figure.

Nick nodded and Liz said "Hmm" as they both made a show of considering the staggeringly low price.

"Mind if we have another look around?" Nick asked casually.

"Of course not. Take as long as you like."

When they were alone again in the enormous bedroom Nick turned to Liz, wide-eyed with amazement. "Bloody hell, did we hear that right?"

Liz felt dizzy, like she'd just been told she'd won the lottery. "It's got to be worth a lot more than that. Why hasn't anyone snapped it up?"

"Well, I guess it's like she said – it's too quirky for most people. It's wildly impractical. It's a bit isolated. And it does need a hell of a lot of repair work."

"Not much."

Nick frowned. "I don't think we're looking at the same house, Liz. The one we're standing in now is a serious fixer-upper."

Puzzled, she tried to recall anything beyond the odd nick or scratch that needed doing. "So it needs a bathtub," she said with a shrug. "That's not such a big deal."

"It needs a lot more than that. Half the stained-glass windows are cracked and the floor's certainly seen better days." At Liz's pleading expression he added, "Still, I suppose there's nothing urgent or life-threatening."

"It doesn't leak."

"We'd have no neighbours."

"It's not family-friendly," Liz added with a wicked grin.

Nick laughed. "That was cruel of you. What in God's name made you say that anyway?"

"Oh, she just hit a nerve. As if I don't get enough of that from my mother. Why does everyone assume that no woman is complete without a bloody baby?"

"Hey, I'm just as keen to stay child-free as you are," he said, "but that was a cruel blow."

She bowed her head and grinned up at him sheepishly. "Sorry," she said. "Forgive?"

Nick wrapped his arms around her and kissed her. "Always. And after dinner we can revel in the freedom of not being tied down."

Liz giggled. "Well, perhaps *you* can," she said. "*I* rather like being tied down." She drew his hands down and pressed them against the front of her jeans. "Imagine the fun we could have in this room."

"No need to stifle your cries," he said, biting her ear. "I wanted to have you on the staircase. And in the bathroom by the stained-glass window. I was picturing you naked the whole time."

She turned, surprised. "So you *do* like the house!"

44

"Liz, I *love* it. I was just playing hard to get with her."

"Oops. Guess I missed that trick."

"You wear your heart on your sleeve, Hedgehog. You need to learn how to keep things back sometimes. Gives you more bargaining power."

She blushed. "I know. You're right."

They looked up at Carson Menrath's plaster head, the blank face staring silently out into the room. Outside the rain turned the lights of the town into magical splashes of colour. A crescent moon peeked out from wispy clouds high above.

"A place like this comes along once in a lifetime," Liz said. "If we don't take it we'll always look back and regret it."

Nick nodded. "And even if we don't stay here forever we'll always be able to say, 'Remember that amazing half-house we lived in?'"

Liz's eyes filled with tears. "God, I love you."

"I love you too."

The deep kiss that followed was interrupted by Sylvia, whose exaggerated gasp was so phony that Liz suspected the woman had been spying on them.

The happy couple turned to her, smiling. "We'll take it," Nick said.

CHAPTER 3

Their friends had warned them that buying a home was a notoriously convoluted process. At times it seemed like there would be no end to the paperwork, property surveys and solicitors' fees, but finally – after weeks of what seemed like pointless machinations designed to make everyone else lots of money – the house was finally theirs. They heard the first cuckoo of spring on the day they went to collect the keys and both took it to be a good sign.

They'd packed a week's worth of clothes and toiletries to see them through until the removal men delivered the rest of their things. And that morning they'd purchased an air mattress. Their lease on the Bristol flat didn't run out until the end of the month, but they were too excited about the house not to spend their first night of ownership there.

They sat in the window seat of the bedroom with a takeaway pizza and a bottle of champagne as a slice of moon rose over the Somerset hills. Although the spring night was mild, they'd been unable to resist the romance of the fireplace. Flames crackled in the hearth, making the outline of the vast room jump and shiver. There was just enough light to see shapes and shadows. The striations in the oak panelling gave the room an otherworldly feel, as though they were deep in the woods, surrounded by trees. Perhaps even *inside* a tree.

"This is our home," Liz said blissfully, not for the first time. "This is where we live now."

Nick closed his eyes. "It's so quiet."

Outside they could just hear the hiss of cars passing by on the roads below like gentle surf. An owl hooted somewhere in the nearby trees. A log popped in the fireplace. But there was no stampede overhead, no slamming of doors, no wail of sirens outside. As much as they both loved the excitement and culture of the city, there was no substitute for such tranquillity.

Liz looked over at the air mattress, its tiny inflated form utterly swamped by the scale of the room. "I wonder if it will be scary sleeping in such a big place?"

"I'll protect you," Nick said, reaching over to stroke her thigh.

She stretched her leg out, placing her bare foot in his lap. He stirred beneath her touch but he calmly finished his champagne and set the glass on the floor beside the empty pizza box. His eyes shone in the moonlight. "Are you still hungry?"

47

"Always," she purred.

He cradled her foot in both hands and gently lifted it to his lips, kissing her polished pink toenails.

Liz shivered as he drew his fingers over the arch of her foot and up along the swell of her calf. She extended her leg, hooking it around Nick as he pulled her firmly towards him. She arched back on the cushions as he unfastened the buttons of her blouse one by one and kissed every inch of warm flesh he uncovered. When she was naked he carried her to the air mattress, and she couldn't suppress a laugh as it jostled them like a rocking boat. She had to grab his shoulders so she wouldn't fall off.

"Sex on a bouncy castle," Nick said, grinning. "This might be a bit of a comedy sketch."

After some awkward manoeuvring they found a reasonably stable position and Liz gazed up at Nick. "This is the happiest night of my life."

"You've said that before," he said with an indulgent smile.

"I know. But they keep getting better and better."

Nick lowered his mouth to hers and she giggled as the slight motion threatened to spill them onto the floor. But he held her tight and soon they found an easy rhythm, and Liz lost herself in the taste and the touch of him. Afterwards they fell into a twilight sleep, lulled by the warmth of the fire and the soothing crackle of flames.

***

Liz dreamt of jagged cliffs and crashing surf somewhere far below.

She was standing naked on a snow-crusted hilltop. Her breath steamed in the icy air but she didn't feel the cold. It seemed vitally important that she reach the other side of the hill, that she find a way underneath the snow to get there, but no matter how far she walked, she remained trapped and exposed in the centre, like a tiny specimen under a microscope. The only sounds were the waves and the soft crunch as her bare feet punctured the snow. Her footprints circled back to the same spot again and again. She felt watched.

All around her the world seemed to have vanished in a fog. Something was waiting for her beneath the snow, something she was meant to find but try as she might, she couldn't get to it. Her distress became fear and she began to run blindly. It was like trying to move through treacle. The heavy snow tripped her up and she fell, sprawling, into the white expanse. She scrambled to her feet, spitting out frozen mouthfuls that tasted like chalk.

The nearby rolling waves pounded like thunder, as though

they crashed in the sky instead of on the rocky beach. There was such a sense of menace in the sound, a feeling like the world itself were growling. Reluctantly she looked up, expecting to see her watcher. Or watchers. There was nothing but blank, empty sky, bleached by the fog.

She was desperate to find the way down, the way in, the way *through*. But the snow was fathomless. She dug with her hands, burrowing into it like an animal, slowly hollowing out a tunnel. The labour seemed to last for hours but she worked tirelessly, driven by the sense that something was waiting for her, something that *needed* her.

That was when the ground began to rumble. Snow shivered from the walls of her tunnel, pouring down onto her like grain filling a silo. There was the eerie sensation of being watched, and she peered up towards the opening. It was so high above now it was barely a pinprick. Her stomach plunged and a sense of vertigo made her press her hands against the sides of the tunnel. There was no way back up. As the tremors grew more forceful, the cascading snow became a deluge. It would soon fill up the hole and trap her inside, burying her alive.

She tried to scream, but her mouth was full of snow. But it was all wrong. The snow tasted putrid, rotten. All she could do was watch helplessly as the lurching ground made the icy walls crumble around her. Snow surged down on her with relentless speed and then all was dark and silent.

***

Liz's eyes flew open and she blinked in the darkness, not knowing where she was. She pawed at her lips, spitting, but there was nothing in her mouth. The dream was fading and with it, the anxiety. The edges of the room began to define themselves and she remembered with a sigh of relief that she was home. In *their* home.

Then she saw it. The pale cold face that was looming over her. She sat up with a startled cry.

"What? What is it?" Nick asked, clutching at her to stabilise them both on the rocking air mattress.

Instantly she felt foolish. "Oh, just me being silly," she said with an embarrassed laugh. "I thought I saw a ghost." She pointed up at the plaster head, just visible in the glow of the moon and the fading firelight.

"I guess you did," said Nick, relaxing. "Hey, I don't mind you watching, old boy, but she's mine, you hear me?"

Liz giggled. "It does feel a little weird. And good lord, what a vulgar thing to do – have your own face carved on the wall."

"Don't forget Vanora," he said, pointing to the ruin directly above them. "Wonder what happened there?"

"Maybe hers wasn't a good likeness and she chipped it away in a fit of pique."

"Or he caught her in bed with the stable boy one night and destroyed it himself in a jealous rage."

"It does make you wonder," she said. "I've never lived in a place with so much history. I must do some research."

"Yeah, I don't buy that load of old rubbish Sylvia told us." He threw off the duvet and stood up, his naked body gleaming in the moonlight as he went to get the champagne bottle. "Like some tedious sentimental costume drama. 'Oh, Mr Darcy!'"

Liz admired his form as he stood silhouetted before the window. "How can anyone so gorgeous be such a philistine?" she asked.

"Philistine? Hey, this is Tesco's finest champagne!"

She laughed. "You know what I mean, Mr Anti-Romantic. And technically it's sparkling wine, not champagne."

"Said the pedant to the philistine." He held the bottle up to the window and peered at it. "There's a tiny bit left if you want it."

"Yes, please."

He upended the bottle into one glass and handed it to Liz.

"Anti-Romantic," he scoffed. "Whose idea was the air mattress?"

Liz drained the glass and, although she tried to resist, her gaze was drawn back to Carson Menrath. The blind eyes seemed to be fixed on her and she fancied that they would follow her if she moved around the room.

Nick had returned to the window, where he stood admiring the view.

"Master of all he surveys," Liz murmured sleepily. She'd meant Nick, of course, but she was suddenly unnerved that her comment could refer to the plaster head as well.

Nick turned to her and his smile glinted in the moonlight. "*All* he surveys," he said in a deep voice that filled the room. He crawled carefully back underneath the duvet without bouncing it too much and Liz nestled her head into the warmth of his chest. She wanted to make love again but she couldn't shake the uncomfortable sensation of being watched. They drifted off to sleep in each other's arms and when Liz woke later needing the loo, a strange unwillingness to reveal her nakedness to the room made her hold it in until morning.

CHAPTER 4

"So when's the party?" Rachel asked.

"The what? Sorry?"

Liz's mother clucked her tongue at Nick. "The house-warming party?" she queried slowly, as though they'd just been discussing one.

"Oh." He blinked in confusion. "Erm, well, we–"

Liz rolled her eyes at her mother and rescued him. "The removal men aren't coming for another week," she said patiently, "and we're not filling the house with drunken revellers until they have somewhere to sit."

"A week? How long does such a thing take? Honestly!" She took a delicate sip of her wine, as though personally affronted by the wait.

Rachel Barber had been less than thrilled with the house, presumably because its family-unfriendliness only further quashed her dream of grandchildren. She refused to be convinced that Liz was as happy and fulfilled as she claimed. How *could* she be without realising her full potential as a woman? The last time they'd had the tired old "you'll change your mind" argument, Liz had stormed out, slamming Rachel's door hard enough to crack a window.

That was how it had always gone with them. Rachel would push and nag and bully to get her way until Liz finally lost it and blew up at her. Then they wouldn't speak for weeks. Finally, Liz would feel guilty and ring her mother on some friendly pretence and they would go on as if nothing had happened. In this case the friendly pretence had been Wintergate.

The morning after their first night in the house had turned into a farce when the air mattress finally exploded underneath them as though objecting to their exertions. They had reluctantly returned to the Bristol flat and Liz was now counting the days until they could move in properly. In the meantime, Rachel had insisted on taking the train from London to see the place, no doubt simply so she could be the first to do so.

That was another thing Wintergate had in its favour: there was no guest room. Rachel could stay in whichever overpriced hotel in Bristol she wanted (Clevedon had no five-star establishments) and Liz and Nick could retreat to their own space, their home, their haven. Liz smiled at the thought. *Haven*. Yes, that's exactly what it was. They had planted the first seeds of the beautiful garden that would be the rest of their lives.

"A week isn't too long," Nick said cheerily.

"What about the boys?" Rachel asked. "Have you told them about the house yet?"

"I emailed them all the day the sale was finalised," she said, knowing it would gall Rachel that Liz's brothers had got the news before she had.

"I haven't heard from any of them in ages," Rachel sighed.

Liz ignored the implication of neglect. "They're fine as far as I know. Jack's got a new girlfriend apparently, but he didn't want to say more for fear of jinxing it. He said he'll come and see the house sometime next month."

"Said? So you talked to him, did you?"

"No," Liz said, trying not to grind her teeth. "I sent him an email and he texted me back. You know how difficult he is to get on the phone."

Rachel gave a huffy little snort. "I don't understand all this *typing* when one could simply be *talking*."

Her refusal to embrace technology meant she was often behind the curve. Not that that was such a bad thing; Liz had no desire to be in constant reach of texts or instant messages from her mother.

"My parents are keen to see the house too," Nick said, topping up Rachel's glass. Liz slid her own half-empty glass within range and pleaded with her eyes for more as well.

Rachel pressed her lips into an approximation of a smile and forced herself to ask how Charles and Olivia were. Liz suspected that Rachel's dislike of them stemmed from nothing more than petty class rivalry. She was the kind of conniving social climber Jane Austen could have written. One of those catty women who noticed – and remarked upon – people's accents and other such "character flaws". In less charitable moments Liz had to wonder if Rachel hadn't driven Sam, Liz's father, to his early grave with her histrionics. She'd certainly played both her Grieving Widow and Suffering Single Mother roles to the hilt. Liz was only eight at the time, but even then she recognised her mother's tendency towards melodrama.

Charles and Olivia Holland, by contrast, were absolutely lovely and Liz entertained a childish fantasy that they were her true parents. Some mix-up at the hospital had landed her with Rachel instead. Perhaps she'd even been kidnapped by the calculating woman who so adored babies and little children – except of course when they were messy or noisy or otherwise inconvenient.

"Oh, they're fine," Nick said, pretending as always that

nothing was amiss. He had the enviable ability to let Rachel's irritating habits wash right over him. "They send their love."

"Olivia offered to buy us a bathtub," Liz said delightedly. "Isn't that sweet of her?"

But Rachel was far better at this game than Liz. With a put-upon sigh she took another sip of her wine and said it was all well and good for some, she supposed, who'd had more opportunities, and oh how she wished she'd had a university education so she could have got a better job to buy fine things for her children.

Liz stared at her flatly for several seconds. "I need the loo," she said, and pushed back from the table with enough force to rattle the cutlery. She flashed Nick an apologetic grimace although she knew he'd understand. After almost four years, he was used to it.

At the sink she wrenched the tap on and let the water run until it was nearly scalding. She tried to push her mother's needling from her mind but failed utterly. Was it any wonder Liz and her three brothers had scarpered as soon as they were old enough to leave home?

Liz was the youngest. Rachel had always wanted a little girl and she hadn't been prepared to give up. It was easy to imagine her becoming more and more determined with the disappointing birth of each new boy. Liz had no idea whether her father had had any say in the matter, but the fourth time had been the charm.

Rachel had probably envisioned a pink and pretty little girl who would wear dresses and dream of being a ballerina, but she was soon disabused of that fantasy. Any girl growing up in the shadow of three older brothers was destined to be a tomboy. It wasn't rebellion, purely a survival tactic. She couldn't fight back in frills and ribbons, not when she already had so much to prove. Her brothers had a lot to prove too. Once they were fatherless they bound together like a pack of wolves, keen to show the world that they were men, not boys.

It wasn't until Liz reached high school that she discovered that boys could be more than just sparring partners and rowdy mates to have fun with. By then her brothers had begun to see their kid sister differently too and they became fiercely protective of her. No father could have been as intimidating to a potential boyfriend as Liz's three brothers, who frightened away more than one "unworthy" teen Romeo with their police interrogation tactics.

One by one her brothers went off to uni and then into their own lives, leaving Liz behind with their needy mother until the day when she too could escape. Andy, the oldest, had married a Ukrainian girl and moved to Kiev to work as a translator. Simon was a veterinarian in a tiny village in Snowdonia. And Jack was a flight attendant based in London. Liz was closest to Jack, the nearest in both age and proximity, and they got together every couple of months. As for the others, she hadn't seen Andy since Christmas three years before and Simon had gone completely native, only venturing out of Wales for weddings or funerals.

Liz turned the tap off and wiggled her fingers beneath the hand dryer. It came on with a burst of noisy warmth. She couldn't find the right position to make it stay on though, and she soon lost patience and grabbed a wad of toilet paper to dry her hands on instead.

She returned to the mirror to touch up her lipstick, more as an excuse to linger than anything else. She still couldn't fully believe that the house was theirs. It seemed like a lottery win rather than something they had plonked down their hard-earned money for. She still half-expected someone to turn up and say there'd been a mistake, that someone else had actually bought it first, and they were so very sorry, but they had to ask for the title back...

It was silly and neurotic, but Liz had never felt so passionately possessive of anything in her life. All Rachel could see were the cracks in the windows, or the cobwebs that were too high to sweep from the ceilings. No doubt she entertained her own neurotic daydreams of Liz and Nick shivering before the fire in the winter, too poor after spending thousands of pounds on repairs to afford to run the heating. Well, Rachel could fantasise all she wanted about the day that Liz would come running back to her, saying she wished she'd listened. It would never happen.

When she returned to the table she was relieved to see that Nick had steered the conversation into less incendiary territory. He looked like he was boring the pants off Rachel with all the intricacies of the property surveyor's report.

"There's a bit of woodworm but he said that's easily dealt with. And we've no dry rot or anything. The house has been really well looked after."

"That's good," Rachel said. "I must admit, when I first saw it I thought perhaps the rest of it must have fallen into the sea! Are you sure it's *quite* safe there on that little cliff?"

"I'm sure it will be fine," Liz said, smiling. "The house has been there for a hundred and fifty years and the hill itself since we were living in caves and wearing fur bikinis."

Rachel's eyes shone with maudlin affection. "Well, as long as you're happy, Elisabeth. You know that's all I want for you."

"Mother," she said firmly, "I *am* happy. I'm happier than I've ever been in my whole life." She didn't need to add *so don't try to spoil this for me.*

Rachel winced slightly at being called "Mother", a title Liz only used when she was really annoyed. She preferred her children to call her by her Christian name, as though it would somehow break the spell of ageing. After a few moments Rachel smiled, an expression of genuine warmth and sincerity. She took Liz's hands in hers and nodded, acknowledging the telling-off without retaliation.

They drank a final toast and then drove Rachel back to the station. Once they'd seen her safely to the platform and waved goodbye, Liz collapsed into Nick's arms. "Thank God that's over! I swear I'm going to kill her one of these days."

CHAPTER 5

Four years ago Nick had been in Glastonbury with his colleague and best friend Ian Morris. They were there to set up a computer system for an independent travel agency who had specifically requested their firm. However, what should have been a straightforward job was turning into a nightmare.

On top of that, Pauline had rung Nick again that morning, asking when he was going to realise he'd made the biggest mistake of his life and come back to her. Eighteen months after the breakup and she still believed there was a relationship to come back to. He was lonely on his own, but not desperate. Certainly not desperate enough to go back to the woman who'd once flung his iPod into the toilet because he didn't notice she'd cut her hair an inch shorter.

Nick had always considered himself to be fairly easygoing, but the client's woeful ignorance about computers combined with his unrealistic expectations was taking its toll. Ian had seen the shitstorm coming and suggested Nick take off for the rest of the afternoon.

He'd wandered along the high street for a while, enjoying the assortment of quirky shops offering everything from candles and tarot cards to wizard costumes and dragon skulls. There really was no other town quite like it in the whole of the UK. The sun was shining and, since he now had the afternoon off, he thought he might drive over to Wells and see the cathedral.

He was nearing his car when a jean-clad bottom caught his eye. It was sticking out from under his driver's side door. A pair of legs ending in blue hiking boots were attached to it, and when he drew nearer he heard a soft female voice calling to someone. As he watched, she crawled forward and disappeared beneath the car. If he'd turned up a minute later he might not have known anyone was under there at all.

"Um," he said, "can I help you?"

He was half-expecting to hear the clunk of a startled head connecting with the undercarriage but the girl didn't jump at all.

"Shh!" she hissed. "I've almost got him."

"Got who?"

But she didn't reply. Not to Nick anyway. He smiled as he listened to the soothing rise and fall of her voice.

"That's it, come on, you're safe now, I won't hurt you."

There was movement and a tiny animal squeak as she

captured whatever she was after, and then she was still for a moment. Her boots reappeared and then her legs and bottom. She began to twist and rock from side to side as she tried to wriggle out backwards, but now she looked fairly stuck herself.

Nick laughed. "Here, let me help you." He crouched behind her and took hold of her ankles, gently pulling her out.

She emerged in a cloud of dust, smiling and clutching a little bundle wrapped in a red fleece. "Hey, thanks!"

He returned her smile, taking in her rumpled appearance. She looked to be about his age – twenty-eight, possibly a little younger. And she was quite pretty beneath the dirt. Her blonde hair was tied in a sloppy ponytail and the woolly jumper she was wearing looked ruined from its journey underneath the car.

She was the most beautiful girl he'd ever seen.

"Look," she said, opening the bundle to show him.

Wrapped in the fleece was a small brown creature and it took him a moment to realise it was a hedgehog. It was curled tightly into a spiny ball but after a moment it peeked out, its tiny nose quivering as it scented the air. There were flecks of blood on its face, but it didn't seem to be too badly injured.

"He was lying over there by the wall when I first saw him. I thought he was dead. But then these kids came by and started poking him with a stick and I could see he was hurt. He crawled under the car to get away."

"Poor little thing," Nick said, although in truth he wasn't half as interested in the hedgehog as he was in the girl. "What are you going to do with him?"

"Take him to the hedgehog shelter," she said, as though that was obvious.

"Where's that?"

"I don't know but there must be one here. Or at least a vet. My friend would know."

The words were out of his mouth before he could think. "I'll give you a lift."

She hesitated before glancing down at the hedgehog.

"You can't drive with the little fellow in your arms," Nick said reasonably.

"Oh, I was going to walk." But she seemed to be considering the offer of a ride.

It was on the edge of his tongue to reassure her that he wasn't a serial killer before he realised that was probably exactly what real serial killers said before luring a victim into their car.

The girl was peering at his face, as though gauging whether or not she could trust him, and suddenly he was determined not to let her get away.

"I'm sorry about your jumper," he blurted, as though he were somehow to blame. He was just desperate for something to say.

She laughed, a bright, girlish sound. "This thing? It was already wrecked. I've just come down from the Tor." She jerked her chin over at a battered green rucksack lying on the ground by the rear of his car.

He blinked. "The what?"

Now it was her turn to look puzzled. "Glastonbury Tor." She added teasingly, "You know, that big hill you can see from miles away? The one you can't miss because it's-" she pointed "-right there?"

Nick looked over at the famous hill with its little tower at the summit. "Oh, that. Yes, I was wondering what that was."

She stared at him for several seconds. "You're not serious."

After enjoying the bewildered look on her face, he laughed. "No, of course I'm not serious. I've just never been up there."

"Really? Oh, you have to go! The view is spectacular."

"I'm not much of a hiker," he confessed, "and I don't really have a head for heights." That was putting it mildly. Even the view from a high window was enough to make his stomach swoop.

"Oh, but it's not like climbing a mountain. There are steps the whole way. It's perfectly safe. People have been going up there since – forever!"

He shrugged, not wanting her to know just how nervous any sort of height made him. "Well, maybe one of these days... But hey –we have to get your little friend to the hospital."

The hedgehog had begun to struggle and Nick wondered if it hadn't recovered some of its strength just from being in her arms. The notion made him smile.

"I don't think he wants to go," she said, laughing as she tried to hold the creature still.

She was dusty and dishevelled and clutching a wounded hedgehog, and Nick had the sudden crazy thought: *I could fall in love with you.*

"Listen," he said, "do you have any plans? After this, I mean?"

"No. I was on my way home."

"Well," he said, gathering his courage, "if I asked you to have dinner with me, would you say yes?"

She blinked, surprised. Then she blushed. "Oh... I..."

Seeing he'd caught her off guard, Nick pressed his advantage. "Look, I'd love to spend some time with you. And if you'd like our first date to be to the hedgehog hospital, that sounds great to me. My name's Nick."

She smiled again, her face radiant beneath the dust. "I'm Liz. And I'd love to. Have dinner, I mean. That can be our third date."

"Third?"

A mischievous look came into her eyes. "Yes. Our second will be at St Michael's tower, at the top of Glastonbury Tor."

Nick felt panic beginning to blossom inside his chest as he realised what she was proposing. Climbing the hill. The one so high you could see it for miles. The very thought of being so high was enough to trigger a sense of vertigo. But he managed to calm himself. Nothing bad could possibly happen to him in the company of this girl. And even if it could, he realised that he was more than willing to risk it.

"Okay," he said, hoping he didn't sound as nervous as he felt.

Once the hedgehog was safely in the hands of a vet, they walked to the end of the high street and followed the signs that pointed the way to the Tor. It looked daunting and Nick gamely let her lead the way, trying not to imagine what would happen if he lost his footing.

Liz kept up a steady stream of chatter as they made their way up the steep path, asking him all about his job and listening with what seemed like genuine interest when he answered. He was used to glazed eyes and stifled yawns when he told people he was a computer technician, so her reaction was a delight.

They were some way up the rambling steps now and he looked down, surprised at how far they had come already. Something of his nervousness must have shown in his face because Liz instantly distracted him.

"Now you guess what I do," she said playfully.

He laughed. "I have no idea."

"So guess!"

He tried to picture her in a variety of roles to see which one fit. "Tour guide?" he ventured.

"Nope."

"Teacher?"

"Ugh, no! I hate kids."

Her response surprised him. She was so lively and cheerful, so childlike herself. It seemed a given that she would love children.

"Really? 'Hate'?"

"Oh, I don't actually hate them. I'm just not crazy about them. I don't have a maternal bone in my body."

He very nearly told her he didn't either, but then he stopped himself. He didn't want her to think he was already sizing her up for marriage.

He cleared his throat. "Okay, then," he said, trying to imagine other careers for her. She lived in Glastonbury. Perhaps she was a witch. "Fortune teller?" he ventured.

His guess seemed to delight her, but she shook her head. "Actually, I make jewellery." She showed him a Celtic pendant with tiny hands unravelling the knot.

"That's beautiful."

"Thanks. I do a lot of fantasy stuff. Circlets, amulets, crowns." She smiled slyly as she added, "Slave bracelets."

Nick felt his stomach flutter at the realisation that she was flirting with him. He had quite forgotten they were halfway up an enormous hill. As they continued ever upwards, they chatted about books and movies, growing increasingly delighted with each new discovery about the other. Nick had never believed in fate, but surely this wonderful girl couldn't have dropped into his path by sheer accident.

It was the middle of July and the sun was high and golden in the sky. Along the way Liz pointed out various landmarks, most of which Nick had heard of.

"Is that Silbury Hill?" he asked, eyeing a curious-looking peak in the distance.

"No, you can't see it from here. I've been there, though. It's a trip. To imagine cavemen building that! And still no one has any idea what it is or what it was for. I wish I could climb it, but you're not allowed to anymore."

"That's probably just as well," Nick said. "Like Stonehenge. I remember my grandfather telling me that they actually sold little chisels by the roadside when he was a boy, and you could walk right up and chip off a piece for a souvenir."

Liz looked horrified. "That's appalling!"

"Oh, I think we can forgive them. We did eventually evolve a preservationist mindset."

"Yes, but who knows what we might have destroyed before then? Or driven into hiding." She gave a wistful sigh. "You know, sometimes I wonder if the world is full of magic and we've just lost the ability to sense it."

When they finally reached the top of the hill they felt the full bite of the wind blowing across Somerset. It clawed its way through the ruins of St Michael's Tower and seemed determined to convince them it was actually winter.

"Bloody hell," Liz gasped, her teeth chattering, "it wasn't like this earlier!"

"Yeah, it is a bit nippy," Nick said, trying to put a brave face on it. He was cold too, but more than that, he didn't like the feeling that the wind was trying to push him off the hill. He wished Liz hadn't said that about things being driven into hiding. An unsettling memory suddenly came back to him, something he hadn't thought about for years.

He was very young, probably five or six years old, and his dad had taken him to the park to show him how to fly a kite. Nick had been terrified from the moment the brightly coloured eagle soared from his hands into the sky, the twine spooling out so fast it made his heart pound. What would happen when the twine ran out? Would he be pulled off his feet? What if he couldn't drop the handles of the spool fast enough and the kite carried him away over the hills?

The eagle looked far too real. He didn't like its eyes. As the painted bird of prey darted and swooped high overhead, it stared down at him as though he were soon to be its dinner. He didn't know which was worse – the idea that he might be carried away, or that the eagle was alive and waiting for the moment to attack.

He felt watched, helpless, even though *he* was holding the string. The kite didn't feel like a pet on a leash, more like something ferocious he had captured by mistake. Something that was angry with him. He'd seen hawks dive before and he stared in horror at the eagle, expecting it to come screeching down at him any second.

His father shouted with excitement beside him, oblivious to Nick's distress. Seconds later, the twine reached its limit and Nick felt the full length of it yank in his hand. The wind hauled at the kite, hauled at *him*, pulling him up onto his toes. And – he couldn't help it – he let go.

His father gave a cry and made a mad grab for it but the wind was too strong. It carried the eagle up into the sky and out of sight, the spool dangling at the end of what seemed like miles of twine. Nick was instantly filled with relief, but it was soon replaced by an overwhelming sense of shame. He was horrified at the loss of the kite and worried that his father would be angry, or at the very least, disappointed in him. He buried his face in his hands, wanting only to crawl away and hide.

After a while his father spoke. "Well," he said casually, a smile in his voice, "I guess he's flown home to his nest."

It was absolutely the right thing to say. Nick was so grateful it was all he could do to hold back the tears. He couldn't remember the rest of the afternoon, but the eagle had haunted his dreams for weeks. He woke up many times, soaked with sweat, afraid to turn on the bedside light for fear the giant bird would be perched there, eyes gleaming with hatred, beak sharp as a razor, ready to tear him to pieces.

"Hey, are you all right?"

Nick shook off the memory, blinking in surprise. He felt like he'd been dreaming. Liz was looking at him with concern on her face. "Yeah. Sorry." He shook his head. "Weird. I just flashed on something from when I was a kid, that's all. Something I hadn't thought of for years."

She frowned slightly. "Must not have been a good memory. You looked absolutely terrified."

"I'm okay now," he said. For some reason he didn't want to share the episode with her and he was glad when she didn't press him.

They held hands all the way down the Tor. Just before they reached the car, he noticed a kestrel hovering in the air, preparing to dive. He pushed the sight to the back of his mind, where he hoped it would stay.

CHAPTER 6

It was cold in the empty house. Liz wandered from room to room, wondering how they were ever going to fill all the space. The bookshelves in the enormous bedroom gave her a flutter of excitement, but the vast expanses of bare floor had the opposite effect. They made her feel defenceless.

It was hard not to wonder if Vanora had felt the same all those years ago. Had she stood here too, frightened of her new life, worried that she wouldn't belong? The defaced alabaster bust could offer no reply, and Liz found she didn't like looking at it. It made her think of a corpse, nibbled by insects. With a shudder she turned away and headed into the corridor. Her footsteps were far too loud.

It felt strange to be here without Nick. Wrong, even. When they had first seen the house together it had been quirky and welcoming, but now the rooms seemed oddly silent, like breath held before a scream.

When she reached the stairs, she gazed up at the stained-glass window. Pan danced in the centre of the stone circle, attended by fairies and other magical creatures. Liz wanted to imagine that the design had been Vanora's idea, that she had felt the same kinship with the world of fantasy that Liz and Nick did. Only there was something not quite right about the scene. Pan's slitted eyes glowed a deep, unsettling crimson, giving off a feeling of menace rather than mischief. And the fairies seemed less playful than they had at first glance. The stained glass was chipped in several places, giving their wings a broken, bent look. And was that patch of white meant to represent snow? It looked more like a writhing mass of worms.

Suddenly she flashed on her dream of being stranded on the snowy hilltop, exposed to the cold gaze of stars high above in the night sky. She remembered digging deep inside the snow, searching for something. Then there was the terror as the tunnel collapsed, burying her alive.

Liz shook her head, pushing away the weird imagery. What the hell was wrong with her today? She looked at her watch. The removal men were already an hour late. Had they got lost? Surely they would have rung her if so. She paced along the landing as she sent Nick a text update.

Still waiting. Grrr.

As she had already done several times, she found herself

standing before the door at the end of the minstrels' gallery. "The Door to Nowhere", they had dubbed it, and its twin below. The urge to open it was irresistible and her hand trembled with anticipation as she turned the knob, hesitating only a moment before throwing it open. As before, there was only a wall of bricks beyond. And the exact same sight would greet her if she opened the one downstairs. But something in her nature made her keep trying. She smiled as she imagined a portal into Narnia or Middle Earth or Westeros.

The bleep of her phone jolted her back to the present. Nick had texted her a sympathetic smiley and a row of flowers. She stroked her finger over the tiny pictures on the screen and decided to go outside and wait for the van. If she started making her way down the long driveway, it was bound to materialise.

She descended the stairs, enjoying the grand view of the room as she did. She could almost hear the voices from the past, whispering across the expanse of time. The idea of ghosts flitted across her mind, giving her a brief frisson. When she reached the bottom of the staircase, she was half-tempted to turn round, imagining Vanora on the landing. But something kept her from looking back.

The image of the mutilated bust forced itself into her mind

instead, banishing the romantic fantasy and replacing it with snapshots of a nightmare. She saw the charred and mangled remains of Vanora's face, heard the crackle of flames. There were hands clawing at the empty air. The smell of blood and smoke. Voices screaming. And beneath it all, far in the distance, the scrabble of tiny feet.

Liz turned away, pressing her hands to her ears and closing her eyes tightly, shutting it all out. It wasn't real. None of it. She took several slow, deep breaths, trying to calm herself. Her insides crawled.

Go away, go away, go away, she chanted in her mind. She was afraid to open her eyes. But surely nothing in the real world could be as bad as what was playing out on the inner screen of her eyelids.

She whirled to face the room, opening her eyes wide as she did. There was nothing there. Nothing but the empty hall, the empty staircase, the empty landing. Clouds moved in the sky beyond the window, shifting the light through the colourful glass. Pan appeared to be laughing as he danced in the writhing snow.

Liz shook off the chill, wondering at that inexplicable moment of terror. "Vivid imagination" hardly seemed capable of covering it, but what other explanation was there? People got spooked in empty houses, that was all. Even beautiful ones they had just bought and loved with all their heart.

A tiny flash of resentment flared in her mind: if Nick had been here, it wouldn't have happened. The feeling startled her and she pushed it away, baffled. Where had that come from? She didn't resent Nick at all. In fact, she'd been secretly delighted by the thought of being here by herself, of overseeing the process of moving in. She'd imagined herself like a stage designer, directing the removal men as to where to put everything, chatting with them, making them cups of tea. She'd even bought a tin of biscuits to share with them. Where the hell were they? Her watch said it was nearly 11:00.

She pushed open the door and moved through the chilly porch, out into the sunshine. It was one of those rare days the English weather occasionally granted, bright and lovely and rain-less. A day for picnics and walks in the park. The kind of day where nothing bad could happen. The sun warmed her face and only the faintest breeze stirred the leaves. Beyond, she could just make out the gentle sloshing of the waves on the shingle beach.

She wandered across to the barren patch of ground, to the missing half of Wintergate. This was where the fire had been. The fire that had claimed the lives of Carson and Vanora Menrath, and destroyed the entire west wing of the house. It was so sad. She imagined flames licking the sky, blotting the horizon with black smoke. People had died here. The thought sent a little chill through her, but fortunately there was no resurgence of the terrible imagery she'd seen inside.

It was beautiful, in its way. Picturesque. Like the ruins of a tiny castle. She stroked one lichen-encrusted stone spire and was delighted to see a ladybird trundling across a leafy vine. She placed her hand in its way and it happily clambered onto her finger, making no distinction between her and the plant. Its little legs moved ceaselessly, carrying it up one finger and down another, across her hand and up her arm. The ladybird seemed so peaceful, so present and content in the world. It wasn't troubled by nightmares or worries. It just *was*.

When the insect finally unhinged its wings and took flight, Liz closed her eyes and pictured herself in similar harmony with her surroundings. She felt lulled, peaceful. She couldn't wait to explore it all. Poets' Walk sounded like fairyland, a place of glamour and mystery, of endless possibilities. The house would heal, and with it, the ghostly memories. Their happiness would transform it.

She opened her eyes and looked over at the bricked-up

oblongs. While she loved the "Doors to Nowhere", maybe they should turn them into windows. It seemed a shame to be deprived of the view. But there was a flicker of disquiet at the thought. Would it be like peering into a ghost house? What if one day another face should peer back?

With a shudder at the unwelcome thought, she glanced at her watch. And frowned. That couldn't be right. It had shown the same time the last time she looked. She fished her mobile out of the pocket of her jeans and thumbed it on. It was past noon. Had she really been out here for over an hour? Her legs and back felt stiff, as though she'd been standing in one place for ages. Even weirder, there were two new texts from Nick. How had she not heard the phone bleep?

She quickly texted back, letting him know that she was still waiting, but that she expected they'd turn up any second. She hoped that was true. Suddenly the idea of spending the whole day alone here seemed intensely unnerving.

It was so quiet. *Too* quiet. And yet, through the silence, she sensed movement. A tiny pulse, a little throb. There was a feeling of expectation, as if something were waiting. But waiting for what? The air was a void from which anything might emerge. Around her the darkness contracted and swelled, like the shadow of a slowly beating heart.

Desperate to keep the intrusive images at bay, she started off down the hill, moving at a brisk pace. She didn't like the idea of walking away from the house and she found herself glancing back more than once, like a child nervously wandering out of sight of its parents. She couldn't begin to imagine how she'd managed to spook herself so thoroughly.

Halfway down the drive, she stopped. She could hear something – a low, sonorous hum. The ground was vibrating beneath her feet. Her heart leapt with sudden panic as she thought of earthquakes. She wanted to run, but she was frozen where she stood, paralysed with fear and indecision.

But the ominous rumbling resolved itself into the thrum of an engine, and she sagged with overwhelming relief as the removals van came into view, lumbering slowly up the hill.

CHAPTER 7

Nick looked at the clock and wondered how Liz was getting on. She'd been sending him texts throughout the morning, fretting about whether the removal men would turn up and then, when they finally did, whether any of their possessions would be missing or broken. He had wanted to be there with her, to help direct the proceedings, but a work crisis had come up and Greg, his boss, had called an emergency meeting. It was a simple problem, easily sorted, but wiser minds than his felt it needed the input of "the team".

Nick was hardly a part of the so-called team and the meeting was going exactly where he had predicted: nowhere. It was all so pointless, so *tedious*. He knew exactly what everyone would say, what position everyone would take. They might as well be actors in a play, reading from the same stale script that had been underwhelming audiences for years. He wished that one day someone would surprise him, do something mad and unexpected.

But, as the old saying went, you should be careful what you wish for. Liz's last text had lamented the freshly broken door of the fridge-freezer. It had been terrifying, she said, watching the two men (only two!) struggle up the main staircase with it, down the long hallway, and then down the back stairs to the kitchen. They'd grumbled about the house's "crazy layout" and she'd listened to their swearing from the safety of the bathroom, where their new claw-foot bathtub had pride of place before the stained-glass window. As it had been organised by Nick's parents, *its* arrival and installation had gone quickly and smoothly.

Nick knew he should have let his parents treat them to a better removal company too but he was as stubborn as Liz in his own way, particularly about accepting charity. Wintergate was their first home and it was important to them both that they handle everything themselves. They agreed that it wouldn't feel wholly *theirs* otherwise.

Whilst Liz had grown up battling Rachel's smothering influence, Nick had been spoilt by parents determined to give their only child the moon. He'd never been able to make them understand that there were certain things he needed to do on his own. It was a wonder they'd never been robbed blind by con artists, such was their fervent goodwill. If someone needed something and they could provide it, why on earth shouldn't they?

They had already offered to help with any repairs that needed doing, and Nick knew that as soon as they saw the cracked panes of glass and the peeling wallpaper in the bedroom that they would insist. They were generous to a fault but sometimes their generosity made him feel useless. Between them, he and Liz made a decent living, but they were not well off. It was often hard to find the right balance and in this case their bloody-mindedness had clearly not been the best course.

Liz thought Nick's parents were wonderfully gracious but in her unfortunate experience nothing came without a price. Rachel was a merciless scorekeeper, so Liz had been conditioned to expect fallout from any gesture. Nick had worked on her over the years and it had been a real revelation to Liz to learn that not everyone had ulterior motives. Still, her instinctive reaction to gifts was a kind of embarrassed unworthiness. He was pleasantly surprised that she'd accepted his mother's offer of the bathtub so readily. It showed real progress.

The business meeting was going in circles. Greg was rambling on to the others about areas that didn't directly concern Nick, so he stole another peek at his phone. Liz had texted again to say that the bedroom was taking shape. Their bed was now in place and she'd put the sheets and duvet on it while the removal men struggled down the back stairs with the dining table and chairs.

More grumbling. More cursing. They'd tried to pass things in through the ground floor windows but none of the individual panes were large enough to admit the furniture. Now they were complaining about the number of boxes.

"Guys?" Nick said, interrupting Ben's third repetition of his strident opinion. "Mind if I nip out to make a quick call?" Without waiting for an answer he headed for the door, thumbing the button to speed-dial Liz's mobile.

"Oh, thank God," she said at once, "a friendly voice!"

"What's going on?"

She lowered her voice and he could hear her footsteps as she presumably retreated out of earshot. "These guys are *awful!* All they've done is moan and complain the whole time. We have too many stairs. The back stairs are too narrow. The windows aren't big enough. It's like we asked them to do it as a favour and lied about the size of the job. You *told* them there were stairs."

"How far along are they?"

"I think they're done with all the big things. Now it's just boxes. But they're not happy about all the books we own. One guy asked if we'd read all of them and I thought he was trying to be friendly so I gave him that old chestnut, 'Who wants a library full of books you've already read?' Know what he said? 'Then why don't you sell them off?' Unbelievable!"

"Dodgy Removals dot com," Nick muttered. "Sounds like they're more used to removing big-screen tellies and stereo equipment. Through broken windows."

Liz laughed. "Well, I'm not making them any tea."

"Want me to have a word with them?"

"God, no! Then they'll know I snitched! But I'm definitely letting the company know how rubbish they were. I really wish we'd taken your parents up on their offer now."

"I know, me too. I've been thinking about that all morning."

"How's the crisis there?"

Nick sighed dismissively. "Just the usual nonsense. Greg and Ben are going at it while Ian and I make faces and roll our eyes. Certainly not worth me being stuck here while you're putting up with those guys."

"Hey, I'm all right. It's just good to hear your voice. Makes a change from all the swearing. I think the poor house is starting to blush."

"Well, there's about to be some swearing here too. I'll see if I can get away. It's nothing Greg can't handle on his own; he just wants me here as backup. As usual, it's someone else's cock-up but he's trying to put it on all of us. It's like bloody school sports."

Suddenly there was a terrific crash from Liz's end, followed by a distant shout.

"What was that?"

"I'm not sure I want to know," Liz moaned.

They both listened as the shouting grew more and more distressed.

"Shit," Liz said worriedly. "That sounds serious. I'd better go and see what's happened."

Nick made a snap decision. "That's it – I'm out of here. Greg can clean up his own mess. I should have been there with you all along. See you as soon as I can." He rang off and stalked back into the meeting, interrupting a heated discussion about a client somebody had apparently lost. "I've got an emergency at home I need to sort out," he said, "so I'm afraid I'm going to have to go."

Greg's face fell and he looked helplessly around the room. He opened his mouth to protest but Nick held up his hand.

"Sorry, but my wife needs me more than you do. You can ring me if there's anything urgent." With that he turned on his heel and left, his heart pounding from the thrill of having stood up to his boss and been so forthright about it. It was a good feeling and he caught himself smiling as he drove home.

His phone bleeped as he reached a traffic queue at the Clifton suspension bridge. It was a text from Liz.

Broken leg! Ambulance on the way. Chaos! Pls get here soon.

"Jesus," Nick breathed. He flashed his bridge pass at the sensor and crossed as fast as he dared. He found himself stuck behind a trundling Range Rover with a Dutch number plate, frustrating him for a long mile before he could finally overtake. Once free, he floored the accelerator.

He felt bad about the man's injury, but he couldn't help the natural worry that he and Liz would be somehow held responsible. Surely not. Surely removal companies had to have insurance, even dodgy ones. Unless there was some egregious flaw in the stairs or the floor, he didn't see how it could be their fault. Given what Liz had said about them, it was more likely the result of carelessness or incompetence.

Fortunately, the M5 was blissfully free of traffic for once and he counted himself lucky it wasn't Friday afternoon, when the motorway would be bumper to bumper with holidaymakers heading south to Cornwall for the weekend.

As he sped up the hill to Wintergate he saw the flashing lights of an ambulance waiting outside. Liz came running out to meet him. She threw her arms around him and clung to him, trembling. Nick felt the dampness of her tears against his face.

"What happened?" he asked at last.

"It's completely crazy," she panted, shaking her head. "The one guy – Dave – claims there was a loose stair rod that tripped him as he was going up the front stairs. He was carrying a heavy box and he dropped it and fell all the way down to the bottom. His leg's broken. He screamed horrible things at me, saying he was going to sue us, that the house wasn't safe. But his partner and I looked at the stairs and we couldn't find a loose rod anywhere."

"You think he's just trying to put it on us?"

"I don't know. He was really nasty about it. Of course I know he's in pain and I feel terrible about it, but frankly, he's been nasty all day – long before this happened. Do you think we should call the police? Is it even a police matter?"

"No idea. But you said his partner agreed there was nothing wrong with the stairs?"

She nodded.

"Then we're probably in the clear," he said cautiously. "I don't see how they could blame us."

They looked up as the ambulance doors slammed shut and the vehicle drove away, revealing a scruffy young man in faded jeans and a football T-shirt who had been standing behind it. He looked extremely rattled.

"That's his partner," Liz whispered. "Tom."

"I want to talk to him," Nick said. He crossed the forecourt and introduced himself. In his white shirt and tie he felt a bit like a teacher confronting a pupil.

Tom mumbled a greeting and glanced back at the house uneasily, shaking his head. "I'll tell you what I already told her," he said, jerking his chin at Liz. "Our Dave's a good guy. A hard worker. But he ain't never had no accident like this before."

"How badly was your friend hurt?" Nick asked.

"Broke his leg, didn't he? Won't be doing anything for a while."

"I'm very sorry." Nick hesitated before continuing. "Listen, my wife tells me you and she both had a look at the stairs?"

Tom's eyes flashed. "Dave ain't no liar," he barked. "That's his blood on the floor in there, innit?"

Nick raised his palms in a placatory gesture. "Whoa, whoa, I'm not accusing anyone of anything. I'm just trying to understand what happened here. We need to know if it's necessary to involve the police."

At the mention of the police, Tom paled and shuffled his feet. The silence stretched between them for interminable seconds before he spoke. "No, I don't think that's called for," he said, staring at the ground. He chewed his lip, thinking. Finally he raised his head and met Nick's eyes. "I did have a look and I didn't see nothing wrong with them stairs. It's the craziest thing. Can't figure how it happened. Must've just lost his footing is all."

Nick didn't know what else to say so he was glad when Liz took over.

"There are only a few boxes left, right?" she asked Tom, who nodded sullenly. "Why don't you just put them in the hall and Nick and I can take it from there?"

"Yeah," he said, seeming happy with the compromise. Nick supposed he'd been dreading having to face the stairs again after what had happened to his friend.

"Pretty inauspicious beginning," Liz said with a wan smile.

Nick put his arm around her and followed her into the hall. The paramedics must have wiped the floor but the thin spaces between the mosaic tiles were still dark with blood.

Liz shuddered. "There's more on the stairs," she said.

"We'll get it cleaned. I'm sure my parents can recommend someone good."

He took the stairs slowly, bending down to test each stair rod as he went. All of them were fixed firmly in place, holding the runner flush against the steps and risers. Clearly it had been an accident. And while he didn't like the thought of anyone suffering a fall like that, at least he and Liz weren't to blame for it. It had just been their rotten luck to wind up with the world's worst removal men.

"It's the strangest thing," Liz said darkly.

"What is?"

"It was as if the house didn't want them here."

Her words unnerved him and it was a few moments before he could shake the chill.

"Come on," he said, kissing her on the cheek. "Show me what you've done with the place."

CHAPTER 8

Wintergate was home. *Their* home.

It was filled with their furniture, their books and their decorations. Liz had never felt so comfortable anywhere. Even her first flat in Glastonbury, *100% Liz* though it was, hadn't been as satisfying as this. Best of all, even with everything they owned now in place, there was still so much *room*.

For the first time, there were actually empty shelves on the bookcase. And for a true bibliophile, the only thing more beautiful than shelves upon shelves of books was having room for more. They had immersed themselves one weekend in the full-on geeky joy of organising their library. Along the way they found several books they had given up for lost, but which must have only been hidden in the numerous disorganised stacks.

Certain favourite authors had shelves entirely to themselves. The names read like a list of magic invocations: Moorcock, Jordan, Smith, Bradbury, Clarke... Liz's cherished *Elfquest* comics and graphic novels sat on the bottom shelf alongside Nick's *Conan* ones and their small manga collection. And her ancient and battered Tolkien paperbacks had pride of place next to Nick's first editions. *Lord of the Rings* had suffered many obsessive rereads over the years, bearing with dignity the torn pages and chocolate fingerprints of the girl who'd received them as a gift from her father when she was very young. She would never replace them.

Then there were all the non-fiction books: Nick's technical manuals and Liz's arts and crafts texts. And as well as a place for the books, they now had a proper home for all their movies and games. They had designated the downstairs room as the home cinema, media library and dining room.

Scattered throughout the house were all the little figurines Liz had collected or made over the years. Animals, dragons and fairies danced along shelves and mantelpieces, looking not a bit out of place amongst the mythological creatures depicted in the stained glass and carved into the ornate staircase.

And Liz's new workshop was a delight. She had set it up on the minstrels' gallery where it ended at the Door to Nowhere. The area was wide enough to accommodate her worktable and she loved the big airy space with its commanding view of the main hall. The light was perfect and the placement made her feel like a queen. The second bedroom in the leaky Bristol flat had been tiny, with her tools and materials housed in teetering stacks of shoeboxes and partitioned plastic toolboxes. Now all the beads, charms, clasps, chains and crystals were in a little wooden dresser she'd found in a charity shop. And there was still room for more!

Nick always said that her workshop looked like a bomb had gone off in a pixie factory. Liz was sure it wouldn't be long before the whole area was cluttered and disorganised again, but for now at least everything was neat and tidy, with all the bits and pieces tucked away.

"I can't wait to show you the house," she enthused to her brother over the phone. "It's the most perfect place in the world."

"I'm so happy to hear that," Jack said. "I hated to think of you drowning in that tiny flat in Bristol." He gave a wistful little sigh. "I suppose this means you'll never move to London, then?"

"Sorry, but no bloody way. Maybe if our dear mother moved to France. Or America. You know I like having plenty of miles between us. Australia would be ideal."

"Oh, I know," Jack laughed. "Of course she moans about Andy and Simon whenever she gets a chance, like they abandoned her. She's terrified I might meet someone on a trip to New York or somewhere and leave her behind."

Liz shuddered. "Please don't. Then I'd be all she had."

"I told her the other day it wouldn't kill her to go and visit Simon in Wales. Or even Andy in Kiev. But you know how pigheaded she is."

"Well, she's coming to our house-warming party," Liz said.

"Seriously?"

"Uh-huh. Didn't I tell you she's already been out here to see the place? She bullied her way into coming before we'd even moved our stuff in."

Jack laughed. "I guess I shouldn't be surprised. Just pray she doesn't ruin your party."

"She ignored all my hints that she wouldn't enjoy it. Oh, I wish *you* were coming."

"Me too, Liz. But I'm flying all that week and I can't get the time off. Don't worry – I'll see it some other time. And it will be much nicer if I can visit without our darling mother."

Liz couldn't argue with that, although she had been secretly hoping that Jack could keep Rachel occupied at the party and out of Liz's hair.

"By the way, Liz, would you stop pacing?"

"What?"

"I can hear your shoes clacking on the floor. It's really distracting."

Liz held the phone out and frowned at it for a moment. "I'm sitting at my desk, Jack. I haven't moved since I rang you."

Silence spooled out between them while they both listened. Liz heard nothing.

"See? There it is again," Jack said. "Tap-tap-tap. Have you got a neighbour with really noisy feet?"

Liz felt her skin prickle. She rose from her chair and walked to the head of the stairs, glancing nervously along the corridor and down into the hall towards the bedroom. But Nick was at work, and she knew she was alone in the house. She strained to listen but whatever Jack was hearing, it wasn't coming from her end of the phone.

"We don't have any neighbours," she said, "and I can't hear any–"

She froze. There it was. But it didn't sound like a neighbour stomping around. It sounded like someone creeping, moving so softly as to be almost inaudible. Someone who didn't want to be heard. Her gaze strayed to the door. The one that went nowhere.

When Jack spoke again she jumped, then she pressed the phone against her chest to muffle the buzz of his voice while she listened hard, trying to decide where the sound was coming from. The footsteps – if that's what they were – were fading. But she had definitely heard them. It sounded as though they were coming through the wall. She edged towards the door, and it was a long time before she was able to turn the knob. When nothing but a wall of bricks confronted her, she felt a little silly, but no less unnerved.

She lifted the phone to her ear again. "Jack. I heard it. I think maybe someone's outside."

He was silent for a moment. "Do you want to call the police?"

"I don't think so. It's the middle of the day. I can't imagine someone trying to break into a house in broad daylight."

"Is it the postman?"

"He wouldn't be over in the ruins."

"Kids playing?"

She shook her head, frustrated. Every suggestion only reinforced the inexplicable nature of the sounds. What she had heard were footsteps. Footsteps on a hardwood floor. But there *was* no hardwood floor beyond that wall. The sealed doorway led into empty air, and the ground below had only the barest remnants of a foundation. The rest was just grass and weeds. Liz ran a finger over the bricks that covered the recess in the doorway, wondering for just a moment if...

"I can't hear it anymore," Jack said.

"Me neither."

Jack gave a forced little laugh. "Hey, maybe it was on my end after all," he said. "Or the lines got crossed. Or something."

"Or something," Liz repeated, not at all convinced. She knew what she'd heard.

"Anyway, did I tell you I'm going to Hawaii in December?"

The magical word "Hawaii" distracted her from the unease. "Really? Oh my god, now I'm jealous!"

"So is everyone else. Mind you, it'll probably be cold but I'm going to go up to the observatory on Maunakea. I can't wait!"

"Please take a million pictures," Liz pleaded. "I've always wanted to go there."

"Don't worry. I'm taking all three of my cameras. More than anything, I want to get some time-lapse photos of the night sky."

The thought of Hawaii, even of snow-capped Maunakea, made her think of a tropical paradise. It was enough to banish the memory of the phantom footsteps.

When she got off the phone she busied herself with work. Someone wanted a set of Elvish jewellery for a small cosplay event in Brighton. Liz had a few circlets and arm bands in stock but she needed to make a series of ear cuffs to go with them. Those were fun because they transformed a person more than any other element could, giving the illusion of a pointed ear decorated with wire and jewels. Liz had a mannequin head she used for the purpose and she set it in the middle of her blissfully empty table. Now that it wasn't cluttered with boxes full of all her jewellery findings, she had plenty of room to spread out in.

Everything was so easy to find now, she felt like she could weep with joy. She laid out the different gauges of wire, pliers and wire cutters, and began twisting the first cuff into shape, looping it around the mannequin's left ear and forming it into a delicate point. Then she turned the head around and did the same on the right ear. Once she was sure the cuffs were the same size, she removed them and began the intricate decorative work, wrapping each one with smaller gauge wire and twisting it around the cuff with pliers.

It was Liz's personal preference to make one cuff quite plain and decorate the other, so after she finished a pair, she arbitrarily chose one to get creative with. This was her favourite part, doing solo designs that would be unique. She pulled out the hatbox where she kept all the one-of-a-kind pieces. Some of them she had bought, but many of them were simply pretty things she had found over the years and collected like a magpie in the hope of being able to use them someday.

The House of Frozen Screams

She emptied the box and began choosing oddments she thought Elvish role-players would like best. There was a gleaming green ivy leaf that had come off an expensive wall decoration of her mother's. Now at last it would have a home. She could add some glass-faceted beads and a tiny piece of green-tinted chain. For another, she used a grey pearl from an earring whose mate she had lost years ago. She tried on each cuff as she went, enjoying the effect.

She finished fashioning another ear cuff and rummaged through the pile of gems and jewels for something special, stopping short when she saw the dragonfly. She stared at it in disbelief for a while before daring to pick it up. It sat perched on the end of a hatpin and Liz had thought it long gone, lost in the move from Glastonbury to Bristol.

Liz had bought it for herself in an antique shop when she was a teenager. The shopkeeper told her it was Edwardian art nouveau, which sounded wildly exotic. The pin itself was about eight inches long, with a gold-plated dragonfly on the end. Its body was inlaid with a stunning fire opal. The insect looked so realistic Liz was sure she'd heard it buzzing in the shop. It had been marked down to ten pounds because there was a crack in the elaborate gold swirl the dragonfly rested upon.

She had tried to copy it for her own designs but the intricate detail was beyond her humble talents. She had worn it as a scarf pin a couple of times but it really wasn't practical. And as she had nowhere to display it, it had been consigned to the magpie box. Now as she looked at it again she remembered the joy she'd had on first seeing it. She stroked the fire opal, admiring its vivid colours. Within were shades of fire and blood.

Finding it again felt like a good omen and Liz smiled at her surroundings. A purple velvet pincushion sat on the corner of her desk and Liz pushed the hatpin into it. The sunlight caught the opal dragonfly and flashed as if to promise Liz that she would never lose such treasures again – not here.

Her earlier nervousness was now completely forgotten and she barely heard herself as she whispered, "I love this house."

CHAPTER 9

That weekend they went exploring. First they wandered along the seafront, enjoying their new surroundings. There were several places to eat along the way and they vowed to try every one of them, beginning with a pub called the Moon and Sixpence, which sat directly opposite the main attraction.

Clevedon Pier was the very picture of Victorian charm and elegance. The wooden promenade ran along a series of spidery green iron spans that were like delicate legs stepping into the light surf of the Bristol Channel. The planks and benches were inlaid with hundreds of little brass plaques – names of sponsors, gifts, memorials and cryptic inscriptions.

They reached the pierhead, where they had tea and Bakewell tarts at a little pagoda, gazing out across the water towards the south coast of Wales. It was a crisp, clear day and they could see the Severn Bridge to the right and the islands of Steep Holm and Flat Holm to the left. A few gulls cried overhead and there was the purr of a boat somewhere on the water, but otherwise the only sound was the gentle lapping of waves beneath their feet.

Liz found herself wondering just where Carson and Vanora had met. Was it at the end of the pier, where both might have been admiring the view? Or somewhere along the main promenade? She supposed Vanora had been with a chaperone, her mother possibly. Had Carson introduced himself, kissing her gloved hand? Or had they secretly made eyes at one another behind their minder's back?

"Where are you?" Nick asked.

Liz closed her eyes serenely. "A hundred years in the past."

"Ah. Our ghosts."

The word touched something in her mind, a memory, something that seemed familiar. But it was like an aspect of a fading dream; she couldn't focus on it.

Nick laughed. "No need to look so serious," he said. "I was thinking about the Menraths too. I wonder if they walk the halls at night, shaking their fists at the invaders."

"Have you heard them?" Liz asked cautiously, hoping Nick wouldn't think she was serious.

He sighed. "I wish. That would be something, wouldn't it? It's hard not to imagine a house like that full of spirits."

"But you haven't heard any clanking chains?"

"Nothing so dramatic. Just the odd creak here and there."

Liz opened her mouth to say that she'd heard it too. That and something else. Except she couldn't remember what exactly. Her dreams had been more vivid than usual and very weird since moving in, so maybe it was all in her imagination. "Yeah," she said at last. "Creaky floorboards. Only that and nothing more."

Hand in hand they walked the length of the pier again, admiring the view for a while before heading back to the toll house and gift shop, where Liz picked up a handful of postcards to send to her brothers, her in-laws and her friend Gwen in Glastonbury. After some guilty consideration she added one for Rachel to the stack.

A small shelf held books on local history and one title jumped out at Liz: *Clevedon: Through the Eyes of Time,* by William L Pritchard. It was full of old photographs of the town and all its prominent features, including Wintergate. There was one of the exterior of the house, showing how it had looked when it was whole. The west wing had even larger window bays and more extravagant detailing all round.

"Nick, look – our house is in here!"

"Damn," he said, pointing, "looks like that was the best bit."

A stone unicorn sat just above what must have been the master bedroom, facing down a gargoyle that had survived the destruction. "Oh, I wish that was still there," Liz said.

Nick smiled fondly. "I've never lived in a landmark before." Then he laughed, reading aloud. "'Menrath's Folly'?"

Liz peered at the text. It pretty much just confirmed what the estate agent had told them, only she'd left out the far more entertaining moniker the locals had given it at the time.

"Hey, I kind of like that," Liz said.

"We could change it to 'Hollands' Folly'," Nick offered. "That's what everyone else seems to think anyway."

"Ha! Folly or not, it's paradise to me."

The next page had a small interior shot of the main hall and staircase, looking almost exactly as it did now, but best of all was the small grainy picture of Carson and Vanora, presumably a wedding portrait despite its sombre appearance. In a typical Victorian pose, Carson stood beside his seated wife, one hand resting on the back of her chair. He looked exactly as he did in the carved bust, flinty and dour. Vanora was dwarfed by him; she was a slight, frail-looking lady with a melancholy air and big, sad eyes. She was holding a spray of flowers.

"The deliriously happy couple," Nick said. "I can't tell if they're going to a wedding or a funeral."

Liz laughed. "They wouldn't have taken a picture for a funeral, silly."

"Hey, the Victorians used to take pictures of their dead relatives."

"She's carrying a posy," Liz pointed out. "But I agree they don't look overjoyed."

"Poor girl looks terrified."

"Well, she probably was. She was a stranger in a strange land. And if she was as unstable as Sylvia said…"

She had just noticed the caption. It said simply: *The sinister Carson Menrath and his wife Vanora.*

"Sinister?" Nick said. "Why's that, I wonder?"

Liz shrugged. "It doesn't say. I won't argue with it, though. He does look pretty intimidating."

Liz paged through the rest of the book, but there was nothing else about Wintergate or the Menraths. Still, it was filled with wonderful old sepia photos of the town in earlier eras. Horse-drawn carts and early motorcars made their way down streets crowded with the ghosts of people in motion. A Victorian family posed awkwardly on the pebbled beach while the blurs of children swept around them like smoke. At the end of the book was a list of references to Clevedon in literature and, later, in films.

"I've got to have this," Liz said.

Their route home took them past a small arcade and a marine lake that was filled and emptied by the tide. A gently winding path led them through the beautiful wooded area of Poets' Walk, which Pritchard's book told them was so named because Coleridge and Tennyson had wandered there once upon a time. A charming little turret looked out over the Channel, with a fantastic view of the pier. Liz leaned out one of the open stone windows to see better but Nick wasn't tempted by the vertiginous view of the drop down to the jagged rocks below.

"I wonder how far we've walked," he said. "The pier looks miles away."

"We probably *have* walked miles. My feet are killing me. I should have worn different shoes."

Nick laughed. "Well, this is a change. Usually you're the one dragging *me* up the hill. Come on, it's not Glastonbury Tor. It can't be much farther."

"Oh, I'll make it. I really want to see the hill fort. I remember seeing Housesteads and Hadrian's Wall when I was a kid. It was like wandering through an ancient floor plan. No walls – just the patterns where they used to be. I kept imagining I would bump into an invisible wall."

The path branched at a picturesque graveyard full of canted

stone crosses and weathered sandstone, many rendered illegible by the harsh sea air. A ginger cat miaowed at them but it wouldn't stand still to be petted.

"Nearly there," Nick said, clearly enjoying the reversal of roles. "Not far now."

Liz smiled as he took her hand and pulled her along.

They finally reached the top and walked across the lush grassy mound dotted with dandelions. But that was all there was. There were no ruins, not even the stone layout where buildings had once stood. There was no visible evidence of Roman occupation at all. All that remained of the fort was earthwork ramparts and ditches.

"Well, that's a bit anticlimactic," Nick said.

Liz sighed. "Yeah. I was hoping for something more –Iron-Agey. Oh well."

"Can you imagine if they'd let Menrath build the house up here? We'd have had the best view in all of Clevedon."

It was nothing like as spectacular as Glastonbury Tor, but the real joy of it was that it kind of *was* their view. Wintergate was tucked away below, screened from them by trees, but they could see everything else for miles. A concrete pillbox from the Second World War stood on one side and they clambered up onto the roof to make the most of the vantage point. It was beautiful, but something about it inexplicably sent a chill down Liz's spine.

"I can't imagine all this covered in snow," Nick said.

"What?"

"Sylvia's romance-novel story. How Carson and Vanora went for a walk up here in the snow? I was just trying to picture it."

As Liz stared out across the flower-speckled grass, her vision began to blur, smearing everything into a pale haze that made her think of snow. Suddenly she was gripped by a sense of déjà vu so strong it made her dizzy. She could feel the sensation of bare feet slipping through tightly packed snow and there was a disconcerting crunching sound. Her tongue felt coated with a dusty residue. The world tilted beneath her feet and she felt herself sliding.

"You okay, Hedgehog?"

"Huh?"

"I said, are you okay now?"

"Now?" Liz stared down blearily at the grass under her feet. "What do you mean?"

"You don't remember? You mumbled something and stood up but you looked like you were going to fall over. I helped you down off the pillbox. I thought you were going to be sick. My love, you're white as a sheet."

Liz shook her head, trying to clear it. It was like her brain was wrapped in cobwebs. There was something about snow. "I guess I dozed off," she said, baffled, "started dreaming maybe. I think I dreamed about something like that before."

"Like what?"

"Snow. I can't remember it now, though."

"You weren't asleep, Liz. You were wide awake."

Liz had no idea what to say because she had no idea what had happened. "Well, I'm fine now," she said. She wasn't sure she was, but she wanted to be.

Nick didn't look convinced. "Are you sure?"

She ran a hand through her hair and closed her eyes for a moment. She took a deep breath of the warm, flower-scented air and then nodded. "I'm fine. Just hungry. And my feet are killing me." She forced a little laugh. "I think I've got blisters on my blisters."

Nick peered closely at her and the concern slowly melted from his face. "Your colour's coming back," he said, sounding relieved. "Maybe we just did too much walking on empty stomachs."

"I'm sure that's it," she said, eager to agree with his assessment. Anything else was just too weird and unnerving to contemplate. She certainly didn't like to imagine what her gut was telling her – that she'd had some sort of vision. But the mention of snow had definitely triggered something.

"Right," Nick said, "let's go get something to eat. Can you make it down to the house?"

She mustered a smile, shaking off the strangeness of the episode. "Of course. I don't fancy another route march to a pub, though. Could we be horribly decadent and drive the half mile?"

"No problem at all. Let's go."

All through lunch, Liz had a lingering sense of disquiet. Something about the hill fort had bothered her immensely and she was haunted by the thought that, whatever it was, she'd already seen it. In a dream.

CHAPTER 10

By morning, Liz had forgotten all about the weirdness on the hill. Nick was at the office and she was working on a bespoke necklace for a *Doctor Who* fan. She'd baked a small clay TARDIS the night before to be the centrepiece, sculpted the details, painted it blue and set two tiny glass windows into it. It was intricate work but if the prototype was perfect, future incarnations would be just as good.

She laid it in the middle of a scrap of black velvet and began designing the necklace around it, placing bail beads, jump rings and spacers on either side to form a pleasing pattern. Halfway along each side she added tiny clock charms to frame the TARDIS. When she was satisfied with the whole arrangement, she would string them all together, but this was the part she enjoyed most. She couldn't explain in advance what would make it right or wrong; she would only know when she saw it.

Once that was completed she had to start on the backlog of website orders that had built up while they were relocating. The usual dragons, unicorns and more Elvish jewellery, much of which she already had in stock. Some day she was bound to get sick of all the Middle Earth stuff. She'd been making it for years and there seemed no end to the number of people who wanted copies of things they'd seen in the films, but she still found magic and inspiration in Tolkien's world.

A quick check of her email showed an RSVP from her brother Simon, sending his regrets that he wouldn't be able to come to the house-warming party. Liz had known that would be his response, but it would have felt wrong not to invite him. And of course Andy wouldn't come all the way from Kiev. But she was disappointed that Jack couldn't make it. As much as she was looking forward to the party, she was dreading the presence of Rachel among all their friends.

Liz sent a quick reply to Simon and looked back down at the pieces before her. It made her think of excavations, of bones dug up and reassembled to make a dinosaur. Dragon fossils! Now, there was a fun thought. She scribbled a note to herself to sketch out a design for something based on the idea of a dragon excavation. Of course, now that she'd had the thought, she found it impossible to focus on anything else. She indulged herself in a few minutes of surfing the Net for pictures of palaeontological digs before forcing herself to close the laptop.

"Get back to work," she growled at herself. And she did, for a while.

Then the light from the stained-glass window changed as clouds moved in the sky outside. Shades of blue and red washed across her worktable, glinting off the beads. She was finding it hard to concentrate today, but not in a bad way. It was just such a fantastic place to sit and admire the house from. The view of the hall below made her feel like she was in a palace. Someday perhaps, if they had enough money, they could rebuild the west wing of the house. Extend the landing all the way around...

But she mustn't keep getting distracted. As she turned back to the necklace she caught movement in the corner of her eye. She looked to her left, down the long corridor towards the bedroom, but there was nothing there. Of course, the light was bound to play all sorts of tricks with the windows in a house like this. But there was no way anything could have got in. Not with her sitting with the front door in full sight.

It was beautiful, that door, elegant and romantic. She couldn't wait to see people spilling through it in a few days. The peace and quiet of their seaside retreat was wonderful, but Liz nonetheless found herself missing the bustle and excitement of other people. She hadn't seen Gwen in ages and hopefully she would bring

Rowan, her teenage daughter, with her to the party.

When she caught herself staring off into space again, Liz wondered if she should make herself some coffee. But she wasn't sleepy; she just couldn't focus. Another glance at the TARDIS made her think of time, which led to a short fantasy of finding a huge grandfather clock to take pride of place in the hall, one that would bong softly throughout the day and night. She closed her eyes and fancied that she could hear it now. Then she heard another sound. The peaceful clip-clop of horses on a cobblestone drive.

On the screen of her mind she saw a carriage pulling up outside Wintergate to discharge lavishly dressed guests for a masquerade ball. The horses tossed their plumed heads and snorted as their masters and mistresses alighted, ready to sate themselves at the party. Gowns swirled as the ladies showed off their finery, their fantastic costumes far more ostentatious than any modern A-list celebrity's Oscar night dress. Liz could see it all: jewels and feathers, ropes of pearls, and twinkling diamonds.

What would Vanora have worn? Liz naturally imagined her the belle of the ball. Something exotic and historical, she decided, or perhaps mystical. A Russian tsarina? Helen of Troy? Then Liz smiled. No. It would have been more symbolic than that. She knew with absolute clarity. Vanora had been Winter.

She had waited until just the right moment to make her appearance, standing at the top of the stairway and gazing down at the swirling kaleidoscope of colour and gaiety below, listening to the laughter, the clink of glasses, the excited shouts and cries. But once she emerged, every head in the room turned as her guests gasped and pointed, exclaiming over Vanora's Snow Queen costume as she descended the stairs.

It was exquisite, a masterpiece of design. Layers and layers of white silk, studded with pearls and crystals, as though she were snow and ice made flesh. Her face was powdered to match the wintry shades of her costume, so that none could tell where her mask ended and her alabaster skin began. Painted snowflakes danced round her eyes, and a headdress of white peacock feathers swayed above her like spindrift off a mountaintop.

Vanora inclined her head graciously as her guests bowed and curtseyed, indulging themselves in ever more extravagant behaviour at the appearance of their hostess. She smiled, delighted to see so many people there, although she knew only a handful of them personally. A quiver of excitement ran through her at the ravishing decadence of it all. One might be dancing with *anyone* and never know their partner's identity behind the

119

mask. Although she herself was recognisable, she wondered how many would take advantage of the opportunity such anonymity offered.

Tears shimmered in her eyes as she gazed upon the glorious spectacle. Here was a Venetian princess, over there a harlequin, there a medieval knight, and there – Queen Elizabeth! It was as though a history book had burst open and spilled all its figures into the ballroom. Vanora clapped her gloved hands in delight at each new personage she saw. She felt more like a child on Christmas morning than the regal mistress of Wintergate.

"Bravo!" someone cried, and a cheer ran through the crowd.

Vanora looked around for Carson and spotted him at last, costumed as Ra, the Egyptian god of the sun. He was magnificent, so handsome and imposing in his gleaming gold tunic. His mask was a stylised falcon's head, exquisitely detailed, with a large red sun-disk on top.

Her heart swelled as he took her hand and kissed it, and she laughed at what an incongruous pair they must make. Each had kept their costume a secret from the other. But then, very few people seemed to have designed their costumes with a partner in mind – or at least not the partner they had come to the ball with.

"My dear," he said, "you take my very breath away."

"Thank you," Liz murmured, and the scene splintered like glass at the sound of her own voice. Her eyes flew open as she was jolted out of her reverie, crying out as she saw where she was. She had wandered halfway down the stairs.

Confused and a little frightened, Liz clung to the banister, gazing back up at her worktable. What the hell had just happened? Had she been sleepwalking? Surely not. She'd never done that in her life. And besides, it had all been so *real*. It was as though she'd literally slipped into the past. She could taste the champagne, smell the floral perfume worn by the ladies. She had a vivid imagination, true, but this was something else entirely. Where had all that fantastic imagery come from?

Not knowing how to process the strange experience, Liz returned to her desk and stared down through the rails at the empty floor below, half-expecting to see ghosts waltzing there. Her mind still echoed with the sound of their dancing feet, of violins and voices from another age.

Don't be ridiculous, she told herself. *It's called daydreaming.*

But she wasn't convinced. The details had been so rich, so specific. Had there once been such a party here? Could a house have memories woven into its very foundation?

Her eye fell on the little book she'd bought at the pier.

121

Clevedon: Through the Eyes of Time. She flicked to the pages with photos of Wintergate. There was no mention of any masquerade, but that was hardly surprising. Such things were the kind of details that brought the past to life, but they weren't important to local history. Still, perhaps the author knew more than he had put in his book. The copyright date was some twenty years earlier, but Pritchard was bound to be a local and he might still be around. She would ask at the library.

In the meantime she had a necklace to make. As she sat down to work she was half-convinced she could hear cries of "Unmask!" from somewhere very far away. She opened her diary, once more counting the days until the party. Then she smiled as she drew a little doodle of a headdress with sprays of white peacock feathers and pearls.

CHAPTER 11

She was on the frozen hilltop again. As before, she was naked. And as before, she could not feel the cold. Strange trees surrounded her, bending their barren limbs down like grasping, bony hands. Frantically, Liz began pawing at the snow, digging to get away. She couldn't run but she could dig. She could find the way out of here, out of the open.

"Have to find the way through..."

The ground began to rumble, widening the hole she had made, drowning her in snow. With horrible clarity, she realised that she had been here before. She had been buried alive. Once more there was the choking, chalky taste as her mouth filled with snow, the oppressive sense of paralysis. She couldn't scream.

But something else was screaming.

No, it was *calling* to her. Calling her by name.

The trees must have reached her at last because she felt them clutching at her. She fought back, trying to tear herself free. Suddenly a voice penetrated the whiteout.

"Liz!"

She stopped struggling and listened. The trees pulled at her, yanking her from the snow. Her stomach swooped and for a moment she felt as though she were flying. Then there was a flare of light and she gasped at its brightness.

Her eyes were open but it took her some time to realise where she was. Nick was shaking her.

"Liz, wake up!"

"Wha-?"

"Shh! Listen!"

He was sitting up in bed, fiercely alert, his brow furrowed. He had put his bedside light on. The clock said it was just after four.

Her disorientation faded at once and she closed her eyes to listen, straining to hear. The silence was unnatural and absolute. She might hear the footfalls of a spider.

At last she shook her head, mystified. "What am I listening for?"

"I don't know," Nick whispered. "I thought it was a cat at first but then... Maybe an owl? Some night bird anyway. It was weird."

"You were just dreaming," she said, rubbing her eyes as a yawn overtook her. "I know I was."

He shook his head. "It wasn't a dream; it's what woke me up. I've been lying here listening to it and trying to figure out where it

124

was coming from. It almost sounded like it was here in the room with us."

Liz listened again but there was nothing to hear. She lay back and looked up at the ceiling, so high above. "Something in the attic? Bats maybe? Do they even make sounds we can hear?"

Nick gazed upward too, as if he could see through the plaster. "I don't think so."

Liz didn't like the note of unease she heard in his voice. He seemed only a step away from terror. "How loud was it?"

He turned to her, eyes bright with fear. "Liz, it *screamed*. Tore me right out of sleep and I bolted awake and put the light on. It did that two or three times and then it settled into a kind of wailing, like something in agony. I thought maybe an animal had got run over in the road but like I said, it's as though it was *right here*."

"It screamed?"

"Yes. It was blood-curdling. But you didn't even move. You were miles away, talking in your sleep about finding the way or something."

Liz's stomach clenched. Nick wasn't easily frightened, nor was he prone to exaggeration. If he said it had been loud, then it had been loud. And she was an extremely light sleeper, disturbed by the slightest sound. How could she have slept through it? Her mind went back to the hours she'd lost dreaming the day before.

She gave a nervous laugh and clasped Nick's hand. "Wow, I must have been really tired," she said, fully aware that it was a lame excuse. "We can have a look in the attic in the morning. Whatever it is, I'm sure it's nothing to worry about."

He considered this and then nodded gravely. "Yeah. You're probably right." But he didn't look convinced. "I've just never heard anything like that before. It made my skin crawl."

His description of it had done the same to her but she didn't say anything.

Nick was quiet for a long time and Liz was reluctant to break the silence. She felt obscurely guilty, as though she'd done something wrong. When he finally spoke, he unnerved her even further.

"It's too quiet here," he said. "I don't like it. At first I thought it was peaceful but now I just lie in bed at night listening to the blood rushing in my head and watching the shadows swim around the room."

This was news to Liz. "Really? I had no idea. I've never slept so well in my life."

"I know. Your head hits the pillow and you're gone. I

126

remember when you used to keep *me* up tossing and turning all night."

Liz pondered this a while, but could think of no reason why she should feel at home here and Nick so alienated. She remembered their first night in the house, when she'd been startled by Carson Menrath's face staring down at her. She'd put it down to new-home jitters and it hadn't happened since. But for Nick it seemed the jitters were getting worse.

"We could get some kind of white noise machine," she said. "Something that plays sounds like rain or waves."

"That doesn't explain what I heard," Nick said flatly.

Liz didn't want to say it, didn't want to voice the thought she knew they were sharing. Saying it might make it real, make it seem like an actual possibility rather than just a neurotic fantasy. But she didn't want Nick to say it first. If it was her idea, perhaps then he could laugh it off and say she was being silly. She decided to risk it.

"Do you think the place is haunted?"

Nick's thoughtful silence wasn't at all reassuring.

"I'm not sure," he said, choosing his words carefully. "I don't really know what I believe."

She stilled herself against the shudder that threatened to run

127

through her. For whatever reason, she felt it was vitally important to steer Nick away from this train of thought, to remain rational and sceptical. To put the idea entirely out of his mind. It was... safer.

"Look," she said, "neither of us is going back to sleep. The sun's almost up anyway. Why don't we go and look in the attic now? There's bound to be a perfectly logical explanation for what you heard."

A trace of fear remained in his eyes but he nodded. "Okay."

The ceiling in the corridor housed a trapdoor with a pull-down ladder. Until now there had been no reason to go up there.

Nick peered up the steps into the darkness, hesitating.

"I'll go first if you want," Liz said.

"No, it's all right." He switched on the heavy-duty torch and aimed it up into the shadows.

The ladder creaked with each step and Liz felt a little flutter in her stomach as Nick made his way up. It wasn't fear exactly. It was more like anticipation. He reached the top and shone the torch into the space.

"God, it's huge. It must run the length of the whole house."

He climbed up into the space and Liz heard the ceiling creak as he moved away. She followed, eager to see the space. And Nick was right; it was enormous. There was no flooring, only the wide joists to walk on. But even with the angled roof, there was still enough room to stand upright.

"Wow," she breathed. "We could have another whole set of rooms up here."

There were none of the trappings of scary-movie attics: no dressmaker's dummy, no rocking horse, no sheet-draped furniture that resembled ghosts. There seemed to be nothing but dust and cobwebs, and tins of old paint and plaster.

The sun was just beginning to rise, but there were no spears of light piercing through from outside. The only light came from the torch, which must mean that the roof was intact. So if anything *had* got in, it had to be pretty small. Nick swept the torch across the floor but they couldn't see any evidence of owls or bats. Both would leave quite a mess, they were sure.

"Maybe whatever you heard was up on *top* of the roof?" Liz suggested. "Or even in the cliff wall behind us?"

Nick didn't seem reassured or convinced, and Liz felt a stab of sympathy. It wasn't like him at all to be so freaked out.

"Hey, come on," she said, "you know animals can make all kinds of weird noises. Remember that squirrel?"

They had been sitting outside a cafe in Bristol once when a cat had pounced on an unwary squirrel. The ghastly shrieking had sounded like an alien creature. It hadn't just startled the diners, but the cat as well, which immediately released its prey and fled down the street.

But Nick frowned. "It wasn't anything like that, Liz. I swear to God it sounded human. Like a baby."

Liz didn't know what else to say. She hadn't heard it so she couldn't just dismiss his concerns, but it was clear there was nothing human up here.

"Well, I'm sorry we didn't find anything," she said at last, "but whatever it was, I'm sure it's nothing to worry about."

He sighed. "Yeah, you're probably right. I won't say 'maybe it was my imagination' because it bloody well wasn't, but there's certainly nothing up here."

"Come on, let's go and get some breakfast."

As she headed back down the ladder she felt a strange kind of satisfaction, as though she'd succeeded in diverting Nick from... what? If there was nothing hidden, there was nothing to find. Where was this innate secrecy coming from?

Throughout the rest of the morning she watched Nick closely. He would occasionally glance up at the ceiling, a worried expression on his face. Liz did her best to distract him until he left for work. And once she was alone again she felt unaccountably relieved.

CHAPTER 12

"It's amazing!"

The Hollands beamed with pride as each new person exclaimed over the house. It wasn't a large party but the people filled the space. There had been a half-hearted argument about making it a fancy dress affair, but since Liz was in the minority, she acceded to Nick's preference that they keep it informal.

Both Nick and Liz had done the house tour several times so now people were just encouraged to explore on their own. Even so, most of the guests were clustered where guests always cluster at parties – near the bar. In this case the "bar" was their dining table, covered with a red lace tablecloth Liz had found on sale just after Halloween one year.

Ian and his wife Chelle had been among the first to arrive. Liz liked Nick's friend well enough but Chelle had always rubbed her up the wrong way. She was the kind of girl there had been far too many of in school – the ones who were gushingly friendly one minute, but who would turn on you in a heartbeat.

"I have to admit," Ian was saying, "when Nick first told me

about it, I thought he was exaggerating."

"Me too," Chelle chimed in. "I thought the pictures were of some English Heritage place."

"It probably ought to be," Nick said. He filled everyone's glass from the bottle of pinot noir Ian had brought.

Chelle thanked him and gestured around the room with a heavily beringed hand. "You could set up a little gift shop and charge admission."

Liz smiled, although she didn't like Chelle's implication that the house was a tourist attraction. "It's our home," she said serenely, snuggling close to Nick. "Only friends and loved ones allowed."

"And tradesmen presumably," Ian said.

Everyone laughed, even Liz. "Fair enough," she conceded, then excused herself to the kitchen, to check on the stock of nibbles. Someone had already eaten all the sausage rolls, ignoring the smoked salmon and cheese. Typical, she thought with a grin. All Nick's blokey friends would go straight for the pub snacks. She restocked another couple of bowls with crisps and nuts but she didn't want to get trapped downstairs playing waitress all night. She filled two wine glasses and went off in search of Gwen.

She ran into her mother first, in the upstairs corridor. True to form, Rachel had dressed for a much more formal affair and she was sniffily disappointed by the prevalence of casual wear. She looked like she should be having tea with the royal family rather than mingling with the commoners that her daughter and son-in-law called friends.

"I realise things are different these days, Lizzie, but *really!* Jeans? At a house-warming party?"

"Don't be a snob, Rachel," Liz said breezily, refusing to let her mother get under her skin. "Take your boyfriend outside and gaze at the stars if you don't like the company in here."

Rachel bristled. "He's not my boyfriend. Thomas and I are just good friends." She glanced over at the portly little man admiring the stained-glass window, presumably hoping he hadn't heard her. Rachel seemed to have a remarkable number of such friends, and it wasn't the first time Liz had 'mistaken' one for more. A childish game, but always satisfying.

"Whatever you say. But do try to have a nice time."

Rachel gave her the familiar long-suffering smile. "Oh, I'm trying," she said. She swept her gaze around the room, deliberately sipping at her wine, though it was obvious that she wanted to neck it.

Liz abandoned her and continued on in search of Gwen. She

must have arrived by now, though Liz hadn't seen her yet. It was so busy they had given up trying to answer the door themselves and had just left it open for people to wander in and out. It wasn't the sort of gathering they supposed anyone would be likely to crash, after all.

Gwen was in the bedroom, admiring the view from the bay window. She was a youthful forty, with an athletic figure she maintained by a regimen of morning runs, no matter how vicious the weather. She was wearing a purple velvet dress with elaborate criss-cross lacing and long, sheer, medieval-style sleeves. She had woven a matching ribbon through her long strawberry blonde hair.

When Liz entered, Gwen turned to her with shining eyes.

"Oh Liz," she breathed, "it's just incredible."

"I thought I'd find you here." Liz sank down beside her in the window seat and handed her one of the wine glasses. "It's really something, isn't it?"

"I'm so jealous!"

"I knew you would be."

"Well, cheers. Here's to your new home and your new life."

Liz clinked her glass against Gwen's and both drank deeply. "That dress is gorgeous. One of yours?"

Gwen nodded proudly. "I'm taking a class on corset making and I want to do more elaborate steampunk fashions. But I thought I'd do my own twist. Rather than just stick gears and cogs onto Victorian things, I'm going to mix in Arthurian styles. Think 'Mecha Morgan le Fay'."

"Wow," Liz said, unable to fully picture Gwen's vision. "Sounds... different."

Gwen laughed. "Sounds wacky, you mean! But you just wait. I could be on the verge of the next great cosplay wave."

"I'm sure whatever you make will be fabulous, Gwen. Hey, did you see my workshop?"

"I spotted it as soon as I came in. I hope you don't mind but I had a little snoop too. Those fairy sketches are brilliant! Boy, do I miss you at Hill of Dreams."

Liz gave a wistful sigh. "I miss you too. And the shop. I miss people in general – the buzz and the craziness. But then I look around at this place and remind myself why we left Glastonbury, and then Bristol. And I find myself being seduced by the silence."

"It does get to you," Gwen agreed. "They say a quieter life will keep you sane."

"I hope so. Now if I could just get my mother to do the same..."

Gwen chuckled. "Remember that day she actually came to the

shop? I thought she'd wandered straight out of some BBC drama!"

"Yeah, she was a little out of her depth. I'd only told her I made jewellery so she must have been expecting Tiffany's."

"And we almost had her convinced that Tolkien was a fashion designer."

"Almost!"

They shared an easy laugh at Rachel's expense before moving on to more pleasant topics.

After they'd caught up properly Gwen said, "We shouldn't let so much time pass."

"I know," Liz agreed. "You're only an hour away; it's hardly a cross-country trip."

"Hey, it's my fault too. I hate driving but it doesn't mean I can't do it. I never even saw your place in Bristol. You always came to me."

"You didn't miss much, trust me. It was a sweet little flat at first but it didn't take long to become a nuisance." She shuddered at the memory of the leaky ceiling. "I wouldn't go back there now if you paid me."

"I still feel bad that I never saw it. Your first place together and all."

"Never mind. It's heaven now, living somewhere that only

rains on the outside." She finished her wine and set the glass down. "How's Rowan? I'm surprised she didn't come with you."

Gwen shrugged and heaved an exasperated sigh. "Teenagers. Who knows what goes through their chaotic little minds?"

When she didn't elaborate, Liz raised her eyebrows enquiringly.

"Oh, you know how it is. Boring grown-up party or clubbing with friends – no-brainer which had more appeal. Only she was acting really weird about it."

"How so?"

"Well, I showed her the pictures you emailed me when you first bought the house. I thought she'd go mad for it. But she just stared at it for a while and then she said it didn't look like a happy place."

Liz frowned. She glanced around the bedroom. It seemed perfectly happy to her. The whole house did. But then, it was *her* house. Of course it would seem happy. Still, she was disappointed. She'd been looking forward to showing it off to Rowan, and especially looking forward to photographing the girl in its gothic rooms.

"Is she still interested in modelling for me?" Liz asked.

"I'm sure she will be. She's just going through a moody phase,

I guess. I certainly had them when I was her age."

Liz hadn't herself, but she made noises of agreement anyway. She couldn't imagine Rowan being anything but sunny and cheerful but she supposed life was full of a different kind of drama at seventeen. Even Rowan would have down days once in a while.

"Well, that's good news," Liz said. "About the modelling, I mean. I've got some fantastic new designs I can't wait to see her in, and this house is the ideal backdrop, a ready-made studio."

The conversation changed direction after that but Liz remained bothered by Gwen's words. Rowan might dress like a goth girl but she had the vivacious nature of a puppy. She wasn't the type to mope around or write morbid poetry and fantasise about death. She was relentlessly optimistic. Her friends were legion and she never passed up an opportunity for fun or adventure. She was also *impossibly* beautiful, with the kind of ethereal, elfin looks that had made her the perfect model for Gwen's clothes and Liz's jewellery. Liz wasn't ashamed to admit that she envied everything about her.

But even if the curse of adolescence had finally caught up with Rowan and turned her into a sulky little madam, perhaps it would fade just as quickly. Liz hated to think of Rowan losing her spark.

"Why don't you come with me and see the rest of the house?"

"Okay." Gwen grabbed their empty wine glasses and shook off Liz's attempt to take them from her. "No, let me do something," she said. "You can pour the next one."

"Fair enough. I ought to see how Nick's getting on anyway. I'm not sure he knows where all the food is and if he–"

Gwen had stopped halfway across the bedroom and was staring up in horror at the bust of Carson Menrath.

Misreading her expression, Liz laughed. "I see you met Carson."

Gwen didn't respond, nor did her expression change. But her hands went limp and the glasses crashed to the floor in a glittering spray of shards.

The sound startled her out of her trance and her look of horror turned to the mess on the floor. "Oh my god, Liz, I'm so sorry!"

"Hey, don't worry about it. We've got plenty of glasses."

"But I don't know what happened. It was so weird! I just felt cold all of a sudden. I mean really cold, like someone had poured ice water down my back."

Liz took Gwen's hands and guided her around the broken glass. "You looked up at the bust and just froze."

Gwen turned back to look at it, but whatever had disturbed her so greatly was gone now. She gave a confused little shake of

140

her head. "I don't know what to say. I just – I have no idea what happened to me. I'm so sorry."

"Stop," Liz said firmly. "It's no big deal. As long as you're okay. I couldn't care less about a couple of wine glasses."

Gwen managed a rueful little smile. "Yes, I think I'm fine. Can't say the same for my pride, though."

"Good enough. Tell you what – you go find Nick and ask him to bring a dustpan and brush up here. I'll stay here so no one else comes in and hurts themselves. Then you can get us some more wine and we'll carry on having a lovely time. Deal?"

"Deal. Back in a tick!"

As soon as Gwen had gone, Liz peered up at the bust, her eyes narrowed in puzzlement. "What did you do to her, you old goat?"

***

As the night wore on people gradually began to trickle away and Liz had the sense that the house was becoming theirs once again. It was probably just the wine, but at times she had been almost certain that the house was holding itself back, stiffly, like a person who doesn't like being touched. Even filled with warm bodies, the rooms had felt... cooler somehow.

Rachel made a rather maudlin goodbye, as though she were going off to war and might never see Liz again. After her sloppy declaration of love she left in a taxi, and Liz watched the tail lights dwindle as she vanished down the hill. Nick's friends and colleagues followed, getting into their cars a few at a time while others left on foot, intent on catching the bus home.

One couple said that they wanted to walk along the seafront and see the pier under the moonlight. Liz had a sudden sense of unease and she had to restrain herself from warning them to be careful, although she couldn't imagine what possible danger they might be in.

Gradually, the forecourt emptied until only one car was left. Liz walked Gwen to the front door and was surprised by the fierce hug her friend gave her.

"Take care of yourself, Liz."

"You know I will."

Gwen pulled away and looked Liz hard in the eyes. "No, I mean it. I worry about you."

Liz didn't know what to say. Things had never been better in her life, so what could there possibly be to worry about? She supposed Gwen was still feeling embarrassed over the broken glasses, and fretting about the change in Rowan.

"I'm the happiest I've ever been," she assured Gwen with a laugh. Then, to lighten the mood she added, "Nick's always there

142

to bail me out if I get into any trouble."

Gwen smiled back but the smile didn't reach her eyes. She glanced up at the house and took a breath as though she wanted to say something else, but in the end she kept it to herself.

"I'll see you," she said at last.

"Not if I see you first."

This earned her another weak smile. As Gwen turned away, Liz couldn't shake the feeling that she would never see her friend again.

CHAPTER 13

Liz peeked through the curtains and stared glumly at the weather. The morning was dark and overcast, the sky threatening rain. Even the birds seemed cowed by the gloom. She hadn't heard a single tweet all morning. She'd promised herself a walk down to the pier while Nick was at work but the ominous sky didn't make that such an attractive prospect anymore. Not that she minded all that much; she didn't really feel up to a walk today anyway and the weather was as good an excuse as any to get out of it.

"Hey, Countess Dracula," Nick murmured sleepily from the bed. "Aren't you going to draw the curtains?"

"No. The view's not worth seeing today."

A sudden cold draught made her shiver and she moved away from the window. The country had been enjoying an unusually mild autumn so far but it looked like that was over now. Even in the height of summer the house had never been very warm. She crossed to the wardrobe and stood staring inside it, half-forgetting why she'd opened the doors. All her jumpers were packed in boxes under the bed, waiting for the onset of winter. Of course, she wasn't going anywhere today, so she didn't have to get dressed at all. She could stay in her flannel pyjamas all day if she wanted to. It seemed a funny sort of luxury, that. As though the house were a colossal comfy bed she could just tuck herself up inside and stay cocooned away from the rest of the world. She didn't have to see anyone, talk to anyone–

"Liz? Are you all right?"

She turned away from the wardrobe. "Huh?"

"Huh?" he parroted. "You looked a million miles away. Is something wrong?"

She shook her head without even considering the question. "Nothing," she said sharply. "I'm just cold."

"Well, you could come back to bed and warm up next to me," Nick said, pulling back the covers. "The alarm won't even go off for another half an hour."

"No, that's all right." Even as she said it she could hear how oddly stilted her voice sounded, as though she'd declined a cup of tea, not the intimacy of sex. She felt the strangest desire to get away before he could show any more concern, ask any more probing questions. "Think I'll just have a bath."

She took her time, hoping that Nick would be gone by the time

145

she got out. Normally she'd have simply wrapped a towel around herself but she felt funny about showing so much skin after rebuffing his advances. Instead she tugged on the fluffy dressing gown she hardly ever used and wrapped her wet hair in a towel.

When she returned to the bedroom, Nick was still there. He was dressed and standing in front of the windows, the curtains drawn and tied back. He looked at Liz curiously.

"What do you mean, the view's not worth seeing today? It's gorgeous. You used to get up at the crack of dawn to go hiking on days like this."

Liz glanced at it but she wasn't impressed. The sky still looked leaden to her, the clouds hanging over the countryside like wool soaked in muddy water. "Please yourself," she mumbled.

"Wow, you are out of sorts today. Did I do something or did you just wake up on the wrong side of the bed?"

She couldn't tell if he was making light of her grouchy mood or trying to be sympathetic. Either way, she felt herself bristling. The sound of his voice was grating on her nerves. All she wanted right now was to be left alone. The sky was grim and horrible. Why was Nick telling her it wasn't? She felt mocked and belittled.

It took an astonishing amount of willpower to make herself smile and offer him the very lightest of apologies. "I'm sorry,

Nick. I guess I'm a little distracted. I've just got so much to do." That wasn't true of course, and he must know it, but he was good enough to let it go.

"Well, all right, if you're sure nothing's wrong," he said, sounding doubtful and a little hurt. "I'll stay out of your way, then."

She couldn't think of anything to say to that and her silence only served to underline the awkwardness of the moment. She unwound the towel from her hair and began patting it dry, hoping he'd take her actions as a dismissal and leave.

He did turn to go, but then he hesitated in the doorway. "Oh, and before I forget," he said, "Greg wants me to go to Manchester next week to meet some clients. It'll only be for a couple of nights. I meant to tell you yesterday."

It sounded like a suggestion he hadn't seriously considered before. Now it must suddenly seem attractive to him.

"Okay," she said.

Her short answer clearly wasn't what he'd wanted to hear and she had the sense that she'd failed some kind of test. Now he was starting to look annoyed. "Okay? That's it?"

She shrugged. "What do you want me to say? If you have to go, you have to go."

"Well, for starters, you usually ask if you can come too. If not, then you start fretting about being on your own overnight."

"So I'm less neurotic now. Isn't that a good thing?"

His expression told her it wasn't. "It's just not like you, Liz. I don't know what it is, but you've been acting strange the last few days. You always seem like you're somewhere else, somewhere far away. Is there anything going on I should know about?"

"Why would anything be going on?"

"I don't know. You just seem so – cold. So unfriendly. You're talking about the weather being ghastly when it's not. You've been wandering around in a daze since you got up, and now you're not even the slightest bit concerned about me going to Manchester. So yeah, it feels like there's something you're not telling me."

Liz lay back on the bed, not caring that her wet hair would soak through the bedclothes. "I'm just tired."

Nick went to her and clasped her hand. Liz resisted the urge to yank it away.

"What can I do, Hedgehog?"

"Nothing." She sighed and offered the time-honoured excuse that would explain everything away. "It's just that time of the month, I guess."

Predictably, he relaxed at once. Ah yes, the mysteries of female hormones. Always the perfect alibi for any kind of weird behaviour.

She gazed up at the pale face of Carson Menrath and felt a shudder of revulsion. She dug deep inside herself and forced another smile for Nick. "Everything's just so different since we moved here. But *good* different. Maybe I don't need to worry about you going away anymore. I feel safe here."

That seemed to do the trick. The clouds lifted from his eyes and Nick beamed down at her, then bent to kiss her. She closed her eyes and let him, resuming her smile as soon as he pulled back.

"That's great," he said. "I never thought you were in any particular danger in the Bristol flat but I'll be a lot happier knowing you feel secure."

Liz squeezed his hand. "Wintergate will protect me," she said. She had no idea where the words had come from.

CHAPTER 14

The hotel room was awful. The sort of place a student would turn his nose up at. The company had booked him an "executive" room and Nick supposed the plastic chair and the rickety little table crammed in next to the window were a luxury not provided in the standard rooms. There was the usual soulless corporate art, the usual drab bedding and curtains. He appeared to have a roommate too; a large spider had built a rather impressive web in the darkest corner of the ceiling. Clearly she was a long-term resident. Nick left her alone, trusting her to protect him from other invaders in the night.

He wasn't fussy when it came to hotels, but this place had all the charm of a Dickensian orphanage. He hardly dared investigate the bathroom, but as long as there wasn't a body in the tub he decided he could probably cope. There wasn't a body as it turned out, just the previous guest's wet towels. At least the toilet itself looked clean.

His phone sprang to life with the *Batman* TV theme song and he smiled as he answered it.

"Hello, psychic lady."

"Oh, have I timed it right?" Liz asked brightly.

"Just walked in the door this minute. And wow, you should see this place."

"Is it nice?"

"Pure luxury. Four-poster bed, gold-plated bathroom taps, complimentary champagne. I may never come home."

Liz laughed. "Oh dear. Sarcasm alert. Is it a real dump?"

"Appalling. I was just about to ring housekeeping – assuming the maids haven't all run away screaming."

"Don't stay if it's terrible. Make them find you a B&B or something."

Nick shook his head, remembering the long queue at reception. "No, that's more trouble than it's worth. It's only for two nights, and I'm not paying anyway."

But Liz didn't want to let it go. "Exactly. You're their guest so they shouldn't put you in a rat-hole. What does that say about their company?"

"I'm sure they had no idea it was this bad. It's one of those grand old Victorian places. Probably the height of luxury in its day but it's gone to seed now." Then he added with a chuckle, "Bit like our place, really."

There was a pause before Liz responded. "What do you mean by that?"

"Just the TLC it needs. This room has some of the same symptoms: peeling paint, stained carpet, grubby window. I've got a great view of the alley behind the hotel. Oh, and there's a ceiling repair that looks like some kind of modern art exhibit."

But Liz didn't laugh. Nick frowned at the silent phone for several seconds. "Are you still there, Hedgehog?"

"Yes." Her voice sounded funny. Distant.

"Sorry, I thought we'd been cut off."

When she didn't reply to that either, he sank down onto the bed. "Hey, are you okay? Is anything wrong?"

She waited too long before saying no, and it was still in that cold voice.

"Liz? Talk to me. What's wrong?"

A long sigh came down the phone. Then she laughed. "It's nothing. I guess I'm just a little sensitive about it, that's all."

"Sensitive about what? Some grotty hotel in Manchester?"

"No," she said, sounding surprised that he had to ask. "About Wintergate." When he was quiet for a few moments she added, "Our *home.*"

"Our home. Yes, of course. Sorry." He searched his mind for

something, anything to say. "It's been a long morning," he added hopelessly. He felt like he was talking to a stranger. He had to wonder if his being away for a couple of nights was a good thing or a bad thing for her. She'd told him she was fine with it, that she felt safer in their new home, but she'd been acting weird that day too. She'd said it was her time of the month but she never got that bad-tempered. And anyway, that was last week. She couldn't *still* be having her period, could she?

His instinct was to rush home and put his arms around her. But if she was feeling that moody and on edge, well... maybe the best thing he could do was give her some space.

The silence grew as neither spoke for some time. Eventually Nick capitulated. "Well, then. I guess I'd better go. The meeting's not until later but they want to take me out to lunch first."

Normally this would have prompted playful envy from Liz but she only said okay and told him to enjoy himself. Was she really that upset over a passing comment about the house?

"Love you, Hedgehog," he said softly. She replied in kind but with none of her usual warmth. There was no *I miss you* or *Call me later* or even a word of encouragement about the meeting. She disconnected before he could say anything else.

He tossed his phone onto the bed and stared at the empty

black screen. It seemed to emphasise her coldness. His thoughts flashed back to their viewing of Wintergate and how Liz had been smitten from the very first moment. She'd seemed completely blind to the flaws that were obvious to him and she'd bristled when he suggested it needed a bit of work.

And hadn't there been other times when she'd been weird about the house? Oddly overprotective? She'd practically bitten Rachel's head off at the first word of criticism. But since Liz was always at odds with her mother, he'd simply ignored it. Now he was starting to wonder whether she was becoming a little obsessed.

That might explain the dreams. She often woke him up in the night, thrashing around, kicking the duvet off, then yanking it back. She mumbled words he couldn't make out, but in the morning she could never remember what had disturbed her.

Of course, maybe she was feeling out of sorts for some other reason. The silence and isolation of Wintergate was such a vast change from the hectic pace of Bristol. Liz had always thrived on energy and excitement but perhaps the house was dampening some of her extroverted spirit. Perhaps she was simply mellowing with age.

Or what if...

The thought struck him like a blow. What if she was pregnant? Neither of them had ever wanted kids. Indeed, they'd both called it a deal-breaker in the early days of their relationship, and not even jokingly. But things happened to women over time. They were at the mercy of crazy hormones that men couldn't even begin to fathom. His own mother had told him she'd never wanted a baby, then one day it just "felt right". And here he was.

He shook his head. No, not Liz. If anything, she was more anti-breeding than he was. She was less tolerant of noisy kids in restaurants, and their previous neighbours' litter had driven her up the walls. Still, he thought, it would explain an awful lot.

The strangest thing of all was, now that the idea of children had crossed his mind, he didn't find it unpleasant. In fact, when he looked up and saw himself in the mirror, he realised he was smiling.

CHAPTER 15

Liz laid out the new pieces she wanted Rowan to model, then wandered through the house as she waited for the girl to arrive. She tried to imagine how the place would look to her for the first time. She remembered her amazement when she and Nick had first seen it, but now that they were settled in, the immediate wonder seemed more distant. It certainly was for Nick, who always seemed to find fault. Liz couldn't help taking every comment personally.

It was hardly a dilapidated old shack. It was a piece of history, a place built with love and affinity with the ancient landscape. Its eccentricity only added to its charm. Liz had never felt so connected to a place before.

She was brushing her hair in the bathroom when she heard a car coming up the hill. A blue Citroën lurched to a stop in the forecourt and she heard the wrenching of the handbrake from where she stood. She took some pleasure in watching Rowan emerge from the car and gaze up at the house, looking suitably awed. Liz hurried down the stairs and threw open the door before

Rowan could ring the bell.

"Hello you!" Liz cried.

"Hey," said Rowan. "Wow, this place is really posh!"

It was impossible not to swell with pride, but Liz was learning how to rein it in. She shrugged. "What can I say? It's home. Come on in."

Rowan scuffed her Doc Martens on the mat before stepping onto the mosaic tiles, peering down at the design. Her thin frame was draped in a V-necked dress of distressed black lace, the better to show off her pale throat.

Liz imagined they would just have to get used to the slowness of visitors from now on. No one could just stroll into a house like Wintergate; there was too much to see on the way. Rowan stared up at the stained-glass window, the stairs and the minstrels' gallery, her kohl-rimmed eyes wide with reverence.

"I like your hair," Liz said, admiring her brilliant red tresses.

Rowan smiled at the compliment. "Thanks. I got bored with the blue."

The last time Liz had photographed Rowan, her hair had been petrol blue with streaks of black. Striking, but she supposed it was the kind of look you got tired of pretty soon. When Liz was her age, she'd coloured her hair jet black, then managed to turn it pink while trying to return to her natural blonde. The novelty of changing colours had worn off very quickly indeed.

"Well, come on up and I'll show you the rest of the house."

Liz led her up the stairs and then along the corridor. She pointed out the bathroom and continued on to the bedroom. Throughout the tour the girl was uncharacteristically quiet. She followed along, looking slightly anxious, her wide eyes taking everything in.

"Are you cold?" Liz asked.

"Huh? No, I'm fine." Rowan let her arms drop, apparently unaware she'd wrapped them around herself.

"Because it can get chilly in here."

Rowan shook her head curtly and Liz abandoned the interrogation. The girl must have something else on her mind, that was all.

They reached the bedroom and Rowan turned as she gazed up at the vaulted ceiling. She stared, open-mouthed. Speechless.

That's how we must have looked the first time, Liz thought fondly. *Gob-smacked.*

"You really live here?"

"We sure do."

Rowan gave a little shudder as her eyes met those of Carson

Menrath. "I don't think I could sleep under *that*."

Liz laughed. "Yes, well, it did take some getting used to." Gwen had been right about the change in Rowan. Normally the teenager was bubbly and outgoing. But Wintergate seemed to have shut her up. "Want some tea? Coffee?"

"Uh-uh," Rowan murmured, touching her forehead.

"Hey, you okay, sweetie?"

"Dunno. Bit of a headache."

"Poor thing. Do you want something for it?"

"No, I'll be fine. Let's just do the pics. Is this the new stuff?" Rowan brushed aside her discomfort and turned towards the window where Liz's jewellery was displayed on a table. "Oh, I love this one."

Rowan was holding up an elaborate beaded collar of imitation rubies, trailing in uneven drops. It was just the sort of thing Liz knew Rowan would love and she had actually anticipated giving it to her as a bonus after paying her for the shoot. But Rowan's tone was flat and lifeless. It was clear there was something bothering her, something she was trying hard to keep Liz from seeing.

Helpless to do anything but play along, Liz picked up her camera. "Shall we start with that one, then?"

"Sure."

Rowan hadn't seemed to notice the window or the view and Liz felt a wave of uneasiness, as though she were keeping the girl here against her will. For a moment she considered calling off the shoot. Maybe she should take Rowan into town for lunch or something instead, get her to talk, to open up about what was bothering her. She couldn't imagine Gwen would mind her playing go-between.

"Is this okay?"

Rowan had fastened the collar around her neck and was looking at Liz expectantly.

"It looks gorgeous on you," Liz said. "But then everything does. Listen, are you sure you're up for this today? Only you don't really seem like yourself."

Rowan smiled, a feeble echo of her mother's smile on leaving the party. "I'm fine, really." There was a pause while she thought for a moment, but she seemed unable to come up with anything to add.

Liz sighed and forced a smile of her own. "Well, all right, if you're sure..."

Rowan nodded, the false smile turning to a rictus. Her eyes flicked up to Carson Menrath for a moment and then she looked away.

"All right, why don't you stand against that wall?" Liz nodded towards the east wall, where the light from the window was best.

Rowan moved with unconscious grace to the spot and raised her head like a ballerina to lengthen her neck. The red beads lay against her throat like drops of blood. Liz usually had to tell her not to smile but today Rowan was the very picture of tragic beauty.

"Can you turn your head to the left? That's good. Down a bit? Perfect."

Normally these shoots were great fun for both of them. Rowan loved to perform for the camera and Liz loved seeing her creations exhibited to such great effect. But ever since Rowan arrived she had seemed... haunted. Yes, that was the word. And with each piece she modelled, her discomfort became more and more apparent. It was as though something in the air was sapping all her energy.

Finally Liz couldn't keep it in any longer. She lowered the camera and met the girl's eyes. "Rowan? Look, I know something's bothering you. Please won't you talk to me? If it's something at home–"

"It's nothing like that," Rowan said. Her eyes darted up to the plaster head again; she seemed to be caught in an agony of

161

indecision.

"It's okay, Rowan. Whatever it is, you can tell me."

The girl sighed heavily before capitulating. "I don't want to sound rude but – well, it's the house."

"The house? What about it?"

Rowan hesitated for a moment, reluctant to speak. Then she blurted it out: "I hate it."

This was the last thing Liz had been expecting and she was completely at a loss for words. For several seconds she stared at Rowan, then up at Carson Menrath's effigy. "Wow," she said, uncertain what else to say. "I know it's a little unusual, maybe even a bit spooky, but..." She ran out of words and looked back at Rowan.

The girl's eyes immediately filled with tears and she swiped at her face with her sleeve, embarrassed. "Oh Liz, I'm so sorry, but you asked. I've been standing here this whole time feeling *watched*. But it's not just that– I don't know how to say it."

She was silent again for almost a minute.

Liz prompted her gently. "Say what, sweetie?"

Rowan turned to her and the expression on her face sent a chill down Liz's spine.

"I feel *violated*."

The word hit Liz like a slap and she sank down onto the bed, staring at Rowan.

Rowan shuddered and rubbed her arms, huddling into herself. She looked utterly wretched, like a little girl lost in the woods in some dark fairy tale.

"I can feel him," she said softly. "His eyes, his hands. I can feel him touching me."

It was a long time before Liz could speak. Gwen had been unnerved by the bust too, but nothing like this. "Rowan," she began at last, "you know he's not real." She felt like someone trying to convince a child that there was no monster under the bed.

But if Rowan heard her she gave no sign. Her voice seemed to come from far away. "He wants to get inside me." Then she winced as if in pain.

Liz could only stare in shock as Rowan's hands slipped down her body, down her thighs and then between them. Then she thrust her hands up against herself, rubbing hard. "No, please," she whimpered. "Please..."

This snapped Liz out of her shock and she flew to Rowan's side. She peeled the girl's hands away and tried to hold her but Rowan wriggled away violently. She covered her face for a

163

moment with a sob of shame and when she looked back at Liz her eyes were wide with abject fear. "I'm sorry," she gasped. "I don't know what– I just can't..." She darted a glance up at the bust once more and gave a small cry. Then she fled.

Liz ran after her. "Rowan, wait!"

But the girl was fast. She pelted down the corridor and then down the stairs, taking them two at a time and only stumbling slightly on the last few treads. She reached the door and pawed frantically at the handle until she got it open and raced outside. Liz stood at the top of the stairs, staring open-mouthed through the doorway after her.

A few seconds later, she heard the car start and there was the violent grinding of gears as Rowan gunned the engine, whipped the Citroën around and then sped down the drive, kicking up a cloud of dust that billowed in her wake and trailed into the hall.

Liz stood where she was for several minutes, her thoughts a whirl of confusion, pity and fear. The door was open onto a bright sunny day but she might have been standing naked in the snow for all the warmth she felt. It was a long time before she was able to descend the stairs and close the door, leaning back against it with a sigh of resignation.

She didn't remember returning to the bedroom but she found

herself standing at the foot of the bed shortly after, gazing up at the alabaster face that had so frightened poor Rowan.

"What did you do to her?" she asked. "What did you do?"

Voicing the question made her feel a little funny, but not as funny as the thought that had crossed her mind during Rowan's upsetting display. She was sure Carson Menrath had been smiling.

CHAPTER 16

It felt strange to have the house all to herself that night. Liz sat in the window seat with a glass of wine and admired the view as the sun sank out of sight. The lights of the town seemed very far away, as though she were on a tiny island adrift from the rest of the country. Once the thought of such isolation would have disturbed her; now it felt comforting.

The merlot warmed her throat and she closed her eyes, savouring the rich taste. She felt a little funny about Rowan and Nick, neither of whom had seemed like themselves today, but she put them out of her mind. Rowan was just a wide-eyed teenager spooked by an old house and Nick – well, he was just missing her. That was the only reason she could think of for why he'd have said such a terrible thing about the house. He hadn't meant it. He'd be back the next day and everything would return to normal.

She finished the glass and poured herself another, enjoying the mild flutter of decadence that drinking alone always brought. The distant motorway twinkled like a string of fairy lights and Liz found her thoughts straying ahead to Christmas. They could get a real tree this year, a great towering skyscraper of pine to fill the entrance hall. One so tall they'd need ladders to decorate it. All at once she could smell the heavenly aroma of pine and wood, of mulled wine and Christmas pudding. As she downed the second glass of merlot she could almost feel herself getting drunk on the vision of spices and brandy.

Liz lay back on the cushions and gazed up at the ceiling. The shadows thrown by the crackling fire danced across the beams and cornices like revellers at a ball. How lavish everything must have been all those years ago.

What must Christmas have been like for Vanora? Would she have brought her family over from America to celebrate it with her? Or was she all alone? Was she pining for the children she would never have, mourning the Christmas gifts she could never give them?

She saw Vanora sitting at the window in a froth of velvet skirts and petticoats, gazing out into the lonely night. How alien this country must have seemed to her. How cold and wet. Of course, Americans of that period played their little society games too, but they didn't have the vicious class divide that pervaded Britain. Did the servants feel their master had married beneath him? Did they feel they could get away with things because their mistress was a foreigner and ignorant of their ways? Liz suspected that they did. And how much worse must it have been for a woman of that period who couldn't have the child she so desperately wanted? She must have felt cursed.

Liz had tried on a corset for the first time at a steampunk convention a couple of years ago. She had loved the look at once, the way it whittled her waist down to nothing and exaggerated her meagre bust and narrow hips. It gave her the enviable hourglass figure coveted by women throughout many periods of history. It also made it impossible to slouch; one always had perfect posture in a tightly laced corset. But after wearing it for about ten minutes she began to feel constricted. She missed the freedom of movement, the ability to bend at the waist. Mostly she missed being able to take full, deep breaths. As soon as she realised she couldn't breathe deeply, she felt anxious, and she could imagine that anxiety escalating into a full-blown panic attack if she didn't do something. It only took a minute to unlace the corset and free her chest to inflate fully once more and she'd been left feeling silly over her minor fright.

The image returned to her vividly as she imagined Vanora sitting where she was. How stifled and confined she must have felt. How *caged*. Especially with the heartbreak of a stillborn child

168

fresh in her mind. How awful it must have been having to smile and be polite to all the people who would take advantage of her hospitality and then whisper about her behind her back, treating every little social *faux pas* like a capital offence. She could never have known any real friendship, any real love. All she had to look forward to was another day of gliding through her life, keeping up appearances and pretending that inside she wasn't screaming like an animal in a trap.

Liz sat up suddenly. Stillborn child? Where had that come from? And all those other details... was she daydreaming again?

She stared at her empty wine glass, unsure if it was her second or her third. She felt a little woozy and she stumbled when she tried to get up. Laughing at her clumsiness, she made her way to the bed and collapsed. The shadows cavorted above her. She could almost hear their voices – talking, laughing, whispering...

One stood out in particular. A man's voice, deep and resonant. She looked up at the plaster head. The pale eyes were fixed on her, the play of light animating them, giving them the illusion of life.

"No wonder you freaked Rowan out," Liz said, trying not to be afraid herself. She remembered how uneasy the effigy had made her feel at first, how she hadn't liked the thought of being watched throughout the night. She hardly gave it a second thought anymore. But now...

Was it just her imagination or did the head seem larger? Nearer?

She tried to tell herself it was just the wine. She'd had a bad day and drunk too much to drown her sorrows. But being drunk didn't explain the smell. She was sure it wasn't her imagination. Her nose was full of the scent of wood, musty and sharp. And underneath it, the hot wet reek of sweat.

The fire was dying. Liz had no idea how long she had been lying there, immobile. The room grew slowly darker as the flames burned away to embers. Now the shadows took on nightmarish proportions, reaching for her like the fingers of demons. Liz tried to turn away but she found she couldn't move. Her limbs felt heavy, as though a great weight were pressing down on her, pinning her to the bed. Her skin was alive with the prickling of gooseflesh and a violent shivering overtook her. The room was icy cold.

She tried to tell herself not to be ridiculous, not to be scared, but the feeling had taken hold of her. It was just like the mounting panic she'd felt that time with the corset, the terror that she wouldn't be able to breathe, the idea that she would gasp and pant and suffocate as the laces drew tighter and tighter and squeezed the life out of her.

She opened her mouth to scream but nothing came. Nothing but the stench of rotting wood and sweat.

And then came the pain.

It hit her deep inside, like a cramp. As though her insides were a wet rag and someone was wringing it out. Liz gasped and the word "no" came from somewhere. It was whimpered several times more before she realised it was her own voice, meek and strangled. But the pain didn't stop.

Tears filled her eyes, blurring what little she could see. There was nothing in the room but shadows. Soft flickering shadows from the dying light of the fire. And the shadows were of nothing. Nothing but the hard edges and angles of the room.

And Carson Menrath.

Now she was certain of it. The white face *was* closer. Too close. Had it broken away from the wall and fallen on her? Was she going to die crushed beneath it? She sensed laughter around her and inside her and then an even crazier idea popped into her mind: the head hadn't moved; *she* had. She was floating, hanging in the air before the solemn face, with the hard oak floor a long way below.

Her insides wrenched again and she recognised the sensation for what it was. Splinters raked along the delicate inner walls of her sex. Back and forth, in and out. Unpleasant thoughts flashed through her mind, a hard rain of ugly images. A pair of glaring, angry eyes met a pair of frightened ones. A voice pleaded. There was more wrenching, more cramping, more *penetrating*. Then something took hold, something tiny. A parasite. A monster. It grew within her, warping and distorting her, leeching away her blood, her fluids, her life.

It had only lived in her nightmares before but now it was free. It had clawed its way out of her. It was here. Alive. Hideous. *Real*.

A cry of disgust, of humiliation and rage. Then despair.

From somewhere far away came the sound of hammering, of splintering wood. Then the smell again. Mouldy, musty, decaying. Wood. Sweat. Loathing.

Liz tore free of the vision and found her voice at last. She released a long blistering scream, a howl of anguish that seemed to come from another world. With her voice came movement and she broke the spell of paralysis, flailing her arms desperately as though to stop herself from falling. But there was only the bed beneath her. Her eyes flew open and she stared up at the ceiling. She heard the sizzling embers of the dying fire and saw the flickering shadows. High above her, Carson Menrath stared solemnly at nothing. A plaster head, nothing more.

Tears pricked her eyes and she wondered if she was losing her mind. It couldn't have been a dream. It was too real, too vivid. Too painful.

It was still there, that hot burning deep inside her. Then she felt the dampness. She sat up, crying out at the raw ache in her abdomen as she moved. The bedsheets were soaked, painted bright scarlet with blood.

For a moment all she could do was stare, transfixed. A part of her knew what had happened, that deep primal part inside every woman. She'd heard that some women knew from the very first moment, an idea she'd always laughed off as cloyingly sentimental. But she understood it now, understood it with the full horror of realisation.

He wants to get inside me.

Rowan's haunted words drifted back to her.

I feel violated.

Liz opened her legs carefully, hissing at the pain. She slipped her fingers down into the bloody gash and began to probe gently. The spicy odour of blood didn't quite mask the other smell. The woody scent was still sharp in her nostrils. And when she found

173

the splinters she calmly plucked them out, one by one, and wrapped them in a tissue. Then she allowed her eyes to travel up along the wall, knowing exactly what she would find. Even so, the sight made her insides clench with horror. There was a damp, dark stain on the wall just below the plaster head.

A scream twitched in her throat, impatient to be given voice. She choked it down. Then a single thought took hold and held fast in her mind: *Nick must never know.*

PART TWO

HOSTILE WOMB

CHAPTER 17

It was a week since the Manchester trip and neither one of them had mentioned their strange little fight. You could hardly even call it a fight, Nick thought. Not really. Just one of those funny misunderstandings. A clash of moods. When he got back, Liz acted as though nothing had happened and they seemed to be in some kind of silent truce. Nick wasn't about to upset the balance by dragging it up again, and he didn't feel the need to extract any kind of apology from Liz.

For her part, Liz had been very affectionate on his return, and he supposed she felt guilty about the whole thing. Maybe she was simply trying to make it up to him without acknowledging that they'd had a row. If that was the case, he was happy to forget all about it.

Several times it was on the tip of his tongue to ask her about the other thing – the elephant in the room – but he never did. Besides, if he was right, she'd bring it up herself when she was ready and if he was wrong... Well, he didn't want to upset her.

So he'd kept quiet.

In the past he'd occasionally wondered what might happen if one of them had a change of heart. People with kids always seemed to think that was a given. Rachel had certainly hectored Liz enough with that smug old prediction. *You'll change your mind.* In other words: *You'll come to your senses one of these days.*

Nick's parents were far more easygoing. They made it known that they'd love grandchildren, but only if Nick and Liz wanted them. There was no pressure. He'd just never been all that interested. Babies were terrifyingly helpless, and children in general were so needy. He hated the thought of being tied down, of losing the luxury of spontaneity. Besides all that, he supposed he had a deep sense of insecurity about what kind of father he would make.

More than anything though, he hated the idea of something coming between him and Liz. While they certainly had their differences – and Lord knew they'd had their share of fights – it had always been him and Liz against the world.

But now...

He lay in bed staring up at the ceiling and wondering what it would be like to have a kid. A baby. The idea still filled him with fear. The noise, the mess, the disruption, multiplied by his own

177

fear of inadequacy in the face of it all. There were a million selfish reasons not to have kids, and he and Liz had always agreed that their lives were full and happy enough without the added chaos that a little Holland would bring. Now that it seemed a possibility, however, he was finding the idea more appealing by the day. Maybe all those other people had been right; maybe one day you *did* just change your mind. Or maybe you had to wait until you were faced with the reality before knowing how you would feel.

Hadn't that been Ian's reaction when Chelle announced that she was pregnant? The couple had been going through a rocky patch and then one morning she had simply dropped the bombshell, along with the news that she'd secretly stopped taking her birth control pills several weeks before. Ian had been livid at first, more at the deception than at the consequence. Nick took his friend out to drown his sorrows where, after several pints and a lot of soul-searching, Ian admitted that Chelle's announcement had made him see her in a whole new light, one he thought he could grow to love even more. Nick had been less optimistic. After all, having a baby was supposedly one of the worst ways to attempt to save a marriage. But they were still together now, as happy as ever, and their six-year-old son was a great kid. It seemed to have worked.

Nick couldn't imagine either him or Liz being so deceitful, but what he *could* imagine were the myriad ways in which such a sudden reversal would change a couple. Parenthood had transformed his friend's relationship for the better; what might it do for him and Liz?

He looked over at her, sound asleep beside him, and reached out a finger to touch her hair. Lost in her own world again. She'd been sleeping so *deeply* lately. And that was just one of many things that had changed about her. When they'd first moved into Wintergate it had felt like a second honeymoon. Now there was a gulf between them, secret and unspeakable. He rolled over, unable to look at her any more right now. It hurt too much.

He thought back to the day she'd insisted that the weather was awful when it hadn't been. She'd been so snappy and grouchy that morning, blaming it on her period. And Nick had believed her. Then came that weird phone call and more snappishness from Liz. Her whole personality seemed to have changed and there was only one explanation he could think of for such a complete transformation. He just didn't dare ask her about it.

And that was the worst thing of all, wasn't it? That he couldn't even talk to her. That he was actually *afraid* to talk to her. He felt a sudden flash of anger at the unfairness of it. What had happened

179

to her, to *them*?

He lay there for a long time, his thoughts chasing round and round. Finally, he decided he couldn't take it any longer. He rolled back over and nudged Liz.

"Liz? Hey, please wake up."

She didn't respond.

He took her arm and shook it, calling her name. It was some time before her eyes at last fluttered open. She looked lost and bewildered, even frightened, as though she had no idea who might be shaking her awake.

"It's only me," Nick said, smiling. "You remember me? Your husband?"

She didn't laugh at his feeble humour but her lips did twitch in an attempt at a smile. "Nick," she mumbled.

"Yes. Listen, we need to talk."

That got her attention. It was a phrase that never signalled anything good.

"What is it?"

And so he told her what was bothering him. The way she'd been acting, her strange new reclusiveness, her sniping, his confusion. Then, when he felt he'd made his case, he found the courage to ask the question.

"Liz, are you pregnant?"

Her eyes went wide and for a moment she looked truly frightened, as though he'd told her that he was dying. Emotions battled across her features for a moment and Nick shrank back, sure he'd just ruined everything. But then Liz gave a comical grimace and laughed.

"Fuck, no!"

After the suspense of the past week, it wasn't what Nick had been expecting – indeed, even hoping – to hear.

"Oh," he said.

The fact that he didn't immediately share in her revulsion at the prospect wasn't lost on her. Her eyes widened again and she drew back from him, as though he had some contagious disease.

"You sound disappointed," she said, her eyes blazing.

He didn't know what to say, so he stayed silent.

"Were you hoping I was?"

He shrugged. "I guess. Maybe a bit. I just couldn't think of any other explanation for why you were acting so weird and then – well, I guess the idea didn't seem so terrible after all."

The expression on her face was one of absolute horror. He may as well have told her he wanted to amputate her legs.

"Liz, would it be the worst thing in the world? I mean, we're

181

settled now. We have a house that you – that *we* – love. Business is going well for both of us. Maybe it's time to think about it. You know I love you more than anything."

She didn't even respond to his declaration. She pulled away, snatching her dressing gown from the chair beside the bed and covering herself up, spitefully denying him the sight of her body. When she finally spoke again her words were vicious.

"We always said it was a deal-breaker. You say *I've* changed? Take a look at yourself. You're the one who's changed. I don't even *know* you anymore. I can't *believe* you would do this to me!"

As her diatribe continued, Nick tried to interrupt, to calm her down, to make her stop. But she didn't want to hear it, didn't want to listen, didn't want to be near him at all. Tears spilled down her cheeks and she scrubbed at them angrily, like a child in the throes of a tantrum.

"I'm sorry," he said. "Okay? I'm sorry. I haven't just changed everything on a whim. It's just – I thought maybe you already *were* pregnant and – well, like I said, it suddenly didn't seem like the end of the world and–"

If she heard anything he said, it wasn't apparent. She batted away his attempts to touch her and stormed out, slamming the big oak door behind her.

Nick sat on the edge of the bed, absolutely shell-shocked by her behaviour. They'd had arguments in the past, but this was in a league of its own. A week ago she'd blamed her testiness on her period. He'd seen the bloodstained sheets in the bin when he got home from Manchester, so he hadn't questioned it. But now he had to wonder if there was something else going on with her.

Right now she clearly wanted her space and there was nothing he could do but give it to her. Once she got whatever it was out of her system she'd be back to normal again. Hopefully.

CHAPTER 18

After a couple of days of being frostily cordial with one another, Liz began to warm up again. She didn't exactly apologise, but she made it clear she was feeling bad about how she'd acted.

"Do you fancy a walk?" Nick asked one Sunday morning. They'd slept in and he was surprised at just how late it was. The view from their window was as magnificent as ever. It looked chilly but the sky was a vibrant blue with only the slightest wisps of white cloud. "It's a beautiful day. We haven't been to the pier in ages."

Liz burrowed deeper into the bed. "It's cold."

Nick frowned. "It's gorgeous! Just wear a coat."

"I bet the Channel is frozen over," she mumbled, pulling the bedclothes over her head.

He couldn't tell if she was joking or not. The house was never exactly warm, no matter how hard the sun beat down, but it certainly wasn't freezing. Perhaps she just wasn't fully awake. He shook her again. "Come on, Liz. Autumn's nearly over and I really want to enjoy the sunshine while it lasts. I'll take you out to lunch. We can go to one of those pubs on the seafront."

She was silent for so long he thought she'd gone back to sleep. Then she gave a resigned little sigh and peeked out from beneath the duvet. Something in his expression softened her and she sat up to kiss him. "Okay," she said. "If you want to go, we'll go."

"I'm sure it will make you feel better. You've been cooped up in here ever since we moved in."

"I haven't got cabin fever," she said, an edge creeping back into her voice. She caught it herself and smiled. "But yeah, lunch would be nice."

"Great! Don't forget to wear trainers this time."

She gave him a mock salute. "Yes, sir."

The day was as sunny as Nick had promised, although Liz seemed to keep looking up at the sky in surprise at the fact. She didn't even need to button her coat. They retraced the path they had taken before, up to the hill fort and then down past the graveyard at St Andrew's church.

"Look," Nick said, pointing. "It's that same cat."

The ginger tom they had seen before was waiting for them by the churchyard gate, as though he'd never moved. This time he did allow himself to be petted. He walked in a drunken figure of eight, tail curling like a frond as Liz stroked his back. His purring was noisy enough to be heard over the crashing surf and he positively yowled when they made to leave him.

"Demanding little chap," Liz said with a laugh. "He must belong to the vicar."

"Maybe he *is* the vicar."

Liz laughed at his joke, which cheered Nick further. It felt as though things were going back to normal.

They ate on the verandah at the Moon and Sixpence, admiring the view. People were down on the beach in shorts, in defiance of the season, and the smell of barbecue wafted up from there. Sunlight glinted off the waves and several sailboats were dotted around the Channel. There were even a few swimmers in wetsuits, though the water couldn't be any sort of friendly temperature. After eating, they walked the length of the pier and then headed for home.

At the marine lake a little boy was sailing a remote-controlled boat. Or rather, trying to. A man, presumably his father, offered words of encouragement. The little boat moved in fits and starts, yawing wildly from side to side before crashing into a floating mass of seaweed.

Nick couldn't help but smile and something twisted in his

heart, a sudden and powerful sense of envy. He'd had a remote-controlled car as a child and he'd been no better at operating it than this boy. The man stood behind his son, covering the boy's tiny hands with his own, guiding the boat back into the open water. Nick's father had done exactly the same thing. The memory was so poignant that for a moment he thought he might cry.

"Ground Control to Major Tom."

Nick tore his eyes from the scene. Liz was looking at him strangely.

"Sorry," he said, nodding towards the boy. "Just a flashback."

"Ah. Well, I hope he's got enough lifeboats on board. Those passengers are going to need them."

Any other day he might have laughed at her harmless jest but just now he felt oddly vulnerable. He recalled her crass response when he had asked if she were pregnant. *Fuck, no!* He drew back from her a little, feeling inexplicably wounded once more.

Liz seemed to sense she had done something wrong. She edged closer to him and slipped her hand into his. He squeezed it but it still felt as though something had moved between them.

That morning, as he'd stood before the window in nothing but his pants, he had rather hoped she might be aroused enough to make love. In the past she would have been. But it had been *weeks* now. Liz just never seemed to be in the mood anymore. He felt unwanted.

"I love you."

He was so surprised by her words that for a moment he thought she'd been reading his mind. He kissed her. "Oh Liz, I love you too. So much."

They didn't speak the rest of the way, not even when the cat greeted them at his usual station. Nick leaned down to give him a half-hearted scratch behind the ears but Liz didn't wait for him.

Back home, Nick broke the awkward silence by suggesting they watch a movie. He picked a comedy they both loved, hoping it would lighten the mood. It only seemed to raise the occasional smile from her, though, and she seemed distracted the whole time as though listening for something in the bedroom overhead.

CHAPTER 19

The necklace was awful. She'd mangled the end clips with her pliers and crushed two of the spacers as well. Liz glowered at it before sweeping the whole ruined mess off the table towards the bin. Beads and charms clacked against the rim before bouncing off and rolling away in all directions on the floor, many of them sprinkling down under the banister into the hall below.

"Great," she muttered. "That's just great."

It was that bloody cat's fault. Would it ever stop yowling? It had seemed content just to sit in the same spot day after day. Why was it suddenly here? Had it followed them home the last time they were out there?

There was no way she was getting any work done today. A quick check of her email showed her a handful of new orders and a couple of notes whose subject lines suggested unhappy customers. She had already refunded one woman who'd complained that the tiara Liz had made for her daughter's "sweet six" Disney Princess birthday party was too dangerous for a child. *Too many sharp edges.* What the hell did the bloody cow think

189

crystals were made of – marshmallows? Clouds? Angel snot? It had taken all her willpower not to send the scathing note that kept composing itself in her mind.

It was just one of those days, she supposed. She couldn't please anyone or do anything right. And now that cat was here to make sure she had no peace. She stalked along the corridor to the bedroom and parted the curtains, sweeping the forecourt with a piercing gaze. There was nothing there. Then she heard it again. Louder this time.

She cocked her head, listening intently. It was a high, thin cry, muffled as though coming from just outside the house. From *behind* the house. Maybe it was somewhere up on the hill. Or even in the archway below. Perhaps it wasn't the cat at all but some bird with an especially unlovely call. A hatchling that had tumbled from its nest?

When the sound came again she furrowed her brow. Odd. It could almost be coming from somewhere in the room. She closed her eyes and focused on pinpointing the source of the cry, standing absolutely still. She was so absorbed that when the phone rang, she jumped as though electrocuted.

She snatched up the handset. "Hello?"

After a small pause Nick said "Hey, you all right?"

"What do you mean?"

"Just that you sound out of breath. And a bit testy. Anything going on?"

She sighed and dropped into the window seat. "Just some stupid crow or something. I can't figure out where it's coming from. It sounds like it's in the room."

"Probably starlings," Nick said. "They build nests in the wall, don't they?"

Liz sighed with relief. Of course. No wonder she was hearing them in the house. "That must be it," she said.

"Always happy to help a damsel in distress. But listen, the reason I'm calling is – we finished early today and Ian asked if we'd like to have dinner with him and Chelle."

Liz stared at the wall. Now that Nick had put the idea in her head, she was certain she could hear the bird inside the wall. It sounded weird, almost like a human voice. "Dinner?" she repeated blankly.

"Yeah. They suggested Myristica. Sound good to you?"

"Myristica."

"Liz, are you sure you're all right?"

"What? Yes, I'm fine. Sorry. Just this bird..."

"Well, forget about the bird for a minute, will you? Do you

want to meet us there?"

In truth she did, but her knee-jerk "yes" became a stilted silence as her mouth worked to frame a "no".

"Liz?"

"Oh, I don't know," she said at last, wearily. "I've got a lot of work to do here and I don't really feel like going out."

Nick was quiet for so long she thought he'd hung up. When he spoke his voice was low and concerned. "Are you sure nothing's wrong? We haven't been to a nice restaurant in ages and you don't seem like yourself lately."

"What's that supposed to mean?"

"It's not supposed to mean anything, love, it's just the truth. You're acting like some shut-in old spinster. You never want to leave the house anymore. You're moody and you've got a really short fuse these days. Is there something going on you're not telling me?"

Her heart swelled at the concern in his voice and she yearned to be held, to be taken in his arms and squeezed tightly and told that everything was all right, that he loved her, and all was right with the world. But even as she knew the feelings were there, it was as though some other force prevented her from actually expressing them. Her emotions seemed distant, like memories she should put aside for the moment to deal with the present problem, which was getting out of an unwelcome invitation.

"I'm sorry," she said, forming the words carefully. "I'm just not feeling well. I buggered up a project today and I'm a little stressed about fixing it."

"Then a nice meal is just what you need! Come on, Ian and Chelle said they haven't seen us in ages."

"They were at the house-warming party."

"Yes," he said, drawing out the word, "and that was nearly two months ago. Come on – don't you want to go out?"

"No. Really. You go ahead. I've got a headache."

He sighed. And this time it sounded a little exasperated. "Liz, this is crazy. What's happened to you? It's like you're a different person."

The thin cry cut through the air again and Liz raised her head. It had come from the area behind the bookshelves, she was sure of it now. She carried the phone across the room, waiting for the sound again.

"Liz?"

"Yes?"

"Are you listening?"

"Yes," she snapped. "I just heard it again. It's behind the

bookshelves. You don't think it's damaging the house, do you?"

Nick was quiet for several seconds, as though listening for it too. When he spoke again he sounded very unhappy. "I'm worried about you, Hedgehog. Something's happened. Something's going on that you're not telling me. Whatever it is, I can help. But you have to talk to me."

"I don't have to do anything! Why don't you just say what you mean: you think I'm going crazy. Or I'm already crazy. Oh, wait, I get it. You've been talking to my bloody mother, haven't you? Did Mommie Dearest give you some brilliant insights? Right – get this through your thick skull: there's nothing wrong with me! I'm perfectly happy and I'll continue to be perfectly happy so long as people *leave me the fuck alone!*"

Her outburst had shocked him into a stunned silence. All she could hear was his breathing. Then he said, calmly and coldly, "Fine. If that's how you want it, you can have all the space you want." And the line went dead with a click.

"Good," Liz told the handset. "We don't need you anyway."

Her hands were trembling as she set the phone down in the charging dock, where it emitted a little beep. Well, that was that. Nick wouldn't be coming home tonight. He'd stay in Bristol with his friends and the three of them could talk about her all they wanted. It wouldn't be the first time. Besides, Liz had seen the way Chelle looked at the house, seen the pinched little frown as she noticed each flaw, each bit of untidiness. Honestly, sometimes the snooty little bitch reminded her of Rachel.

Her heart was pounding with the stress of the argument but something else was gnawing at her mind. She didn't want to be around Nick right now but she was also strangely anxious about being left alone overnight. Something had happened last time, hadn't it? Only she couldn't seem to remember what.

In any case, there was no way she was ringing back to apologise. Nick was the one being unreasonable. Wasn't he? What had he even said to set her off? Oh yes – dinner. She *did* want to go. What on earth had possessed her to bite his head off and say no? It was as though something wanted her to push him away. Her harsh words came back to her, bringing with them a wave of guilt. She reached for the phone with an unsteady hand but by the time she had picked it up again, she couldn't think who she wanted to ring.

None of her thoughts seemed to make any sense. A burning line of pain was slowly stitching itself along the side of her head. She had to swallow down a wave of nausea as the dial tone swelled and swelled and finally began to bleat with robotic urgency. She threw the phone against the wall with a cry, clutching the sides of her head and rocking with the pain. It felt as though her head was splitting open.

Then, as quickly as it had come on, the pain subsided. Liz found herself kneeling on the floor, staring at the scattered, broken pieces of the handset. She picked up the largest piece and held it to her ear, listening.

"Who's there?" she asked.

But there was nothing, not even a dial tone. Of course there wouldn't be; the phone was in bits. But someone *had* called her. Hadn't they? Her gaze was drawn to the bookshelves against the back wall. The room was silent, but she knew it wouldn't be for long. Yes. Something had been calling her.

She listened, knowing the sound would come again. It was louder when it came this time. As though whatever it was knew that it now had her undivided attention.

Without even being aware of it, she moved towards the bookshelves. The source of the sound was level with her head and she pressed her ear against the spines of the books. In addition to the cry, she could hear the friction of something moving, scratching. For a moment she imagined a hedgehog trapped back there, its spines rubbing against the inside of the wall as it tried

196

to get free. But she was certain they didn't cry like this.

She began removing the books, starting with the collection of battered paperback fantasy novels she'd been accumulating ever since she was a child. At first she was careful, keeping them in order and laying them down gently to one side. But as she cleared each shelf she grew more impatient until she was simply tearing the books away, oblivious to how they landed as she flung them to the floor.

In no time she had emptied half the bookcase. Now it should be light enough to move. She rocked it from side to side, walking it out to expose the wall. The space behind was covered with dust and cobwebs. In the process of moving the bookcase, she disturbed a large brown spider that scurried across her hand. She gave a little squeal of disgust and flailed at it, raising a cloud of dust that made her cough.

She didn't want to put her head against the filthy wall to listen as she had with the books, but she found she didn't need to. The sound was coming through loud and clear. It was a distinctive cry, soft and yet piercing. Horribly mournful. It sounded anguished, like something forsaken, abandoned. A profound feeling of sorrow came over Liz.

"It's okay," she murmured. "I'll help you. I'll get you out."

At some point she must have gone down to the kitchen to retrieve the toolkit from underneath the sink. She began using the claw of the hammer she found herself holding to lift and peel away the paper. It was heavy Victorian stuff, and it didn't come up easily. Behind it the cry grew louder and more desperate, as though whatever was back there knew she was getting close.

Plaster dust clouded the air as she scraped at the wall – first with the hammer, then with her hands. It got in her eyes, nose and mouth, making her sneeze and cough. She hissed with pain as a fingernail broke, and then she began to use the hammer in earnest. The first blow showered both the floor and the books with dust, and it took several to break through the outer crust of plaster. There was some kind of primitive insulation inside the wall cavity, and she could see evidence of insect life between the joists, as well as mouse and rat droppings.

She wrinkled her nose at the sight, unaware that the sound of crying had stopped. She had the sense of having come into a room with some specific purpose, only to forget it once she was there. Staring into the exposed cavity made her feel ill at ease. At the same time, the sight was somehow familiar. The arrangement of upright wooden posts and their crossbeams. The dust. The spider, watching her from the high vantage point it had escaped to.

She knew this place. She'd seen it before.

"Where are you?" she heard herself whisper.

Closing her eyes, she reached up to a crossbeam just above her head. Her fingers moved along the length of the wood before coming to rest on something small and hard. Her first thought was that the tiny gnarled thing was a twig. So it was a bird after all, and she'd disturbed its nest. But when she stood on a chair for a closer look at the space it had come from, she saw that there was no nest. There were, however, several more of those strange-looking twigs.

She turned them over and over in her hands. As she stroked their coarsened surface, she could almost fancy that they were moving. Then one twitched.

She was sure it had done so of its own accord. And if the first one might have been her imagination, the second certainly wasn't.

Twitching, moving, with new life they flexed and reached, telling her by their movement what they were.

Abomination.

When Liz closed her eyes she saw an infant's hand grasping hers, only to be pulled away. But the tiny hand wasn't right. The fingers – there were too many of them. From somewhere deep inside herself she heard another cry, and this one had something of madness in it. Gently she stroked the desiccated little fingers, trying to soothe the creature they had belonged to. But the other cry, the one that was inside her head, the one she knew to be that of the creature's mother, would not be stilled.

CHAPTER 20

"I think we need some time apart."

Liz nodded, even though Nick couldn't possibly see her over the phone. After ringing the land line the next afternoon and getting no response, he'd tried her mobile. Fortunately, she'd heard it and answered. She didn't like to think what might have happened if he'd been unable to reach her at all and had come home in a panic.

"Nothing drastic," Nick added hurriedly. "I'm not talking about splitting up or anything. It's just that I can't seem to do anything right these days. Everything I do seems to irritate you and you just keep pushing me away and–"

"You're right," Liz agreed, seizing upon the suggestion like a lifeline. "A few days on our own might be good for us."

As she spoke, her eyes flicked towards the ruined wall. She had only the vaguest memory of tearing it open. She'd woken in the early hours to find herself lying sprawled over the scattered books and rubble, her neck and shoulders aching from exertion, her fingers raw and bloody from where she must have been

201

clawing away the wallpaper. The pain was coupled with a deep sense of shame, as though she'd got drunk and trashed a hotel room.

There was a long silence on the other end of the phone. "I'm really sorry if I've done anything that's made you so upset," Nick said, "but I just can't take the chaos. You've changed, Liz. And whatever's wrong, whatever's happened, it's obvious I'm making things worse. So whenever you're ready to sort things out with me..."

She wanted him desperately. She wanted to tell him everything. And to be reassured that she wasn't crazy, that everything would be okay again. But the words just wouldn't come. All she could see around her was the evidence of some kind of madness, the destruction she'd caused last night yet had no memory of. She had to clear the mess away, hide what she'd done. Then she could tell him how sorry she was. Then he could come back. Then things could go back to normal.

Her throat felt full and she blinked back tears as she resisted the words of love she so badly wanted to speak. If she said them, he would hear her cry for help. He would come home. She felt her heart swell at the thought of how easy it would be to end the terrible little war she had unwittingly started.

Say it, she urged herself.

But something held her in check. Some insidious voice inside her head whispered terrible consequences.

If he comes back now, he'll see what you've done. He'll know you've lost it completely. Then he might leave you for good. He might even have you sectioned.

The idea was too much to bear. All she needed was time to sort things out. So, instead of speaking from her heart, she drew herself up and imagined she was addressing her mother, adopting the most aloof tone she could muster.

"Yes, that's fine. A few days."

It was all she could manage. She put the phone down before Nick could hear her crying.

CHAPTER 21

"Whom did you say you were after, pet? A preacher?"

"No," Liz said patiently. "Pritchard. William L Pritchard. The author of this book." She held up her copy of *Clevedon: Through the Eyes of Time*. "I was wondering if he lived around here."

The librarian stared at Liz for several moments as though she'd spoken in another language. She had one of those ancient, lived-in faces you saw lovingly preserved in artsy monochrome portraits. There was nothing monochrome about her hair, though. It was the glaring yellow of a DIY bleach job. Suddenly her eyes widened and with a sharp intake of breath she clapped her bony hands together.

"Oh! You mean our Will!"

Liz shrugged. "I guess so. I want the man who wrote this book. If that's Will, then that's the man I'm looking for."

"Well, of course he lives here, dear."

When no further information seemed forthcoming, Liz looked around, wondering if she should look for someone else to help her.

But the old lady was busy scribbling something on a slip of paper. She pecked at several keys of the antique computer before her, and squinted at something on the screen, presumably checking it against whatever she'd written. When she was satisfied, she passed the note to Liz.

"What's this?"

"His address," the lady said, as though that were obvious.

"His *home* address? No, you don't understand. I don't know him. I couldn't possibly just turn up on his doorstep."

The woman waved away her explanation. "Oh, he won't mind. You know what writers are like."

"I'm afraid I don't have any idea what writers are like. Look, have you got an email address for him maybe?"

This earned her another blank look. The woman probably hadn't used any new technology in the past thirty years.

"All right, then," Liz said patiently, "what about a phone number?"

"You could always nip down to the Moon and Sixpence. That's where you're most likely to find him." She giggled like a schoolgirl sharing a secret.

Liz sighed with immense relief. "Thank you," she said. "I'll go and look for him there."

She remembered the pub. It was the one directly opposite the pier, where she and Nick had eaten the last time they'd gone for a walk. Her heart twisted at the thought of Nick. She told herself this would all be over soon. She just needed some answers. There was a mystery here and she was determined to solve it. Something was very wrong with Wintergate, and she hoped that Will Pritchard could help her figure out what it was.

It had taken a lot of effort to get moving after the wrenching call from Nick but she had done it. Her brain felt stuffed with cotton wool and she moved like someone weighed down by stones. Nevertheless, she'd forced herself to clean up and get dressed. She'd put her coat on and grabbed an umbrella, but once she was outside, she'd been surprised to see that the sun was out. Her head also began to feel better. The thought crossed her mind that the house wanted her to stay there, but she dismissed it. It was just more craziness from that sick place in the back of her mind. Well, she would soon close the door on it forever.

The ground floor of the pub was like a cave, dark and cool. At first she thought it was empty but then her eyes adjusted and she realised that there were several patrons inside. Which one was the writer? she wondered.

In the farthest corner sat a tubby little man with enormous

glasses. He was staring intently into a pint glass as though trying to decide whether it was half-full or half-empty. At the bar stood two men in high-vis safety jackets, probably taking a break from working on the roads. She could certainly rule out the young woman eating lunch, but what about the man in the flat cap scowling down at his feet, no drink or food in sight?

She was just about to make for the bar to ask the publican for help when she spotted someone else. An elderly man sat by one of the windows, a glass of what looked like whisky in front of him. At his feet lay the largest dog Liz had ever seen – a wiry grey giant of a beast. The man wore an old-fashioned tweed jacket and, although he looked thin and frail, she could see the determination in his features. There was a fierce intelligence in his steely grey eyes. He was writing in a leather-bound notebook and Liz noticed that he used a fountain pen. Ah yes, she thought with a smile, this was what a writer looked like.

The dog lifted its head when she turned towards them and watched her with interest, but nothing like aggression. Still, she approached with caution until she stood before the table. The man didn't seem to notice her at first but the dog made a soft chuffing sound. Presumably its way of saying, *Hey, we've got company.*

"What is it, Hyperion?"

The dog chuffed again and his tail moved back and forth, sweeping the floor. The man looked up, blinking as though surprised to encounter another human being.

"Oh, hello," he said pleasantly.

"Hi. I'm sorry to disturb you, and I know I'm being terribly rude, but are you by any chance William Pritchard?"

She could see by the light in his eyes that he was. He smiled, a warm, grandfatherly smile she couldn't help but return. "I am," he said.

"Then I wonder if you could help me." She wasn't sure where to go from there, but as she searched for the right words to phrase what she wanted to say, Pritchard gestured at the empty chair across from him.

"Please," he said. He closed his notebook and capped his pen, signalling that she had his full attention.

"Thank you." Liz sat down gratefully, glancing warily at the dog.

Pritchard gave a soft laugh. "You needn't worry about Hyperion. Titanic he may be, but he wouldn't tread on an ant."

He was what Nick would call "a proper dog", not one of those little yap factories.

"Gentle giant, eh?" she said, reaching out a tentative hand for

208

the animal to sniff. Hyperion's cold, moist noise quivered and his tongue flicked out in a little kiss across her knuckles. She smiled and scratched his ears.

"Now then," Pritchard said, "what can I do for you, my dear?"

"My name's Liz, Mr Pritchard."

He winced at her form of address. "Please. I'm just Will."

"Very well," she said, smiling. "Will. I was hoping you might have some information for me about my house. I'm sure you know it. You mentioned it in your book. It's called Wintergate?"

His eyebrows climbed to his thinning hairline. "Oh? You've bought the place, have you?"

Liz nodded. "My husband Nick and I – we've been living there now since May."

Pritchard looked thoughtful as he finished his drink. "Menrath's Folly."

"Yes, that's what you called it in your book."

He lowered his head modestly, like one humbled by the words of a fan. Liz supposed he probably didn't get many people chasing him down to tell him they loved his work.

"Would you like a drink?" he asked. He looked sheepishly at his half-empty glass. "I realise it's probably a bit early for you, but–"

"That would be lovely," she said at once to put him at ease. It was a little early, but she'd had a terrible night and the offer of a drink was too tempting to refuse. "But please let me get it. I'm the one barging in on you, after all."

Pritchard gave a little laugh. "Don't be silly. I wouldn't dream of it."

Liz found herself charmed by this show of archaic manners and she relented. "All right," she said. "A glass of chardonnay. But I'm getting the next round."

He nodded acceptance of her terms and headed off to the bar. The spring in his step suggested that he was delighted to have company. She hadn't noticed a wedding ring and she wondered if there had ever been one. While he was gone she stroked Hyperion, marvelling at his size. If he stood up, his head would probably be level with her chest. Still, while his height might be intimidating, she imagined he wasn't much of a guard dog.

Pritchard returned with their drinks and settled in. "Now then," he said, "Wintergate. First, tell me what you know about it."

"Only what the estate agent told us. That Carson Menrath built it for his wife Vanora. She was from America. They lost a baby and she never recovered, and then they both died in the fire that destroyed most of the house."

Pritchard sipped his whisky, listening. Liz felt as though she were reciting facts to a kindly schoolmaster.

"Then there's what you said in your book. That he wanted to build it on the hill fort and had to settle for building just beneath it instead."

"Yes, he was obsessed with Wain's Hill. He actually funded quite a few archaeological digs himself. You can see a lot of the artefacts they found in the Bristol Museum." He smiled. "No doubt you've wondered why that archway leads directly into the hill?"

"We have, yes."

"Well, at one point Carson wanted to put a tunnel through it. He was never happy with what the archaeologists dug up. He wanted to go deeper."

"What was he looking for? Gold?"

Prichard shrugged. "No one knows. But whatever it was, he never found it."

Something about that made Liz feel uneasy. She'd had a taste of that obsession herself. She covered the broken fingernails of one hand with the other. "In your book," she said, "there's only the two pictures of the house and another one of Carson and

211

Vanora. You said he was 'sinister' but you didn't elaborate."

"Yes, that's right," Pritchard said. "It's funny how stories develop a life of their own over the years. Usually it's the mundane ones that get embellished and turned into horror stories. A widow dies and years down the line people claim her spirit walks the halls of her derelict house, pining for her lost love. Or a child drowns in a stream and people feel a ghostly presence there forever after. Well, in this case, the horror story got usurped by the tragic romance."

Liz didn't like the sound of that. "Horror story?"

"I'm afraid so. You see, Carson Menrath wasn't quite the besotted Romeo that local history has made him out to be. I don't doubt that he married for love. He was the youngest son, so technically he was of little use to the family. That is, he didn't have to shoulder the burden of the family empire. He still wanted an heir, though. And Vanora couldn't provide it."

"Uh-oh. He was impotent?"

"Worse. Bad genes." Pritchard swirled his glass and Liz watched as the light reflected off the amber liquid. It made her think of rust, of things rotting and going bad.

After a few moments he spoke again. "The first baby was born. It just wasn't what Carson wanted."

"It was a girl?"

Pritchard shook his head. "It was an abomination."

Liz flinched.

"Carson's word," Pritchard said. "Abomination."

The wine was cold but that wasn't the source of the chill she felt. She'd heard that word before. Hissed in her ear, whispered in her mind. In *Vanora's* mind.

"Jesus," she murmured.

Pritchard laid a reassuring hand on hers. "Oh, I'm sorry. I didn't realise it would upset you so much."

"It's not that," Liz said. "Please continue. I have to hear the rest."

He eyed her uncertainly.

"Please. I have to know. Then I'll tell you why."

Pritchard didn't look at all sure about continuing. He downed the last of his whisky and reached down to stroke the dog. Following his lead, Liz took a big gulp of wine. The chill numbed her throat for a moment before fading to a pleasant burn. She placed her hands flat on the table before her, waiting.

"The nineteenth century wasn't the most enlightened of times, you see," Pritchard went on, "and Carson wasn't the most enlightened of men. The baby wasn't born completely normal. It

213

had–"

"Extra fingers," Liz finished.

Now it was Pritchard's turn to look startled. "That's right. And extra toes. How did you know?"

Liz didn't hesitate. She reached inside her bag and gently withdrew the little bundle she'd wrapped in a handkerchief. She passed it across the table to Pritchard.

He took it from her and stared at it for several seconds before opening it. He didn't seem surprised by what he saw.

"That's very sad," he said at last. "Such a shame."

"Carson cut them off, didn't he?" Liz asked.

Pritchard met her eyes. "Yes."

"And the baby died."

"I'm afraid so. I don't imagine he actually meant to kill it. He probably just wanted to 'cure' it of its deformity. But Vanora never recovered from the horror of what he'd done."

"Why wasn't he arrested?"

"Babies frequently died in that period, and Carson's family helped to cover it up. After all, a son in prison would be even more of a scandal than a deformed grandchild. As far as the record is concerned, the baby died at birth from a heart condition. It's buried somewhere in St Andrew's churchyard. When I was researching the book, I had access to some private correspondence between Carson and a local doctor. Quite a bit of money changed hands, which is what made me curious in the first place. These days a thing like that would be front page news, but back then..." He gave a sad little shake of his head. "Where did you find the bones?"

"Inside the wall." The memory made her shudder, but again Pritchard didn't seem too surprised. "Why would he do that?" she asked. "Why not just throw them out? Or bury them with the body?"

Pritchard steepled his fingers and stared down at the bones as though reading a set of runes. "Time is a mirror," he said. "It reflects both the present and the past." When Liz looked puzzled, he continued. "There's an old folk tradition of concealing objects inside the walls of a house. Clothing, jewellery, food, bones. Anything people thought would bring luck or ward off evil. And yes, some people even walled up living things."

Liz thought of the mewling cry she had heard and imagined the horror of some poor animal trapped behind a wall, howling and clawing desperately to get out until it weakened and eventually died there.

Pritchard looked down at the bones again. "I suppose a baby's

215

fingers and toes seemed as good a talisman as any to Carson Menrath."

"What happened to Vanora after that?"

"Well, history paints her as one of those melancholy souls who just couldn't handle the grief of losing her child, but that's a very modern conceit. Infant mortality was high back then and parents just didn't have the same sort of bond with their children that they have now. Babies especially. In wealthy families they were pretty much the nanny's responsibility until they were old enough to be shipped off to boarding school."

"Unless they were girls," Liz added.

"In which case they were taught to be good little prospects for marriage. Foreign wives were welcome if they came with a family fortune attached, as Vanora did. I don't believe Carson married her solely for her money, but I doubt he'd have been as smitten with someone less well-heeled. In any case, he wanted a son and she didn't give him one. At least not one to his liking."

He paused in his telling and refolded the handkerchief around the tiny bundle.

"Did he think the bones would bring him luck?" Liz asked.

"I suppose he thought they would bring him a son. He still wanted an heir, you see."

Liz did see. All too clearly. The wine turned to vinegar in her mouth as she pictured the scene: Carson taking what was lawfully his, while his obedient little wife did her duty. She hardly dared to ask, "Was there another baby?"

To Liz's relief, Pritchard shook his head. "Not that there's any record of. She did get pregnant again some time later, but her health had deteriorated by then. She had some sort of accident and she didn't just lose the baby; this time she lost the use of her legs. She never left the house again."

"The poor thing," Liz said. "I can see why you didn't put any of this in the book."

"It's a little too grim for a tourist guide to a lovely seaside town."

They shared a companionable silence for a while, gazing through the window at the pier and petting Hyperion whenever he rose to politely request attention. As Liz finished her wine she wondered whether or not to tell Nick what she'd learned. But he had already expressed a growing dissatisfaction with Wintergate. She didn't want it to turn to hate.

After a little while she pushed back her chair and got to her feet. "Well, thank you so much for your time."

"It was my pleasure, even if the story wasn't particularly

pleasant. If you ever need anything else, you know where to find me."

"I still owe you a drink."

Pritchard smiled. "Next time."

Liz returned his smile, enjoying the promise of a future meeting. Outside the sky had darkened and she felt chilled as she headed home along the seafront. A young couple was just setting out along the pier. Liz watched them through eyes glazed with tears as they linked hands and kissed deeply. The girl wore a bright red jacket that blurred into a scarlet smear. Once upon a time that had been her and Nick, so madly, desperately in love that they couldn't bear to be apart for a single minute. Had it been that way for Carson and Vanora once? The tiny bones felt heavy in her bag.

She turned away and continued on her walk. The wind had picked up, but there were still people all along the rocky beach and the arcade. She looked across to the pier, her eyes searching for the young couple. Above her a line of flags snapped in the brisk wind, their ends tattered and torn.

The marine lake reflected a leaden sky and Liz didn't notice the little boy at first. It was the same child they'd seen before, sailing his boat. This time he was by himself. The boat's battery must have died because he wasn't using the remote this time. He guided the boat across the ruffled surface of the water with a long stick, steering it back towards the edge when it went too far out. Something about that seemed profoundly sad to her and her heart wrenched at the sight of him crouching there all alone. Liz was halfway along the concrete shore when the boy stiffened and whirled round to stare at her, his eyes wide with fear.

"I'm sorry," Liz said, "I didn't mean to scare you."

The boy didn't answer. Instead he snatched up his boat and ran, leaving Liz standing alone by the cold water. Far out on the pier, Liz could just make out the girl's red jacket. They were at the pierhead, huddled together, cocooned in a world all their own.

She stared at them for a while, lost in her own thoughts, then, collecting herself, Liz followed the now-familiar route up the hill to where she knew the ginger cat would be waiting. She paused long enough to pet him and then carried on, back to the beautiful house that concealed an ugly history.

***

Will Pritchard stared after the young woman until she was out of sight. Beside him Hyperion whined and Will stroked him absently.

"Poor girl," he said. "I'm glad she doesn't know the rest of it."

CHAPTER 22

Nick sat staring at his computer screen, reading and re-reading lines of code that might as well be in Swahili for all the sense he could make of them. He'd had a terrible night and he'd been sleepwalking through most of the morning. How well he could remember shambling through work after an hour of sleep in the past because he and Liz had spent the entire night making love, or talking, laughing, just – being together. Were those days over now? Forever?

His mum had called and left a message asking him to ring her back but he couldn't bring himself to do it. He wouldn't be able to bear it if she asked how Liz was. He didn't want to share his misery with anyone else. It was bad enough that Ian and Chelle knew. He didn't intend to live in their guest room any longer than necessary, though. He missed Liz terribly. He couldn't think about anything else. What if she were ill? Or having some kind of breakdown? Shouldn't he be there for her no matter what?

Chelle had said some rather harsh things that first night, but he knew there had always been friction between them. They could be pleasant enough to one another, but they weren't friends. Liz was just being selfish, Chelle had said, selfish and childish and dramatic. Nick had listened, nodding but not agreeing. She didn't know Liz like he did. She needed her space sometimes; so did he. They had always understood that about each other and respected it. She truly had become another person but he refused to believe it was forever.

He picked up his mobile and retrieved Liz's number. He had snapped his contact picture of her one afternoon on the train to London. Liz was crouched on her seat, holding her wedding ring up and eyeing it like Gollum. She'd been doing the voice and Nick remembered thinking to himself how lucky he was to have such a mad wife.

Now the madness had taken an ugly turn. His finger hovered over the CALL button but, as he'd done several times already, he switched the phone off instead and put it away.

He didn't know what to do, but one thing was certain. He wasn't going to get any more work done today.

He saved the files he was working on and was just about to shut the computer down when his desk phone rang. For a moment he considered not answering it, but then he relented. It might be Liz.

"Nick Holland," he said warily.

"Hi, Nick. It's Gwen."

It took him a moment to place the voice and the name. She had never rung him before. "Hi, Gwen. What's up?"

Her words came in a rush. "I don't know where to start and I really hate to call you like this, but I'm worried about Liz."

So that was it. Now the call made sense. He sank back into his chair. "Join the club," he said ruefully. "What'd she do to *you*?"

"Sorry?"

"Did she bite your head off? She's been going through a pretty weird phase. She hasn't been herself at all."

Gwen sighed as though he'd confirmed her suspicions. "Oh dear. I'm so sorry. I don't mean to add to your worries but now it's even more important that I talk to you. It's about this email she sent me this morning. Or rather – the sketch."

Now he was confused. "What are you talking about? What sketch?"

"Yeah. I mean, I knew she was working on some new designs. She seemed really excited about everything and she was wanting to branch out into larger pieces. Figurines and garden sculptures, stuff like that. I was expecting something along her usual lines. Fairies, hobbits, animals, you know? Not this."

This was all news to Nick. Liz had never said anything to him about branching out and he felt obscurely hurt. He was always happy to look at the things she made and was very proud of her when one of her creations took off. Why wouldn't she have shared it with him if she was moving in a new direction? How long had this been going on?

"Well," Gwen continued, "she emailed me this morning and attached a picture of a sketch. She said she'd done it in the middle of the night. Just woke up and couldn't go back to sleep. I'm not surprised if this is what was in her head. Have you seen it?"

"I didn't even know about it," he was forced to admit. "What was it?"

Gwen was silent for a few seconds. He heard her take a deep breath before speaking again. "Nick, it's very disturbing. Can I forward it to you?"

Something fluttered in the pit of his stomach. He didn't want to see it but he knew that he had to. "Yes, of course." He gave her his email address and promised to ring her back as soon as he'd seen it.

What could she have drawn to upset Gwen so much? The woman sounded really shaken. He refreshed his email page and within a minute the inbox showed that a new message had arrived, forwarded by Gwen from Liz. He hesitated only a moment before clicking on it.

Hi Gwen. This came to me in the middle of the night. Couldn't sleep for thinking about it so I got up and drew it. Could be a big sculpture – 2 or 3 feet. Moveable parts. Do you know someone who could do it? Liz

Even the email sounded wrong. It was too clipped and impersonal for Liz. The attachment was called "Radiant". His finger hovered over the little icon, wondering what he would see when he clicked the link to view it. Then he told himself he was being silly and tapped the mouse button.

A window sprang open, revealing the sketch. And he felt like someone had doused him with ice water. On the screen, rendered in scratchy, violent pencil strokes, was the most nauseating picture he'd ever seen.

It was a woman, naked and horribly swollen. She was lying on her side in a mockery of a sexy glamour pose, one fleshy arm cocked behind her head, her smiling face upraised. The features were smudged and indistinct and the eyes were dark, empty hollows. He couldn't help imagining that they'd been pecked out by the sharp beaks of carrion crows. But it was the rest of the image that really made him shudder.

The woman's bloated body was riddled with large holes that went all the way through her belly, her chest, her throat, her legs. The detail was meticulous. The edges of each hole looked ragged and inflamed. Diseased. Worst of all, wriggling through the holes like worms in rotten cheese, were dozens of tiny babies. Malformed babies with snarling faces and cold, beady little eyes. He was convinced he could see them moving, squirming like a sea of maggots.

Suddenly he felt transported back to his childhood, when he and a friend had found a dead fox in the bushes. They'd flipped it over to reveal a teeming mass of pale larvae, writhing over each other in a struggle for the juiciest bits of rotting flesh. Nick had been sick first, falling to all fours as his stomach lurched and contracted, spattering his school uniform with vomit. His friend quickly followed suit.

The ripe, pungent stench had been trapped in his nose for days after seeing the fox and it made his stomach quiver again now as he looked at Liz's sketch. It was foul.

"Jesus," he breathed, turning away from the computer. Had

Liz really drawn this? He couldn't imagine such an image even occurring to her in a nightmare, let alone inspiring her to want a sculpture of it. Perhaps she'd simply attached the wrong file. But then where had it come from in the first place? Could her computer have been hacked? Infected with a virus?

The thought of infection made his stomach lurch again. He could see every detail of the sketch as though it were seared into his retinas. No. As sickening as it was, it was unmistakably Liz's work. He knew her style. She could draw a simple square and he'd know it was her work. Where the hell had this thing come from? And - moveable parts? She had imagined those babies *crawling* and Nick could see that clearly too, their tiny fat bodies moving jerkily through the gaping wounds in the woman's body, devouring her as she lay there eyeless, smiling her vacant smile. *Radiant*.

He switched the computer off and put his head in his hands.

CHAPTER 23

The house looked cold and unwelcoming. The sun was just beginning to set, casting a pale, sickly light over the stone angles and curves. Although Nick had only been away for three days, it felt a lot longer.

Liz's green Peugeot was parked in the archway and he was happy to see that she hadn't put it in the middle to stop him parking beside her. He took that as a good sign. Likewise, his front door key still worked and he shook his head sadly that he could even imagine her changing the locks to keep him out.

"Liz?" he called. Then, not knowing what else to say, he added, "I'm home."

When he got no answer he made his way up the stairs. His eye was drawn to her workshop in the minstrels' gallery but he resisted the temptation to look too closely at it. He didn't want to see any more sketches like the one Gwen had shown him. The table was pure chaos, as was the floor. Glitter, beads and baubles were scattered everywhere. Liz's desk was always a mess but he couldn't tell whether it was more cluttered than usual.

As he turned away and headed down the corridor towards the bedroom he thought he could hear voices. Did Liz have company? It seemed unlikely. And there was only her car outside. It took him a little while to realise that the only voice was hers. She was talking to herself.

The bedroom door was closed and he didn't want to startle her, so he knocked softly and called out again. "Hello? Liz?"

Her voice fell silent and he stood outside the door, listening. There was a thump and then the clatter as some heavy object hit the floor. Then the scramble of feet. A few seconds later Liz opened the door, peering out like a wary animal.

"I was hoping we could–" He froze at the sight of her. She was filthy, covered in dust and cobwebs. In one hand she held a hammer and in the other, a splintered board. For a second he flashed back to the day they'd met, when she'd been dusty from crawling underneath his car to rescue a hedgehog. This Liz looked like her evil twin. She stared at him, *through* him, as though she didn't recognise who he was.

At last he found his voice. "Liz, my god! What happened?"

She blinked at him, hearing but not comprehending. Her eyes were bloodshot and swollen. It looked like she hadn't slept at all since he'd left. There were streaks of blood on her face.

"Nick. It's you."

"Of course it's me. Jesus, what have you done?"

"I buried them in the garden," she said. Her voice was flat, her face expressionless. "I didn't like to leave them in the house, in the wall. I didn't think it was right. Not when Will told me what he'd done. But I couldn't fix the hole. I didn't want you to see it."

He was listening to the ravings of a madwoman. "Hold on. Slow down. Who's Will? Buried what? Oh Hedgehog, come here."

He pulled her into his arms and held her tightly, not caring how filthy she was. She stood stiffly for a moment as though she wasn't quite there, as though she had no idea who he was. Then she relaxed and let him hold her. The hammer and board fell to the floor with a loud bang. It made him jump but he didn't let go. Her arms slipped around him and then she was sobbing against his chest, pouring out a litany of things that made no sense at all. But some of them were apologies.

He stared over her shoulder into the room to see what she'd been doing and he was shocked at the destruction she'd wrought. She'd torn one of the bookcases away and smashed a hole into the back wall. Books were scattered all across the floor and amongst the debris. In a way, that was the most disturbing sight of all. Knocking a hole in the wall – that he could see her doing. But not destroying their cherished books.

"What have you done?" he murmured again.

It was some time before Liz came back to her senses. They sat on the floor amid the rubble and Liz told him the whole story: the sounds she'd heard, the nagging sense that something was calling to her, the almost trance-like experience of breaking through the wall to make that grim discovery. At times she cried, looking at all the books that were most likely ruined, her childhood volumes of *Lord of the Rings* among them.

Eventually she recounted the story Pritchard had told her. Nick held her and comforted her as she unburdened herself, and slowly she began to seem like her old self again. There was no sign of the cold, calculating Liz that had pushed him away so viciously, only his warm and loving wife. It was like a spell had been broken. Whatever the explanation, she'd emerged from the fog of bitterness, and if smashing through the wall had done the trick, then great. He wasn't going to complain.

After her meeting with Pritchard, she'd gone back to searching the wall cavity, wanting to be sure she'd found everything there was to find. Then she'd carried the tiny bundle outside and buried it.

"I didn't know if I should mark the spot like a grave or not. It seemed a bit morbid. I put them under some flowers instead. I hope I did the right thing."

Nick kissed her. "I'm sure you did."

She looked up at the hole in the wall. "Maybe now I'll stop hearing it. Now that it's laid to rest."

Nick didn't believe in ghosts and he still couldn't wrap his head around the idea that she had heard the cries of a baby, dead for more than a century. But there was no easy answer to such a puzzle. How else had Liz known exactly where to find the mummified fingers and toes? After a while, a logical explanation came to him.

"Maybe what you heard was just some animal trying to get to the remains."

"No way. You didn't hear it, Nick. It was a baby."

"I don't doubt that it *sounded* like a baby. Remember the scream I heard that morning? That sounded human too."

Her brow furrowed as she thought about that. "You're probably right," she said, but without much conviction. "I want to believe that's all it was. But anyway, what Will told me really happened. There's no denying that."

"Yeah," Nick agreed, "that's properly horrible. Not exactly a little anecdote we'll be telling friends and family." He'd been about to add "or prospective buyers" but checked himself. He was still reluctant to test her hypersensitivity to any criticism of the house. Besides, if a ghost had been laid to rest, even an imaginary one, maybe things could finally go back to normal.

He took Liz into the bathroom and got into the tub with her. They'd made love in it the day it was installed, but there was nothing erotic about this shared bath. It was a cleansing, a rebirth. It took a while to scrub away all the dirt and grime but he stayed with her until she looked human again. And once she did, her confusion seemed to melt away.

"Oh Nick," she said, tears standing in her eyes. "I'm so sorry. I've been awful to live with, haven't I?"

"Shhh. You just had a bit of a rough patch, that's all. Who knows why these things happen? All that matters is that you're here with me."

"But the wall... I can't believe I did that. And our books!" Tears slipped down her cheeks and she scrubbed them away. "What could make me do something like that?"

"Hormones?" he offered with a shrug. And as soon as he said it, everything fell into place. Liz saw the change in his expression at once and understood it too.

"Oh my god," she whispered. "I'm pregnant, aren't I?"

CHAPTER 24

They did the test twice, just to make sure. And there was no mistake. As she stared at the mark on the little test stick, a wild succession of feelings raced through her. Her gut reaction had been pure horror, followed by the *eureka* moment. In a way Liz was almost relieved. At least it was an explanation for her strange behaviour of late. Nick seemed oddly timid about the result and that was hardly surprising. She remembered that horrible fight when he'd first suggested the possibility, the way she'd lashed out at him and pushed him away. All just for asking. It made her cringe in shame to think about it.

Foremost in her mind was sheer incredulity. How was it even possible? She took her birth control pills religiously and those pills were supposed to be something like 99.9% effective.

But there was something gnawing at the back of her mind. Some kind of vague memory, like a remnant of a dream. Something secret, something shameful. A sudden sharp pain made itself known and she thought of splinters. Blood and chalk. The smell of sweat. For a moment she almost had it, the memory.

Carson Menrath. Those tiny bones. Had she found them all?

She kept her face steady, giving away none of the madness that was struggling to surface. She was just freaked out by what she'd learned from Will, that was all. Anyone would be. Now that she knew what had happened to Vanora's baby, how could she not imagine the same thing happening to hers?

She caught herself quickly. *Hers?* What was she thinking? There would be no baby. There couldn't be. A little frisson of horror swept through her at the thought and she immediately heard an inner voice justifying itself. Just because she didn't want children didn't mean she could do what Carson had done.

Nick was watching her, clearly waiting for her to say something. Was he still thinking it might be nice to have a baby? If so, what the hell was she going to do? The silence was becoming unbearable.

As hard as it was to say the words, she knew she had to. She mustn't let him think there was any chance. "I'm not keeping it," she told him softly. "I just can't."

The words were like barbs. Although he tried not to let it show, she saw the hurt in his eyes. He didn't respond.

"Nick, I'm sorry, but even if *you've* had a change of heart, I haven't. It wouldn't be fair to either of us and especially not to the baby. I'd only resent it and then we'd have a fucked up kid that would hate me as soon as it was old enough to."

He gave a long, deep sigh and met her eyes. When he spoke his words sounded considered, as though he'd been rehearsing them in his mind for some time. "Is there absolutely no possibility at all that this could be a good thing for us?"

She chewed her lip. It was the nightmare scenario she never imagined she'd have to face. Of course it was Nick's child too, and in a perfect world there would be a way for the father to have more than just a token say in a situation like this. But the bottom line was that it was her body and her choice.

He must have been reading her mind. "I know ultimately it has to be your decision, but could you do something for me? Could you at least wait a little while? Give yourself some time to think about it before you do anything rash. Can you do that?"

She felt herself bristling at the request, especially at the word "rash", but she didn't snap at him.

"Nick, I-"

"Please? Time is on our side. If you decide you really don't want it, I'll support you every step of the way. But will you at least consider it first?"

He was right about time; she had plenty of that. Surely she

owed him that much – the simple promise that she'd think about it. It was difficult, but she forced herself to agree.

"Okay. I promise I'll wait a little while," she said, and her guts clenched at the way his face lit up.

CHAPTER 25

Nick was happy. He couldn't remember ever feeling quite so happy. So Liz had gone a bit mad and smashed through a wall. So what? She was pregnant. Didn't pregnant women do mad things?

Even more than happiness, his overwhelming feeling was one of relief. They had an explanation for everything that had happened. No wonder she had felt so hostile and confused lately.

He'd been unable to focus at work because of all their problems, but now he had a different reason to be absent-minded. A *good* one. He'd poured tea into his coffee that morning at the office and laughed like crazy about it. They were *pregnant!*

When the phone rang he picked it up with a smile, expecting it to be Liz. It wasn't.

"Nick? Hi, it's Gwen."

He had been so lost in thought that it took him a moment to place her. "Oh," he said, disappointed. "Hi."

"Hi." There was an awkward pause, as though the next move were his. He found himself resenting the intrusion.

"What can I do for you, Gwen?"

"You- um, you never got back to me. The other day." When he didn't reply she added hesitantly, "About the sketch?"

Sketch. What sketch? It took him a moment to remember. "Oh yes," he said. "That." He was annoyed that she'd brought it up. "What about it?"

Gwen seemed taken aback by his response and was silent for a while. Nick was surprised at his own hostility, but then, she had interrupted his pleasant thoughts. He wondered if he could simply put the phone down, but then that might raise even more suspicion in her nosy little mind.

"Well, I just thought it was... disturbing," she said, sounding baffled. "Didn't you?"

He could barely remember it, to be honest. Something to do with babies and a sculpture? Oh yes. "Radiant". That's what Liz had called it. And it *had* been pretty ugly.

"Not really," he said coldly. "Liz has always drawn stuff like that. Obviously she's just never shown you before."

He could visualise Gwen's frown as she pondered that, could almost see it deepening on her face. It took her a long time to formulate a response.

"No," she was finally forced to admit, "she hasn't. But I'm confused. I thought you said she wasn't herself, that she'd been

238

acting strangely."

Why wouldn't the bloody intrusive woman leave him alone? Nick realised he was grinding his teeth. He closed his eyes to calm himself. "Just female stuff," he said at last, hoping that would be enough for Gwen. No such luck.

"What are you talking about? Nick, did you really look at the sketch? Liz has *never* drawn anything like that before - never. And it's not just the drawing. She said she'd *dreamed* it, and she wanted to make it into a sculpture. Our Liz! How can that not worry you? It was like something a psychopath would draw."

"Hold on a second, Gwen. 'Our' Liz?" It was all he could do to keep himself under control. He couldn't remember the last time he had felt such rage. "First of all, she's not 'our' Liz. She's *my* wife. And second, she's simply found a way of working stuff out that you don't approve of."

"Nick-"

"No, listen. She's got a lot on her mind and she scribbled it down in picture form as a way of facing her fears. I'm sure the bit about making it into a sculpture was just a joke. I'm not even sure why she sent it to you at all, since it was obviously too much for your delicate sensibilities."

Gwen was silent. Nick listened to the sound of her breathing and his own heartbeat swelled in his ears. He felt as though he were watching himself from a distance, trying to pick a fight for no good reason. Surely Gwen was just concerned. Why on earth was he lashing out at her like this? Even knowing he was doing it, he couldn't seem to stop.

"Liz already has one overbearing mother," he added. "She doesn't need another one."

The words stung him almost as much as they clearly stung Gwen. He heard a sharp little intake of breath on the line and then something like a sob. She tried several times to speak but in the end she just sat there, waiting. Was she afraid to hang up on him?

"Goodbye, Gwen. Don't call here again. And don't bother Liz either. We don't need you." He didn't slam the phone down. He placed it gently in the cradle and gave it a little tap of finality. And he smiled.

CHAPTER 26

Liz woke in the night, her stomach growling. She was absolutely starving. The clock told her it was only 2:30. Breakfast was a long way off.

A thin beam of moonlight pierced the darkness, shining like a spotlight on the back wall. It was like looking at the scene of a crime. Together she and Nick had sorted through the books and tidied up as best they could. Nick's signed copy of *The Martian Chronicles* had been flung halfway across the room but the slipcase had protected it from harm. Likewise, all the valuable comics were in plastic bags. But quite a few of the paperbacks had broken their spines.

"Sorry, Elric," Liz murmured, gathering up the damaged volumes of the series.

"Oh, he's tough," Nick said, giving her a reassuring squeeze. "And mass market. We'll buy new copies."

She knew he was as gutted as she was by the destruction, but it was wonderful of him not to make her feel any worse for the temporary insanity that had wrought it.

Once they had cleaned up the books, they'd stuffed the cavity with foam insulation and nailed plywood over the hole. Then they'd put the bookcase back in front of it to hide the unsightly repair.

Nick had tried to make light of the whole fiasco, joking about the National Trust police who must never know of their amateur attempt to put in a window, but Liz felt haunted by the whole endeavour. She knew he was only trying to keep her spirits up, but all she could think of was the last time boards had been hammered into place there, and why.

She had avoided looking at the plaster effigy since making the grim discovery. It made the ruin of Vanora's one seem even uglier. Had Carson destroyed it because of what had happened? He had probably been too blinded with sick rage to realise whose tragedy it really was. Liz couldn't shake the feeling that there was something else, something important that she was forgetting. Whatever it was, she knew the truth now: Carson Menrath had been a vile man.

He wants to get inside me.

Who was that? The voice in her head seemed familiar but it took her a long time to place it. Rowan. Yes, she'd been meaning to invite the girl out to model some of her...

She sat up. Hang on. She'd done that, hadn't she? Rowan *had* been here, when Nick was away in Manchester. But something had happened. Why couldn't she remember? The murky images kept sliding away from her as she tried to fix on them.

I hate it.

Had Rowan actually said that? About Wintergate? She could remember Gwen telling her something at the party, something about how Rowan didn't think the house looked like a happy place. But had she really said she hated it? Liz couldn't think why.

Her mouth was horribly dry and she could taste something like chalk, something with a distinctly mineral tang. It was probably just the endless clouds of plaster dust raised by her recent adventures. The room had been hazy ever since, as though the dust would never settle. The powdery taste brought with it Menrath's face. His cold eyes, his vicious manner. Her insides churned as a wave of nausea came over her.

Nick was sound asleep beside her and she knew what he would say about it if she told him. Morning sickness. The very idea of it, that she of all people should be suffering from that particular affliction, made her feel both queasy and angry. Breathing deeply, she forced herself to climb out of bed. The floor was icy but she didn't think to put her slippers on.

She stood staring at the bookcase for a moment, feeling ill. The revisionist version of Carson and Vanora's story was obscene in light of what she now knew to be the truth. The thought made her stomach lurch and she hurried down the corridor, reaching the bathroom just in time to fall on her knees before the toilet.

"Thanks for that," she grumbled. But the embryo inside her couldn't hear her, couldn't empathise, couldn't know anything. And it wouldn't be capable of doing anything at all for a long time. That was the worst thing for her about the thought of a baby. Not its disruption of her life, but its total dependence on her. The sacrifice of self required to take care of it. That she should be tied for years and years to something so helpless, so demanding, so *needy*, filled her with an unbearable dread. She knew deep in her heart that she wasn't capable of it. Not every woman was. Certainly her own mother hadn't been, though she'd selfishly had Liz and her brothers anyway. And there was another horrific thought; she might become just like Rachel.

Never.

A dissenting voice spoke up. Wasn't that all the more reason to do it, then? To prove that she was not her mother? To show that she could love someone more than herself? To bring something pure into the world and fill it with love and joy and so many other good things?

She shook her head. No. She wanted her life the way it was: her and Nick against the world. Having children was a job for others who had the aptitude.

Liz gulped water from the tap and splashed her face, glancing in the mirror as she did so. She looked wretched. Hardly surprising, given everything. Her eyes were red and puffy from crying, and she felt a little stab of guilt. Poor Nick. He didn't deserve all this craziness. She'd been so hateful and resentful ever since he'd first suggested that a child might be nice. She'd felt betrayed, but she had no right to feel that way. The truth was that he'd changed his mind because he was a better person than she was. He had a bigger heart.

She was meant to be considering the idea herself. She'd promised him that she would. Well, she certainly had enough guilt to go around. At least she was a good enough person to feel bad about not wanting the baby. She'd always imagined that in such a case she'd have no qualms or hesitation at all about getting rid of it. But now she felt its presence. There was life inside her. And nothing seemed easy about the decision at all.

Oh, it was too late – or too early – to be thinking about all this. There was plenty of time to do all the soul-searching and agonising she needed to before she made a decision. And yes, it was *her* decision. In the end no one but Liz could make it. She also knew unequivocally that, no matter what she had promised Nick, there was no way she was having this baby.

A yawn overtook her and for a moment she considered just going back to bed. But her stomach growled in response, rejecting that idea for her. She was even hungrier now that her body had purged itself. The phrase "eating for two" sprang into her mind and she grimaced, feeling even more resentful.

Barely awake, she tiptoed down the stairs to the kitchen and opened the refrigerator. The chilly air hit her and she realised she'd forgotten her dressing gown as well as her slippers. Well, she could curl up beside Nick and soak up his warmth as soon as she'd put something inside her empty stomach.

There was a platter with the remains of a roast chicken in the fridge. She was so sleepy she couldn't even remember having cooked it, but she carried it to the table and set about carving off a slice. Or rather, trying to. The meat was incredibly tough. That or the blade was dull. It took a lot of sawing just to make the first cut but after that it slid through the flesh easily.

The slice fell onto its side. Liz grabbed it with both hands and started to eat. It didn't taste right. It didn't feel right in her mouth, either. The meat was too stringy to be chicken, and the taste was completely alien. She remembered Nick telling her once that he'd inadvertently eaten rat meat from a street food vendor in China. What lingered most in her mind was his description of the smell. "Distinctly rodent-y," he'd said.

The mouthful of meat Liz was chewing smelled pungent and tasted foul. She supposed that was what he'd meant by "rodent-y". It wasn't something she could have put into words. And she must have carved off some bone as well because suddenly, something very sharp pierced the back of her throat. She gave a little cry and spat out the chunk of meat. There was something embedded in the roof of her mouth and she gagged as she pushed her hand inside to pry it loose. But it wasn't the only one. It was as if she'd eaten a mouthful of nails. Some of them felt loose inside her mouth and she spat them out. They lay on the plate like a scattering of burnt and bloodstained pine needles.

With a cry she backed away from the table. By now her eyes had adjusted to the gloom and what she saw on the platter turned her stomach. It wasn't a rat, and it wasn't a chicken. It was a hedgehog. Its little body was sliced open like an anatomy specimen. Tiny dark spines outside, gleaming red muscle inside. She'd cut lengthwise through its body and part of its head.

She scrubbed at her mouth in horror, desperate to rid herself of the taste of it. The spines had cut her and she could feel the blood oozing down the back of her throat, warm and salty.

Movement caught her eye and she turned back towards the table. The hedgehog – what was left of it – was moving. It shuffled its fat little body around until it was facing her. Then it lifted its mutilated head, turning it sideways to fix her with its remaining eye. She had no doubt that it *saw* her. Saw her with crystal, baleful clarity.

Liz screamed. And screamed.

At once she heard the thunder of Nick's feet overhead as he raced towards the stairs, but she couldn't stop screaming. Not even once he was there with her, holding her, soothing her.

It took her a while to calm down. Her throat was raw and sore from screaming, and from what she'd eaten. She wiped her mouth with the back of her arm, streaking it with blood. "Oh god, Nick," she whimpered, "what have I done?"

He looked at her, bewildered. Then he followed her gaze to the table. He got to his feet and approached it nervously. He stared at what was on it for a long time and then slowly turned back to Liz. She knew by his expression that something was very wrong.

"What?" she asked, the word barely a croak in her ruined

throat.

"It was supposed to be a surprise," Nick said. He sounded wary, guarded. "I don't know what you think you saw, but you must have been dreaming."

What she *thought* she saw? Could he not see the poor creature? The bloody spines she'd pulled from her throat and spat out? Or had the hedgehog dropped down from the table? She certainly wouldn't have heard it with all the noise she was making. What if it had crawled off into the house somewhere, was even now hiding and waiting? But no, she could just make out the shape of it on the table. It was still there.

She rose shakily to her feet and made herself look. A cry of dismay escaped her. It was a cake. A cake in the shape of a hedgehog. She hadn't sliced into a living animal at all. There were no blood-stained spines, just a mushy lump of sponge and icing.

"But..." She didn't know what to say. There was no explanation but the one Nick had given her: she'd imagined it. "I thought it was... I was so sure." She stared at the blood on her arm, on her fingers, under her nails. The evidence didn't lie. "Look, I'm bleeding!"

Nick answered her unspoken question. "Whatever you imagined, you must have hurt yourself some other way."

She felt as though she were standing alone on a beach, watching the waves recede, reality and sanity melting with them. And once all the water had been sucked away, it would gather and swell and come racing back with all the force of the ocean behind it, to crash down over her and cover her completely and drown her with madness. For one wild moment she felt like screaming again, just throwing back her head and letting loose a savage animal howl that would go on forever.

She could still taste the warm pink flesh of the hedgehog, still taste both its blood and her own. It had been *real*. It had been *alive*.

It was too much. She sank to the floor again and curled into a ball, losing herself in her tears as Nick tried to hold her and comfort her.

"Real," she said in between sobs. "It was real."

CHAPTER 27

It was raining, hard and relentless, pounding against the sides of the house like gunfire. Liz had managed to make herself smile and pretend to laugh off the previous night's misadventure, with suitable apologies to Nick for ruining his surprise. So she'd spoiled the cake – that didn't mean it wasn't still edible, did it? She'd even gamely eaten a bite this morning and made the appropriate noises of pleasure.

"Delicious," she'd said. And Nick had looked as though he believed her.

But as soon as he was gone, so was the charade. Now she was alone again. Alone with her thoughts and the rain and the horror of her condition, which was far worse than any nightmare or delusion. Something was trying to worm its way inside her mind, just as it had wormed its way into her body.

Outside the wind lashed the barren trees and drove rain against the house as though it were a storm-tossed boat. So much for her idea of going back to see Will Pritchard. At a loss, she decided that work might be the ideal distraction. In fact, hadn't she had some fantastic idea the other day, some new design? She could start on that. She hadn't heard from Gwen in ages, which was odd. But she probably had her hands full with Rowan. Poor girl. Liz remembered her own teen years with nostalgia. She didn't miss them and she wouldn't go back there for all the world, but the march of time was so unforgiving. She was only twenty-nine herself but she remembered how old that had seemed when she was Rowan's age. You became more and more aware of your mortality the older you got. Your body started making its own strange demands. And sabotaging your plans.

She glanced up at Carson Menrath's face. It stared down at her with an imperious expression that made her shudder. *Sinister.* Across from him, the remnants of Vanora's carving jutted from the wall like a stump from which something vital had been cut. She wanted to ask Will if he knew the story behind it. Had Carson done it? Or Vanora herself?

Her worktable was a mess. It was always in a bit of a state, but this was different. Somehow it didn't seem like her normal chaos. Had Nick been rooting around for something? She couldn't imagine that there was anything he'd need from her assortment of beads and wires and charms. There were bits scattered all over the floor and the chair and down on the floor of the hall, where they'd fallen between the balusters of the minstrels' gallery or bounced down the stairs. When had that happened?

As she swept them up she thought she heard voices. Raised voices, as though people were arguing. Neighbours, she supposed with a shrug. Then she caught herself. They didn't have neighbours, not anymore. They weren't exactly cut off from the world here but they were isolated enough. Unless there were people standing right outside.

Liz closed her eyes and listened, trying to make out what they were saying. A chill went through her at a single word she heard repeated. *Abomination.*

There was a female voice, crying. Pleading. *My child, our child...*

Liz shook her head to clear it. It was just her own wild imagination, animating the story Will had told her. The house affected people strangely. Maybe Carson wouldn't have done what he had if they'd lived somewhere else, if he had built some other house for Vanora. Maybe the child would have been normal.

Such a thing belongs in a freak show, not bearing my name.

It was only a child.

Liz felt her hands move, pushing something away from her, something she couldn't see. Her eyes burned as though she'd

253

been crying, and her body ached dully.

No, stay away, don't touch me...

A chill slithered through her limbs and Liz began to tremble. She closed her eyes to shut out the images, but they were worse behind her lids. She saw Nick, his face twisted into an ugly snarl, his hands clutching at her dress. There was the sound of tearing fabric, then a scream. She felt her legs forced apart, smelled blood and the hot, heavy stink of sweat.

"No, please, Carson, no!"

She gasped and her eyes flew open. She covered her mouth with her hands, startled by the words she had spoken. There was no one there. She sat alone at the bottom of the stairs, bathed in the coloured light from the stained-glass window high above.

It took her some time before she could stand again. Her insides burned and she caught flashes of memory, little glimpses of things that could only be from dreams. Splinters, blood, the taste of chalk.

"What's happening to me?" she wondered aloud, staring around her at the great room. The walls seemed to vibrate with captured echoes, the reverberations of voices from the past. She knew what some of those voices were saying now. She was learning their secrets.

The nearer she drew to the past, the more she would find out. And she *had* to find out what had happened. She felt driven to learn the truth, if only to pacify whatever restless spirit was tormenting her. She'd found the remains of the butchered infant in the walls, but clearly that was not the end of it.

Carson had wanted a son. A *normal* son. And instead, Vanora had produced something he'd called a freak. Did he think he could force her to give him what he wanted? Perhaps in his madness and cruelty he believed it.

Something stirred within Liz. She could feel the tiny unwanted embryo swimming inside her, responding in sympathy with the wretched creature that had died here by its father's hand. Was it asking her for life?

Tears filled her eyes. "No," she whispered to it. "I'm sorry, but no."

No.

It was such a tiny word, but so powerful. It contained so much force, so much confidence. Liz could hear it in her mind, echoing down through the ages. How many millions of people must have said it? How many millions of times? And how many millions of times had it been ignored?

Her stomach twisted and she clutched her sides, wincing at

the cramp. She didn't know the first thing about being pregnant but surely it was too early to be feeling this kind of pain. She'd always told Rachel she had a hostile womb. Maybe that was true. Maybe this was her body's way of telling her there was something wrong with it, that there was something in there that she didn't want. Something she had to get rid of.

Another cramp tightened inside her like a vice and she gasped, sinking to her knees on the hard floor. Bile rose in her throat and she leaned over, ready to be sick. The mosaic tiles swam before her eyes, the patterns shifting as though she were seeing them under water. Small dark spots danced among them, and when Liz finally focused, she realised they were flecks of blood. They must be from the removal man who had fallen down the stairs all those weeks ago. The cleaners had promised there would be no trace of blood left. The sight of it made her feel even queasier.

Her guts clenched again and this time she was sick. Again and again she heaved, vomiting until there was nothing left. Even then, her body kept retching, wringing out every last drop of her stomach contents. She was vaguely aware that there was blood in it. It pooled in the cracks between the tiles, a tiny scarlet river snaking its way around her.

It felt like hours before the sickness passed, and by then she was too weak to get up. She lay on the floor, shivering, pressing her cheek against the cool tiles. Above her the stained-glass colours swirled in her vision, and she was sure the dragons on the newel posts turned their heads to stare accusingly at her. Outside the rain continued to pound.

She thought she could hear footsteps and she listened for a while, too exhausted to move. Then there was only cold silence. She was being watched.

Abomination. Freak.

From somewhere far away came the crying of an infant. Tears welled in her eyes.

No. I found you, what was left of you. You should be at peace now.

As though it had heard her thought, the crying intensified. It sounded both far away and very near. Was it coming from inside *her?* The thought made her shudder and the movement brought on another wave of nausea.

I'm dreaming, her mind insisted. *I'm delirious. Hallucinating.*

But logic and rationale had no place here, not when her mind knew the truth. However much she might wish she were only mad, the crying was not in her head. It was *real*. It was *here*.

There was something alien about it. The tiny voice filled with terror and pain had a sound that was all wrong. It was as though the mouth making the noises was distorted, the lips mangled, the throat constricted. The awful crying echoed through her head like the voice of something sick and dying.

And then she realised what was odd about it. There was more than one voice.

Shapes were moving in her peripheral vision. Her lids fluttered as she tried to keep her eyes open, tried to see. But the room was growing darker. Outside, the rain washed away the world and the crying grew louder as she grew dimmer, fading into grey, blurring into nothingness.

CHAPTER 28

"Look at this thing, Vanora! Look at it!"

Vanora's eyes flew open and she recoiled from the sight. The creature before her was waving two fat pink arms but that was where the resemblance to anything human ended.

The body was slick with blood and fluid. Its legs – too many of them – dangled like the broken necks of birds. The hideous gurgling howls made her flesh crawl, but she forced herself to look at its face. An odd number of eyes rolled wildly in a lumpy, oversized head and two misshapen mouths stretched wide, each voice separate and distinct. It looked like two babies crushed together into one.

Carson was right. It wasn't a baby; it was a monster.

As a child she had once seen a two-headed calf at a fair. Her father had laughed and pointed raucously along with the other spectators in the shabby tent. But Vanora had been profoundly disturbed. The thing had been floating in a tank. The red-eyed man running the freak show prodded it with a stick to make it turn lazily in the murky yellow fluid.

The calf looked nothing like nature had intended. Its body seemed normal enough, the thin legs folded underneath it, a tiny tail trailing behind. But its neck was swollen and it separated at the top into two thick stalks, each bearing an approximation of a head. One of them looked almost calf-like, while the other was monstrous. But even if both had looked perfectly normal, the whole was what mattered. Four milky eyes gazed out at her as it drifted round and round in its watery grave.

"No tricks! No hocus-pocus!" the man had said. "Examine it from every angle and see for yourselves!" Here he leaned down into the faces of the children in the front row and added, "If you dare!"

Her heart swelled with pity. Even though the calf was dead, its indignity would go on forever. It would float in that container until the end of time, its sole purpose to shock and horrify all who saw it. When her father had tried to draw her nearer for a closer look, she had burst into tears and fled. There were some boys outside, peeking in through a hole in the tent, and they laughed when they saw her take fright.

She felt like that child again now, her inexperience of the world having left her wholly unprepared for anything like this. She screamed, overwhelmed by both horror and fear. *She* had produced this thing! It had come from her own body. Then something gave her pause, a realisation that felt shockingly defiant: it was just as much Carson's issue as hers. Carson's son or daughter – or both. His precious heir.

She screamed and screamed, but this time there was no doctor to ease her panic with laudanum, no kindly midwife to take her hand and reassure her. She had been frightened at the sight of the extra fingers and toes all those months ago, but it had been a normal baby otherwise. One she had loved immediately and desperately yearned to hold, to soothe its shock from being torn from her body and thrust into the world. But Carson had stolen it. She had reached for it, pleading weakly, but he had taken it from her, carrying it off in his cruel hands. No one had stopped him.

Through her drugged haze she had heard it crying in a distant part of the house. The sound seemed to go on for hours. Then those cries had abruptly turned to screams. Horrible screams of agony and terror. Vanora had tried to get up, wanting to go to the child, but the doctor wouldn't let her. She had felt the needle pierce her arm and then a curtain descended on the world, shutting out the sound.

When she had woken some hours later, Carson was there. And so was the child. Its tiny hands were bandaged and bloody, and she knew at once what he had done. The child had lain in her arms, pale and limp, not crying, barely moving. The next morning it was dead.

She had told herself that it was a mercy it hadn't lived. She could have other children. Healthy children. *Normal* children. She would give her husband the son he so wanted, and no one would ever know of this. In time this terrible day, this awful experience, would be nothing but a memory. And although she knew what Carson had done, she told herself the child would not have lived in any case. Otherwise the guilt would simply be too much to bear.

Stillborn. That was the explanation they gave. Vanora grieved in her bed, unable to leave and grateful not to have to. She didn't like to think of the intolerable pity she would suffer were she to venture out. The hands that would clasp hers, the hollow words of comfort. Behind the eyes of every sympathetic lady's face would be the glow of relief. Relief that it had been Vanora and not her. Relief that their own babies were not monstrous.

She had mourned that first child, but she would not mourn this second one. Death would be a blessing for it, she thought. Her skin crawled at the memory of its misshapen head, its howling mouths and staring eyes. Two tiny infants, precisely alike, fused together, face to face. Forever and ever, amen. Fingers of madness pressed against her face, teasing her eyes closed, reassuring her that it was for the best. Whatever Carson did with the wretched creature would be a better fate than keeping it alive. What kind of life could it have after all?

Even the most terrible experiences had lessons to teach, and Vanora had learned well from this one. Now a single conviction dominated her thoughts: Carson would never touch her again. She had seen the result of a child made by force. It was both a punishment and a curse. There would never be another one.

Vanora lay in bed, praying for unconsciousness. She could still hear the crying, the twin voices reaching her through what felt like layers of cotton wool, burrowing through the very meat of her brain, slowly eating away at her sanity. At the same time she could hear other sounds. Banging and hammering. Could Carson hear it too? Was he trying to shut out the sound of their crying?

After a while the banging stopped, but the high, thin whine continued through the night. It was muffled but still unmistakably there. Just as the image of it was present behind her closed eyelids. She felt like a child herself, frightened by shadows, trembling before the tiny monster that had crawled from her body. At one point she screamed, hoping to drown it out or frighten it into silence. But the howling only intensified. It could hear her. It was crying for her. *They* were crying for her.

She felt diseased. Tainted. She imagined her reason slipping away with every minute the tiny voices went on. For a while she wondered if she had died in childbirth and now lingered in some horrific purgatory or possibly even Hell. Fervently she prayed, her words random and meaningless, nothing more than desperate animal sounds cast into a void. She wept. Occasionally she slipped into a fitful sleep where dreams dragged her even deeper into madness.

She saw the child drifting in a bottle of cloudy chemicals. There were people clustered around to see it. Carson pointed at it and laughed. Then he turned slowly and looked at her. All the wild-eyed onlookers turned with him, staring. Their faces wore expressions of disgust. She glanced down at herself and gave a cry when she realised she was naked. But not only that. Her lower body was torn, the flesh hanging in bloody shreds like a tattered skirt.

She woke with a scream, surprised to find that she was still alive, still firmly anchored in awful reality.

By morning the crying had stopped and she was forced to wonder if she had ever heard it at all. Had there even been a baby? Her body ached and burned, and the sheets beneath her were stiff with dried blood. The room smelt of death. Once she sensed Carson standing in the open doorway, watching her. But when she raised her head he was gone.

She had no idea how many hours or days passed, how long she lay in the filthy sheets, grieving as much for herself as for the miserable creature with two voices. The skin between her legs was crusted with blood, and she wondered why Carson had not sent for the doctor. He had been even more anxious than she when the first contractions had begun. But it was far too early for the child to be born anyway, so perhaps he'd simply assumed the pain would pass.

The truth teased at her brain like a whisper, a presence she didn't want to acknowledge. He'd known there was something wrong. He'd feared that the baby would be abnormal, and he didn't want anyone else to know. Perhaps the doctor wouldn't be so easily silenced a second time. Vanora imagined herself standing in a room with doors on all sides. Each of them swung open, revealing a long corridor beyond. At the end of every one was an answer. She could sense the darkness of some of those truths already, in the shadows that rustled beyond those portals. One by one she allowed the doors to slam shut, closing her off from their revelations. She didn't want to confront any of them.

The room was foul and the bed was ruined, but she dared not call out. She was frightened of seeing Carson. He had killed the first child and she knew with a sickening certainty that he had killed this one too. Worst of all was her own passive acceptance of it. The poor creature had never been baptised, so it would never get to heaven, never know its Creator.

She prayed in fervent whispers, pleading for the soul of the malformed child and begging forgiveness for wishing it dead. After a while Carson did return. He looked pale and shaken. His eyes were cold and dead and so was the comfort he had to offer. She was too weak to get out of bed and he refused to help her. Instead he brought her liquids, which she drank greedily, only to fall into a fitful, delirious sleep afterwards.

Endless nightmares clawed at her mind, tormenting her with monstrous images. Wounds opened in her flesh, gaping holes through which tiny infants crawled like insects. Their eyes met hers, glaring, accusing. She tried to push them back inside, back through the holes, but more were emerging all the time. They swarmed over her frail and broken body as she lay helpless beneath them.

Distantly she heard the chiming of the clock in the hall. Many hours must have passed but still Carson did not send for the doctor. She woke, she slept, she dreamt.

Finally, after what seemed like years, she was startled fully awake by a young woman's voice.

"God almighty! Miss Vanora!"

She turned her head drowsily. Surely an angel wouldn't sound so stricken. It was a long time before the fog in her head cleared enough for her to recognise her maidservant.

"Jane?" she asked, her voice slurred. "What are you doing here?"

"Oh Miss Vanora, I never should have left. Only Mr Menrath, he said you was taken ill and gone away to London to see a specialist. If only I'd known you was really here, I would've-" Jane caught herself, as though she'd heard a sound. She turned slowly towards the door. Carson stood there, his arms crossed over his chest, watching.

"You would have what, Jane?" he asked coldly.

She lowered her head, shuffling her feet as she stared at the floor. "I'm sorry, sir. I only meant that I could have stayed to look after Miss Vanora. Since she didn't go to London after all."

He nodded slowly, as though measuring her words.

Vanora looked on in confusion, puzzled by the exchange and wanting only to go back to sleep. The voices became indistinct and blurry and she closed her eyes against the intrusion.

Some moments later she was shaken awake again by Jane, who was muttering under her breath as she tugged at her mistress's soiled chemise. Carson was gone.

"It ain't right, Miss Vanora," Jane hissed. "A lady oughtn't to be treated like that, no matter what the gentleman says. You was ill and you needed looking after and I should have been here."

"Where?" Vanora asked fuzzily.

"You mean where was I, miss? Mr Menrath sent me to Bridgwater to see my family for the week. Said he'd got word me mum had taken ill. Only when I got there she was fine. In the very pink of health she was! I didn't think nothing of it so I stayed to visit. But then I come back and find you like this. Oh, miss! I'm so sorry! Come on, now, we've got to get you out of that bed and into a hot bath. Give me your arm, that's it."

The more Jane pushed and pulled her, the more the fog cleared. The first thing Vanora noticed was the smell. It was appalling. A slaughterhouse couldn't smell any worse. Her stomach clenched and Jane held her steady as she eased her feet down to the floor. She had no energy to stand but Jane was a stout girl, strong enough to hold her up and help her undress. Careless of her nudity, Vanora sank back down onto the edge of the bed while Jane ran to the window, letting in a blissful fresh breeze. Vanora breathed deeply, relishing the taste of clean air.

"I think a draught is less likely to harm you than the stink in this room, Miss Vanora. I'll bring up some hot water and you'll be nice and clean soon, I promise."

It was only once she was safely in the tub and Jane was scrubbing her that the full horror of the past few days began to settle firmly in her mind. She realised that none of it had been a dream. Nor was she mad.

As though reading her thoughts, Jane stopped for a moment and looked her in the eye. "Miss, I know it ain't my place to say nothing like this but... P'raps you ought to go away somewhere." She took a deep breath. "Without the master."

Hearing it from someone else was both a shock and a relief. There was nothing in the world she wanted more than to go away, far away, perhaps even back to America. Anywhere, so long as Carson wasn't there. She had married a monster and she would only give birth to more monsters if she stayed here. He would never let her rest. And he would never admit that the depravity was in him, not her. Tears slid silently down her face, and her only response to Jane was a helpless nod.

The girl said no more but she performed her duties with a

gentleness that, by contrast, further highlighted the cruelty Vanora had suffered over the past few months. Yes. As soon as she was well enough to travel, she would go. She would use Carson's own ruse and tell him that her mother was ill and she must return to New York. She would take Jane with her. Once there, she need never return. To avoid any scandal, she could fabricate an illness for herself that would prevent her from undertaking the long voyage back to England. Surely one could purchase the word of a medical man if it was to save a life.

"I'll make up the Chinese room for you, miss, and you can sleep in there. Your own room is..."

Jane couldn't bring herself to finish the sentence, but she didn't need to. Vanora finished it for her.

"Ruined. Just like me." She shuddered at the memory of the awful things that had happened in that room.

"Oh now, miss, you mustn't say such things! You'll be right as rain again soon, you'll see."

Chastened, Vanora lowered her head. "Thank you, Jane," she managed in a hoarse whisper. "I've always liked the Chinese room."

Jane smiled at her and helped her out of the bath. She didn't feel purified but at least she was clean now. Her lower parts still burned dreadfully from the ordeal, and she was weak and dizzy from hunger and from whatever Carson had been giving her. Had he been trying to kill her too? He could just as easily have pushed her off the pier into the sea. He might even have got people to believe she had taken her own life.

But that wasn't Carson's way. It would have been easier if she had died in childbirth, along with the infant. As long as she lived, he would keep forcing her, convinced that it was some weakness in her that prevented him having what he wanted. But if she died, he would be free. Free of the shame and the stigma. Either way meant death for her, but one was far worse than the other. She must escape.

CHAPTER 29

When Liz came to it was dark. She lay still, not knowing where she was. Her back ached and her head was throbbing, but she didn't feel injured. The moon peeked in at her from a high window, but she couldn't make sense of its position. The angles and shadows were all wrong.

She raised her head and sat up, startled to realise she was lying on the floor of the main hall. Images from a horror show swam through her mind as the nausea came flooding back. The sharp smell of vomit hit her and she gagged, putting her hands over her mouth to stifle another wave of sickness. What the hell had happened? Had she fallen and hit her head?

She got to her feet and stumbled to the light switch. The room sprang to life beneath the chandelier. The floor was wet with blood-streaked vomit, and so was she. Her stomach clenched at the thought that she'd been lying in it for hours. And those dreams...

Tears filled her eyes and for a moment she could only stand there, lost. Where did she start? What should she clean up first?

She had a sudden pang of guilty shame, as though she'd done something wrong and must hide the evidence. A glance at her watch told her it was only five o'clock, but winter had dug its claws in and it was already black as night outside. The thought that Nick would be home soon set her heart pounding, and she made up her mind quickly.

Using the banister for support, she hobbled up the stairs and grabbed a towel from her desk. She threw it over the foulness on the floor and went back upstairs. Herself first, then the floor. And she'd take something for her head while she was at it.

As she washed herself, she became convinced she could hear another voice. A woman, gentle and kind. It was as though her dreams had filtered through into the waking world.

That's it, miss. You'll be right as rain soon, you'll see.

She remembered what Will had said, about time being a mirror. It reflected both the present and the past. Maybe sometimes things got trapped between worlds. As she stepped from the tub she peered nervously at her reflection. Her eyes were hooded, haunted.

She got dressed and went to clean up the mess downstairs. She couldn't tell Nick about any of this. But one thing was certain. There was no way in hell she would keep this baby.

CHAPTER 30

Rachel winced as the taxi hit another bump and she nearly smeared lipstick across her face. Her subsequent frown in the mirror only further confirmed for her why she needed makeup in the first place. Time was merciless, and she seemed to find new evidence of its cruel march with every passing day. But there was only so much you could hide with concealers and creams. She wondered how long it would be before she succumbed to the temptation of cosmetic surgery.

With a sigh of disgust she tucked her compact mirror back inside her Louis Vuitton bag. Why was she even bothering? The last person she needed to make up for was Liz, especially since Rachel hadn't even mentioned that she was coming. Besides, if previous unannounced visits were anything to go by, Rachel would probably be in tears before it was over, her mascara running and her nose red.

Once more she took out her phone and stared at it, her fingers itching to push the buttons that would connect her with her daughter. That was assuming Liz even picked up, of course. Half the time she suspected that Liz just sat there coolly watching as the phone rang and rang, waiting for it to go to voicemail, where a computer would ask the caller to leave a message. Which Rachel wouldn't. She would speak to the person she was ringing, not to a machine, thank you.

She caught sight of the permanent frown etched into her features, reflected in the black mirror of the phone's screen, and she snapped the case shut over it. She didn't want to risk Liz telling her not to come, but if she didn't warn her first, Liz was even more likely to be cross. Oh, why did everything have to be so complicated? Why must they always play these games? Rachel knew she hadn't been the perfect mother, but she had always tried to do her best. And in fairness, Liz hadn't been the perfect daughter either. She was the one who was supposed to keep Rachel company when all the boys went away. She still couldn't believe they'd gone so *far*. It made her feel sad and unwanted, as though they were trying to escape or something.

Of course she understood the need for independence, the lure of the exotic and unfamiliar. But surely family should stick together in the end. Surely they should at least be within a few miles of one another. What if something happened to one of the boys? Who would be around to help?

That made her worry about her own situation and what might happen to *her* when she was too old or infirm to take care of herself. She angrily pushed the unwelcome thoughts away. She had plenty of good years left in her and a lot of love to give. It was just a case of meeting the right man. Jack had suggested she join a dating service, an idea she'd found properly horrible. Simon had met his Welsh wife on the Internet, for heaven's sake. That felt to her like only a small step away from meeting at a strip club. There was just something so vulgar about such "connections". People were meant to meet in person, face to face, to exchange smiles and compliments, and then perhaps phone numbers if they got on.

Liz had met Nick in person and Rachel had wholly approved of him, not that her approval had mattered one bit to Liz. In fact, she was surprised Liz hadn't dumped him at the start and gone in search of a man Rachel would find less suitable. No, that wasn't fair. Liz wasn't a teenager anymore. As hard as it was to see her as an adult, that was what she was. She was grown up and free to make her own choices. *Capable* of making her own choices.

She sighed. Still, that *house*. Liz had made some peculiar choices in the past, but that one took the biscuit. She didn't understand what anyone could see in such a place. It was so unlike Liz.

But never mind. It was done and she had to accept it, just as she'd had to accept everything else her children had thrown her way. Andy in Eastern Europe, with a wife who spoke no English. Oksana was beautiful, certainly, but Rachel didn't see it lasting. Age would come for her too one day. And Simon, in deepest Wales. He might as well be on another continent as well, for all the bother it was getting there to see him. Jack had at least stayed in London, but he was always working, always flying somewhere else, touching down just long enough to sleep and then flying off again.

Liz was the only one she could count on, the only one she could go to. But her daughter had stubbornly refused every invitation to come and stay with her in London for a few days. It was the house. She would not leave that house.

The taxi bounced up the single track that led to the top of the cliff, and Rachel steeled herself to face her daughter's ire. She knew better than to think she could get Liz to come back to London with her for a visit, but perhaps she could at least get her out of the house for a little while and take her into Bristol for a nice dinner, just the two of them. Nick was pleasant enough company but Liz was easier to work on when she was on her own. Less... defiant.

The taxi driver let out a long, low whistle as he came to a stop at Wintergate. "Now, there's a spooky house for you," he said, his voice half-amusement, half-awe.

Rachel made herself smile for him. "Yes, it's my daughter's. I'm afraid she has rather-" she searched for the right word "-individual tastes."

"Tell her she should put it on *Most Haunted*," he offered with a laugh.

Rachel's smile thinned at that.

A bracing wind clawed at her as she got out and shut the door. The driver gave her a jaunty wave and she watched as he turned the car around and headed back down the drive. She confronted the grim stone edifice, simultaneously surprised and annoyed to find that she was nervous to knock at the door. She had to fight a sudden urge to run after the taxi and ask him to take her to Bristol instead. Maybe this was all a huge mistake.

But the taxi was gone before she could even finish processing the thought. With a resigned sigh she turned towards the house. The day was viciously cold and the sky had gone white with the threat of snow. She tugged her scarf tighter as she looked up at the façade. It was as solemn and uninviting as a prison. Even out here she could smell the musty odour. Liz had always said she wanted a bright, airy home, a place with huge windows to let in lots of light. Well, Wintergate had the huge windows but from where Rachel was standing, they all looked closed and shuttered. It was the way a crazy cat lady might live, cloistered away in the dark while the rest of the world went on without her. And whispered about her behind her back as well.

Another chill swept through Rachel as she approached the front door. All the trees were denuded, clawing at the bleak sky like skeleton hands. Only a few evergreen shrubs still showed signs of life. Leaves shivered in the rhododendrons, sounding unnervingly like laughter. She reached for the bell, but gasped to see it hanging off the wall, bare wires dangling. It looked like a defused bomb. Instinct made her glance behind her, in case the vandals had only just done their work and were hiding nearby, watching. Then she chided herself for her knee-jerk paranoia. She wasn't in central London or even Bristol. This was Clevedon, as peaceful a little seaside town as one could ever hope for.

The outer door on the right sported a heavy brass knocker in the shape of a mythical creature with a ring in its mouth. Even through her gloves, the brass burned her fingers with cold. She rapped sharply and waited, wondering how well sound travelled through the house. She knew Liz's worktable was up in the minstrels' gallery, but if her daughter was in another room she might not hear it.

She knocked again, and once again got no response. Now she was really starting to worry. She'd tried ringing a few days ago and she'd even sent an email, but got no reply. That wasn't unusual. But there was such an unnatural stillness here, such a feeling of disquiet. Something was wrong. She knew it.

Feeling like a criminal, she decided to try the handle. She could let herself into the porch and knock on the inner door. The huge hinges shrieked as she pulled one of the doors towards her. Her heart fluttered at the sound. It was like opening a tomb. And once that thought crossed her mind, she couldn't shake it.

The chill hit her even harder once she was in the porch, and she zipped up her coat with a shiver. She knocked on the inner door and listened. Nothing.

"Liz?" she called, not liking the way her voice quavered. She pressed her mouth against the split between the two doors and shouted as loudly as she could. "Liz! Let me in, it's Rachel!" Then, feeling foolish, she added "Your mum!"

She listened to the diminishing echo of her voice. It was as though she'd shouted into a vacant cavern. She should have asked the taxi driver to wait. It hadn't occurred to her that she might be stranded here. Finally, she heard footsteps, shuffling and unhurried. For one wild moment Rachel wanted to turn and run, but she checked the instinct and wondered where it had come from. Liz was probably just unwell. There was nothing to be afraid of.

The right-hand door creaked open to reveal a staring eye. Rachel gave a little cry and jumped back before she realised who it was.

"Heavens, Liz, you gave me a turn!"

The eye continued to stare for a few seconds, as though trying to focus. The unnerving thought came to Rachel that its owner was not used to seeing living things. She shook off the feeling, determined to master herself. She was acting like a child, frightened of shadows.

"Come on, Liz, it's me. Aren't you going to let me in?"

"Rachel," came the hoarse response.

"Yes," Rachel said, not liking the strange voice at all. For once she'd have welcomed being called "Mum". "Please let me in."

The blank stare held her for several seconds. Rachel felt her own eyes begin to burn, starving for the moisture of a blink. At last the door opened fully, revealing a dishevelled creature Rachel barely recognised.

Liz's hair hung in her face, unwashed, and a good two inches of premature grey was visible in the parting. It looked like steel wool against the blond. Liz was normally obsessive about hiding it, colouring it as soon as it became apparent. It seemed the least of her worries now. Her eyes were baggy and bloodshot, as though she hadn't slept in days. Her face looked pale and wan, and she was wearing a dingy brown tracksuit that only emphasised her pallor. She could pass for a patient in a long-term mental hospital.

"Oh my god! Lizzie dear, you look terrible."

Liz shrugged. When she gave no sign of moving, Rachel placed a hand on her daughter's shoulder and gently pushed her back so she could enter. For a moment it seemed that Liz would only stand there, waiting to be moved again, but then she closed the door and locked it. The solid *clunk* of the bolt made Rachel feel even more uneasy. She didn't like the thought of being locked inside this place.

Liz was already walking towards the stairs. Rachel followed, unsure what to say now that she was here. She didn't suppose for one minute that Liz was off to make tea and then settle in for an afternoon of gossip and girl talk.

Rachel had been so struck by Liz's face that she hadn't noticed the state her clothes were in. Now, as she walked behind, she saw that the tracksuit was filthy, streaked with mud and paint, and it was torn in several places. What on earth had she been doing?

Rachel's eyes darted around the huge hall as she followed her daughter up the stairs. No, this house was definitely not good for Liz. She'd have to speak to Nick about getting her out. Perhaps the two of them could bundle her up and take her for a walk along the seafront. The cold air would do her good, maybe help to clear her head.

"Lizzie?"

But Liz didn't answer. She just continued on up the stairs. Rachel had the uncomfortable sense that she was following a prisoner to the gallows, and she grimaced, hating the house all over again for the ideas it was putting into her head.

A glance to the left showed her Liz's desk. It looked more like a deathtrap than a cluttered workshop. The floor was covered in beads and wires and debris. It was clearly an accident waiting to happen and Rachel was about to say something when Liz finally spoke. Her voice was flat, with no inflection or emotion.

"I'm working on a new project."

"Oh?" Rachel tried to keep the uncertainty out of her voice, tried to smile and sound interested. "Is it anything you'd like to show me?"

Liz smiled. Or rather, her mouth did. Her eyes remained dull and empty, like a doll's.

"Lizzie?"

"Huh? Oh, yeah." She was quiet for a moment, almost as though she'd lost track of her thoughts. Then she looked up towards the ceiling. "It's upstairs."

Rachel frowned. "Up here, do you mean?"

"No. In the attic."

Immediately Rachel thought of rats. Rats and spiders and cobwebs and dust and all the horrid things people stashed away in attics. No wonder Liz looked such a mess.

"What on earth are you doing up in the attic?" she asked, aware that her voice sounded shrill. She winced even as she said it, expecting Liz to round on her, snapping that she could do whatever she liked, thank you very much.

But Liz only shrugged and looked down at herself as though only noticing for the first time what a mess she was. She plucked absently at her sweatshirt and a bit of dry paint flaked away, falling to the floor.

"I'll show you," Liz said, her voice still devoid of emotion.

She might as well be a robot, Rachel thought. Her heart ached at the sight of the ashen-faced young woman before her. She desperately wanted to grab Liz in her arms, pull her close and tell her that she loved her, that she was sorry for all the bad or selfish things she had ever done, or that Liz had even *thought* she'd done.

"Hey, I've got an idea," Rachel said. "Why don't you let me take you to dinner?"

If Liz heard her, she gave no sign.

"Come on," Rachel persisted, "what's the fanciest restaurant in town?"

"Not hungry."

"Okay, then how about a spa day? We can go have our hair and nails done, the works! I'm sure Nick won't mind."

But Liz wasn't listening. She was still picking at her shirt. Grey flakes fell to the floor like diseased skin.

Tears welled in Rachel's eyes and she swallowed the lump in her throat. "Honey, you aren't well," she said, reaching out. "Please let me–"

At that Liz's head snapped up and her eyes were suddenly sharp and focused. There was something of the fiery spirit that had made their life together so fraught. But the light dimmed almost as quickly as it had blazed and Liz's eyes were muddy once more.

"No," she murmured. "Let me show you first."

"Show me what? Your project? Oh Lizzie, I don't think you should be up in the attic."

Liz cocked her head and another attempt at a smile touched her lips. "It's perfectly safe," she said. "There just wasn't room down here and I didn't want to disturb Nick with the noise."

It was becoming clear to Rachel that she was not going to shift Liz from this train of thought. Very well, if it would make her happy, she'd go and look at whatever Liz was making in the attic. Then maybe she'd be amenable to letting Rachel take her out of the house for a while. The wild thought crossed her mind that she could just kidnap her, take her to Bristol with her, maybe even on to London. Was that what they called an intervention?

"All right," Rachel said with a sigh. "I'll come and look. But only if you promise you'll come and have dinner with me afterwards."

The smile returned to Liz's mouth, a sly, serpentine grin that Rachel didn't like at all. "Good. I haven't even shown Nick yet. I'm glad you're going to be the first."

Rachel didn't know whether to be pleased about that or not but she made herself smile. "I'm sure I'll love it," she said.

The House of Frozen Screams

***

The first thing Rachel noticed was the smell. Paint and mud. Or was it clay? She wrinkled her nose but she pressed on. She had to wonder if this was some kind of test. If Rachel had refused, might it have led to yet another row? Well, she hoped Liz was impressed.

She tried hard not to touch anything as she climbed up the rickety ladder behind her daughter.

"Lizzie, it's absolutely frigid! I do hope you're not spending too much time up here." She knew she was nagging, but she couldn't stop herself. Liz looked terrible and it was little wonder if she was hanging around up here in the cold.

Liz didn't respond. She just moved further into the darkened attic. A fluorescent tube flickered into life, sending the shadows fleeing to the corners like rats.

There was no floor, only a few square white boards laid across the joists in a path to the middle, as though someone had once begun the process of laying floorboards only to abandon it. It was dusty, but it didn't seem to be infested with creepy-crawlies as she'd feared. In fact, the only thing Rachel could see was a large dark shape in the centre of the room. It looked about four feet high and twice as wide. Liz went to it immediately. When Rachel's

287

eyes adjusted to the gloom, she saw that it was covered in a tarpaulin.

"Goodness," Rachel said with forced cheer. "Are you sculpting now?"

Liz stroked the tarpaulin. "It's my masterpiece," she said.

When nothing else seemed forthcoming, Rachel prompted, "Well, are you going to show me or not?"

She was expecting Liz to throw off the sheet with a flourish and reveal some fantastical statue – the caterpillar from *Alice in Wonderland* perhaps, judging from the rough proportions. But Liz shook her head and beckoned Rachel over.

"Uh-uh. You have to come here."

Rachel bit back the exasperated response that sprang to her lips. All she wanted to do was to see whatever it was and then get back down the ladder and out of the damned house. Even though the space was enormous, she felt confined and constricted. The solitary light source made it feel as though the shadows were pressing in on her like walls. Her teeth were chattering and she wrapped her arms around herself. Liz didn't seem to notice the cold at all. Rachel lifted her chin and took a few steps closer to the concealed figure.

Now Liz removed the tarpaulin, not with a flourish but with a gentle tug. It slid off the sculpture with a soft hiss, pooling on the floor like another shadow as Rachel tried to take in what she was seeing. A hand fluttered to her mouth and her stomach twisted.

"I call it 'Radiant'," Liz said, her voice becoming animated at last.

All Rachel could see were the misshapen figures crawling through the holes in the putrid grey-green sculpture. It clearly wasn't finished yet, but it was easy enough to see the emerging female form in the massive lump of clay. The figure had no face to speak of, but it did have eyes. Or at least the hollows where eyes should be. Rachel had never seen anything so terrible in her life.

"My god, Lizzie," she gasped. "What is this thing?"

Now Rachel had Liz's full attention. Her daughter's eyes were instantly bright and clear and as malevolent as those of the hideous sculpture. "What's the matter?" Liz demanded. "Don't you think she's beautiful?"

Rachel couldn't speak. She began to slowly back away. Something was wrong with Liz, *seriously* wrong.

Liz came out from behind the sculpture, her eyes cold and blazing. "Isn't it a perfect representation? Babies make a woman, isn't that what you always said? You can't appreciate the full experience of womanhood until you're a mother? Vanora was a mother. And now so am I."

Rachel gasped at that – not a gasp of delight but one of horror.

"Yes, you heard me. And you know what? You were right. I couldn't understand the power such a tiny thing could have inside me until it was there. Can you hear it crying? Can you? Sometimes I think it talks to me. I wonder what it would say to you if you could only listen?"

Tears spilled down Rachel's cheeks and she held her trembling hands up in a warding-off gesture. "Lizzie, you're scaring me. Who's Vanora? What are you talking about? Oh, Lizzie, you're not well. Please won't you come with me and–"

"Oh no," Liz said, her voice silky and dangerous. "You're staying here with us. You're the one who always wanted babies. You can take care of them. They'll like you."

Rachel felt the blood drain from her face at that. The feeling of being watched intensified and all the tiny hairs on the back of her neck began to tingle. *Us.*

She took a step back but it felt as though the floor had been pulled away. She stumbled and fell, crying out as something cracked sharply in her left knee. Then she was on her side, clutching her leg. The pain washed over her in waves but it was nothing next to her burgeoning fear as Liz advanced. Now she was reaching down to pick something up. At first Rachel thought she was stretching out a hand to help her up. Then she saw the hammer.

Rachel drew a breath to speak, but the word "no" never made it past her lips.

CHAPTER 31

Nick was in a good mood as he drove home. Even the rush hour traffic on the M5 couldn't shake his cheerful demeanour. He crawled along with the other vehicles, lost in his own thoughts. He couldn't find any music that suited him so he left the tuner on a Radio 4 programme about Mount Everest. A climber was talking about his own attempts on the mountain and it reminded Nick of the day he and Liz had met, when she'd just climbed down from Glastonbury Tor. The thought of her made him smile.

Liz was pregnant. *They* were pregnant. He couldn't stop saying it to himself. He was overjoyed and yet it all felt slightly surreal, like a feeling imposed on him by the outlandish logic of a dream. It was impossible to believe that only weeks before, he'd have been horrified at the very thought. Had it been a case of protesting too much all his life? Had he secretly always wanted kids but never allowed himself to admit it? Was he a closeted wannabe dad?

The thought amused him. Certainly the noisy little buggers they'd lived underneath in their Bristol flat hadn't done much to make the prospect of having their own children appealing, but before that? Well, Liz had stated quite categorically on their first date that she never wanted children but he'd been so smitten he'd have gone along with her if she'd spouted neo-Nazi propaganda or confessed a fetish for balloon animals.

Before Liz were the months of frustrated loneliness after he'd left Pauline. His ex-girlfriend *had* wanted a baby, but hindsight told him that his reticence in that case had been more to do with a dread of being tied to her forever than any particular fear of fatherhood.

The phrase "Death Zone" caught his attention, and he listened for a little while. The climber was talking about the highest region on Everest and the lives claimed by the mountain. It was another world up there, he said, an alien landscape in which nothing could survive. And yet something drove people to push themselves through it, for the glory that came from standing on the roof of the world, the highest point on earth.

"There's nothing like it," the man said dreamily.

The very thought of it made Nick shudder. It was incomprehensible. Glastonbury Tor was many thousands of metres lower than the peaks of the Himalayas but he'd still quailed at the idea of climbing all the way to the top with Liz.

Thinking about that reminded him of the episode he'd had up there, when he remembered letting go of the kite as a boy, watching it soar away. Nick had no idea whether his father's casual response had been spontaneous or calculated once he'd seen his son's distress. Nick had never asked. Whatever the case, it was just right. *I guess he's flown home to his nest.* Even at such a young age, Nick understood that it was the perfect response to the situation and he had felt an intense rush of love for his father, both for understanding and for protecting his feelings.

That was the kind of father Nick would be. And once she got over her initial fears, Liz would be just as good a mother. He recalled her selfless behaviour when she rescued the hedgehog, and the patient encouragement she had shown towards Nick on the climb up Glastonbury Tor. Standing at the top in the little tower of St Michael's, gazing in awe at the panoramic view, he had felt invincible. No, it wasn't a mountain, but as far as he was concerned, it might as well have been. He couldn't have done it without Liz. Together they were a force. And their child – or children – would be amazing.

The traffic continued to creep forward inch by slow inch as words from the radio reached him through his daydreams. Obsession. Human remains. Hostile environment.

It was this last phrase that bothered him most. How often had Liz used a similar one? *Hostile womb*. A place where nothing could survive. But surely that was just something she said to annoy her mother. What if Rachel adamantly *didn't* want grandchildren? If all the pressure was off Liz from that quarter, would she feel differently? What if her attitude towards having kids was just stubborn rebellion?

Oh, he didn't mean to trivialise Liz's feelings. He was still baffled himself by his own conversion. But maybe such things only happened in the moment, as it had with Ian. It was all well and good to take a stand on something when it was purely academic. You couldn't possibly know your true feelings until you were faced with the reality of it. Just like the climber was saying about the cruelty of Everest and the suicidal futility of rescue operations. People had to clamber over the dead and the dying on their way to the summit because to do otherwise would be to put their own lives in even greater jeopardy, probably to no avail.

"Everyone knows the risks," the man said gravely, "and at the end you're all alone up there. No one can help you. Leaving a fallen climber behind is common sense, not murder."

Murder.

The word rolled around in Nick's head like a stone. He wasn't religious and he'd never felt that abortion was murder. He believed a woman's body was her own, that she should be the one to make choices about what happened to it. But the idea didn't sit so well with him now. Shouldn't the father have some choice when what was at stake was the life of his own child?

Suddenly he felt confused. He didn't know what was right or what was fair. A chill ran through his body.

It's like being trapped in the deepest, most violent winter imaginable.

Had the climber said that? A few years ago the UK had experienced an unexpectedly brutal winter, with snow blanketing the country for weeks. People had been stranded in their homes, unable to leave except on foot, and only then through several feet of snow. He thought of their curious little house, perched beneath the clifftop. Wintergate.

What was it Liz had mumbled in her sleep that time? Something about the way in? Or the way through? Liz had been dreaming of snow ever since they moved there and he'd assumed it was just an association with the name. Now the settling in of winter felt ominous.

The tone of the programme had shifted into even darker territory, with the radio presenter introducing her next guest, a vascular surgeon who specialised in amputations. He'd taken off six of the climber's frostbitten fingers and all the toes of one foot. The climber himself was oddly blasé about it, and even the surgeon didn't seem to think it odd that people would return again and again to the mountain, no matter how much of them it claimed.

Nick imagined he could hear the crunch of bone as scissors cut through the blackened digits. His stomach churned. There was something about the image that was familiar but he had no idea why. He'd never known anyone with such an injury, yet in his mind it was so vivid.

Snip. Scream.

He shuddered, feeling sick. Surely they weren't playing those sounds on the radio. It was horribly realistic, and he fancied that he could feel the scissors in his own hands. He clenched the wheel, trying to dispel the feeling, but it only intensified the sensation of soft flesh giving way beneath sharp blades. The frostbite must have shrivelled the fingers down to almost nothing because when they came off they were tiny. They were also healthy. And... *pink*.

Something whispered in the back of his mind.

Abomination.

The thought – or had it been a voice? – made him jump. He actually glanced around, as though someone else might be in the car with him. But he was alone. There was nothing in his hands but the steering wheel. His skin was crawling. Unnerved, he switched the radio off.

And he'd never thought he had much imagination! It was just the traffic, he told himself. The long drive. Yet he couldn't shake the idea that Liz was keeping something from him. She had promised him she'd think about it, that she'd at least consider the idea of parenthood. But Nick knew what she was thinking. He'd seen it in her eyes. She was humouring him, nothing more. Telling him what he wanted to hear while secretly planning something unspeakable.

The traffic queue finally rounded the curve and the steel-blue strip of the Bristol Channel came into view on his right. It was normally his favourite part of the drive. Today, however, it felt like a bad omen.

He was certain he could still hear the voices on the radio but when he checked, it was switched off. Other drivers were peering at him and he glared at them until they looked away.

Another ten minutes and he would be home. Yes, Wintergate *was* home. He was finally beginning to feel it. He'd had his doubts at first but Liz had convinced him. Now it was his turn to convince *her*.

They would have this child. He was determined. It was meant to be.

As he drove onto the forecourt of the house, it began to snow.

CHAPTER 32

"You're late," Liz said.

"Yeah, stupid traffic. If only they had separate lanes for commuters and holidaymakers, eh?"

"Why are people still packing off to Cornwall? Summer's long gone and it's been blowing gales all day."

Nick shrugged. "Maybe they're all surfers. Who cares? I'm here now."

Liz arranged her features into a smile, surprising herself at how easy it was. Nick returned her smile and kissed her. If he sensed that anything was amiss, he didn't show it. They could almost be a normal couple, she thought. One with no secrets between them.

"What's for dinner?"

Liz shrugged. "Pizza? I don't know. I just don't feel like cooking."

He moved closer, reaching out a hand to stroke her face. "You do look a little tired."

She'd cleaned herself up and had a shower, but there was

nothing she could do about the bags under her eyes. "I'm okay."

His eyes flicked lower, down to her abdomen, and she felt herself tighten up inside. She knew what he was going to do before he did it and it was all she could do to keep from grinding her teeth as he placed his hand against her belly. She couldn't meet his eyes, couldn't face the awful smile she would see on his face. Somehow she kept from bristling, enduring his touch until at last he pulled away.

"Are you sure you're okay, Liz?"

Again she flashed the easy smile, the lying smile. "I'm fine. Like I said, I'm just tired. I filled a lot of orders today."

He seemed satisfied with that but his eyes remained on her abdomen, as though he could see through her skin to the creature inside, the creature he thought of as his. Barely suppressing a shudder, Liz turned away to grab her coat from the stand by the door. "Shall we go out?" she asked. She didn't really want to leave the house, but it was all she could think of to break the awkward moment.

"No, it's snowing."

"Really?" She glanced through the front window to see fat flakes spiralling down through the outside light. Just seeing them made her feel cold.

"Anyway, I'm not really hungry," he said, to her relief. "Are you?"

She pretended to think about it. In truth, the idea of eating filled her with revulsion. "I guess not," she said, trying to sound casual. Fortunately, Nick didn't seem to find this suspicious and she was thankful he didn't mention anything about her "eating for two".

He stood there for a moment, shifting his feet, looking uncertain about what to do. There was an elephant in the room, eclipsing all other possible topics of conversation.

"Wanna watch telly?" she offered, not knowing what else to say. Their relationship had become like some terrible blind date, an interminable game of tiptoeing around eggshells, with every crunch painfully obvious.

Nick's response was as unenthusiastic as her suggestion. "Sure."

And so they sat downstairs, together but apart. Brightly coloured shows filled with glossy people paraded across the screen, but neither one of them registered what they were watching. All Liz could think of was the parasite within her, and how much she wanted it gone.

They went to bed early because there was nothing else to say and the evening had grown unbearably awkward. Liz eyed the stack of books on her bedside table. She'd been desultorily dipping in and out of the one on top ever since moving in. She had quite forgotten what was happening in the story. Nick looked equally unmoved by his reading prospects and he merely said good night and switched off his lamp.

In the darkness, Liz peered up at the pale glow of Carson's staring face. Even though the bed was warm, she felt a distinct chill. She turned over onto her side, her back to Nick, but sleep would not come tonight.

The weekend stretched before them, two whole days to fill.

CHAPTER 33

Nick lay still, watching Liz sleep. Or rather, pretend to. Her breathing was far too shallow and rhythmic to be the deep breaths of honest slumber. They'd spent the evening like two dangerous animals trapped in a room together, each waiting for the other to make a move. Liz clearly wasn't about to say anything about the baby – *their* baby – but her silence said more than her words ever could have.

His thoughts were confused. At times throughout the evening he had wanted to hold her, but he knew she wouldn't have welcomed it. There was something strange in her eyes, an alien detachment he had never seen before. An owl called to its mate somewhere beyond the walls of Wintergate. The air of the bedroom felt close and stifling. Then the sickly-sweet stink of something rotten filled his nose. He flung the covers back and got out of bed. If Liz were truly asleep the movement would have wakened her, but she continued in her charade, her breathing smooth and level.

Everything was so fuzzy, so mixed up in his head. He stood at the window, peering into the night. The single lamp outside illuminated the snow-covered expanse where the rest of the house had once stood. As he stared into it, something swooped down from the sky. There was a shrill cry and then the phantom was away into the trees, just another shadow.

From where he was standing, Nick was certain he could see a pair of owls, their enormous eyes like saucers. Together they tore into their prey, ripping away skin and lumps of meat with their sharp beaks and talons. Shreds of bloody flesh fell into the snow below. His stomach churned but he couldn't look away. Not even when he saw the tiny fingers they were plucking from the creature's body, from its fat pink arms.

Snip. Scream.

He spun away from the window, refusing to believe he had really seen such a thing. In their bed Liz lay facing him and for a moment he thought her eyes were open. Open and staring at him. Only they weren't her eyes at all. They were cold and yellow and as big as saucers.

He turned away for a moment, and when he looked again she was just Liz. Now he couldn't even be sure if she was faking sleep or not. Her breathing sounded genuine, but he couldn't pinpoint what was different about it. Maybe she really had been asleep all along.

He didn't want to wake her up and so he sat in the window seat. After a while he dared a glance outside but there was nothing to see. The owls were gone, if they had ever been there at all. Maybe he had imagined the whole thing.

One thing was certain: he wasn't imagining the sound. A thin keening assailed his ears and he remembered what Liz had said once before about thinking there were birds living inside the walls. It did seem to be coming from the area she had torn apart. Maybe that was where the owls had gone. After seeing what they had done to their prey he didn't much like the thought of them sharing space with him and Liz.

He crept over to the wall and pressed his ear against it but the sound had faded, if it had ever been there at all. He felt strangely cheated. Liz had been so bothered by the sound that she'd torn the wall open; why wouldn't the creature reveal itself to him as well? It had jolted him from sleep that one morning but he hadn't heard it since.

He listened for what felt like hours but there was nothing to hear. The frustration was exhausting and after a while he was too tired to care. He went back to bed and slipped in beside Liz. She didn't move.

He didn't think he'd be able to sleep but he found himself drifting off almost immediately. When he opened his eyes again he was outside. The sun was shining but it wasn't warm. Icy white light dazzled him, and it took him a while to realise that Liz was beside him.

Come on, she was saying. *I'll be your guide. Nothing will happen to you while you're with me.*

She held out her hand, and as he took it, he realised where they were. At the base of Glastonbury Tor. The crooked path wound up towards St Michael's tower at the top but the steps seemed so much narrower than they ought to be. He knew he had been here before but it hadn't looked like this. Had it? From where he was standing, the tower looked ruined, as though it had been struck by lightning.

They had just taken the wounded hedgehog to safety. Now Liz wanted to show him the view from the summit of the hill. He'd only said he didn't have a head for heights; he hadn't wanted her to know how afraid he really was. But she *had* known. And she seemed to know again, now, and her grip seemed a little firmer than it had all those years ago.

He trudged after her and this time the going was more tiring than terrifying. At least until they reached the edge of the snow and she released his hand. They were still only halfway up.

I have to let you go now, she said. *You have to do it alone.*

He stared at her in horror, part of him frightened and part of him angry that she was changing the memory. This wasn't the way it had happened. There hadn't been any snow. And she'd held his hand until they reached the top. But this time she turned away and continued on up without him.

After a few moments' hesitation, he followed her, worried about letting her get too far ahead. His feet punched through the deepening snow as the wind whipped around them, stinging his skin and burning his eyes. His ears felt like someone had jabbed icepicks into them.

He didn't want to climb anymore but his body seemed to be doing it anyway. Angry clouds roiled in the darkening sky above. It was hard to see the path. Nick tried to place his feet where Liz's had been but the wind filled her footprints with snow as soon as she moved on. He looked down once and his stomach swooped. How could they have come this far, climbed this high?

There was a break in the clouds and a shaft of wintry light fell across Liz's path. Nick blinked furiously to try and make sense of what he was seeing. The snow had given way to rocks, but there was something odd about them. They looked soft and spongy, and he was sure he could hear wet squelching, like the sound of boots coming unstuck from the mud.

A thought came to him suddenly: they mustn't reach the top.

He pushed himself harder, determined to catch up with Liz. He tried calling out to her, but his lips were so numb he couldn't even make a sound. If she sensed his distress, she was unmoved by it. At one point she turned towards him and the smile on her face chilled him more than the weather. He stopped in his tracks, suddenly convinced that he was dreaming. His relief was short-lived, however, as his feet sank into the swampy rocks and he realised what they were climbing over.

Scattered all along the winding path were babies. Many of them were dead but a few still moved, writhing sluggishly in the cold, smeared with mud and blood. Their soft, pulpy bodies were horribly vulnerable beneath his feet but he could see no way around them. Ahead of him Liz continued to advance, raising her knees high and bringing her feet down hard. There was something playful in her movements, something gleefully vicious. She was like a child stamping through puddles.

He couldn't go any further. All he could do was watch helplessly as Liz continued her remorseless climb to the top. He sank to his knees amongst the squirming, mewling infants. Some of them began to crawl towards him, their tiny hands clutching, their mouths contorting with silent demands. It was then that he realised how misshapen they were. Some of them were fortunate enough to only have extra fingers and toes, while others looked as though they had been melted together. Two mouths screamed from a single head of one and another looked as though it had been stitched together from two entirely different bodies. All were grasping at him, clinging to him, pulling him down.

He tried to clamber to his feet, desperate to get away. Liz was at the top now and she vanished inside the ruined tower as he watched. The sky churned hellishly, and from within the monument, Liz began to scream. There came a sound like a sledgehammer against stone and then the tower began to crumble. Stones fell into the sea of bodies, smashing them and then bouncing off down the hill. Nick dodged two of the boulders and turned to run, but hundreds of tiny hands grabbed at his legs. He fell into their mass of flesh and began to crawl, crushing them beneath him as he went.

He managed to reach the snow before the next boulder came tumbling down but this one caught him a glancing blow in the head. His vision swam. There was no pain, only a dull sense of dizziness. The figures around him advanced, surrounding him, reaching for him. Without thinking, he grabbed the rock that had struck him and heaved it into the swarm. It landed with a wet crunch but the others kept coming.

He burrowed into the snow, trying to escape, trying to turn his body so that he could roll down the hill. But the snow impeded him, sticking to him like flypaper. His limbs were weighed down by it and his struggles only mired him deeper.

When the creatures reached him they began to pluck at his face and he could see that their fingers were blackened and shrivelled, as though scorched by the cold. Wildly he flailed at them, grabbing them and breaking them off. They snapped like brittle twigs. If his attackers felt any pain they didn't show it. They just stared at him with owl-bright eyes, accusing and hating, as they kept coming. They crawled over him, pushing him down into the snow, smothering him.

***

Nick burst from sleep with a scream. He clawed at his face, convinced there were hands all over him. It was a long time before he realised it had only been a dream, but he could still feel the cold of the snow and the scratching of those horrible blackened fingers. He sat up and looked around blearily. Liz wasn't there.

He was shaking as he clambered out of bed. The clock said it was well past noon. She must have let him sleep. Something smelled terrible and he wondered if it was him. The sheets were soaked with sweat but that didn't seem to be the source of it. But something else was wrong. It was so dark outside. He stumbled to the window only to see a sky full of stars and a sliver of moon. Midnight then, not noon. Where the hell was Liz?

He stumbled along the corridor like a drunk, assuming she had gone to the bathroom. But she wasn't there. Then he remembered the night with the cake. He was about to head down the back stairs to see if she was in the kitchen when something made him turn.

There was a figure standing at the top of the main staircase.

Nick felt all the blood drain from his face. For long moments he stood staring at the dark shape, his heart pounding. The air felt thick and charged with menace. He didn't dare look away or even blink in case the figure suddenly moved closer. All he could do was stare and wait for it to do something.

When it did move at last, it was only to take a step closer to the banister. Recognition came and then relief flooded him with such force his legs nearly buckled.

"Liz," he said, "what are you doing?"

312

She jumped so violently at his voice she had to clutch the banister to stop herself from falling. Nick rushed to her at once and pulled her away from the steps.

"My god," he cried. "You could have killed the- you could have killed yourself!"

She looked at him as though she didn't know him at all. Her eyes were blank and unfocused. Was she sleepwalking again?

"Liz? Liz, wake up. It's Nick. Wake up!"

He shook her gently and awareness began to dawn in her features. "Nick? What are you doing here?"

She seemed frightened but oblivious to what she had nearly done. He wasn't sure if he should tell her or not.

"Come on," he said, guiding her back down the corridor. "You were sleepwalking."

"I don't sleepwalk," she said with a puzzled frown.

"Apparently you do."

She didn't argue. She merely allowed herself to be led back to bed. Nick climbed in and spooned her, wrapping his arms tightly around her. She was asleep almost immediately but he stayed awake until the sun began to spill its ugly winter light through the gaps in the curtains.

CHAPTER 34

Liz stared into the vortex of the toilet bowl as she flushed away the morning's sickness. She felt clammy and weak and more ill than she ever had in her life. Her head was clanging like a church bell, and it took every ounce of strength just to struggle to her feet.

She rinsed her mouth and looked up at the mirror. A haggard old woman stared back. Her face was puffy and bloated and her skin was pasty, her eyes dull and bloodshot. She'd been breaking out too. Her teenage years hadn't been cursed by this much acne. She looked like a plague victim.

Nick had spent the weekend in what felt like false good cheer, maintaining that she looked beautiful no matter what she said, and being overly affectionate. They'd even braved the snow and gone for a short walk one day, and Nick had insisted on taking her out for dinner in Bristol the next. It all made her feel like a terminal patient, forced into the role of reassuring everyone else that things were normal. She had managed to smile and be nice, all the while seething inside with bitterness and rage that Nick couldn't see through the awful charade. As he left for the office that morning she'd actually heard him *whistling*.

For a long time she stared into the eyes of the pale apparition in the mirror. Where was the glow so many people waxed lyrical about? Where was the sublime inner beauty pregnant women were supposed to possess? Where was the *radiance?* Something about that word made her skin crawl.

Maybe that fabled beauty was only for women who *wanted* to be pregnant. All the others had to suffer turning into hags. Not that she was doing anything to help her appearance. She'd never been one to fuss and preen excessively, but for the past few weeks she had barely felt like washing her hair, let alone putting on makeup or decent clothes.

She'd also started gaining weight. Her abdomen felt swollen and the thought of her body being stretched to accommodate the new life inside filled her with resentment and revulsion. She knew the unwanted embryo had been swimming around inside her ever since Nick's trip to Manchester three months ago. That was three months too long. She'd already lost precious time being in denial since the night it happened.

It wasn't vanity that was pushing her over the edge, but the grim realisation that this pretence wasn't doing anyone any good.

What was the point of waiting any longer to reaffirm her loathing of the idea of having a baby? She would only be delaying the inevitable. Of course, Nick would accuse her of not trying hard enough to accept the idea, and she would accuse him of changing too drastically. It was a fight no one could win and both would be wounded by it.

Worst of all was the certainty that, despite his promise that he'd let *her* make the decision, he was clearly intent on her having it. She'd sensed it at the start of the weekend, known by the way he'd rested his hand over the place where the foetus lay coiled like a worm inside her. The look in his eyes had chilled her. There was something disquieting in that look, something threatening. It frightened her and triggered an awful thought. If she was sometimes in touch with Vanora's memories, might Nick sometimes be in touch with Carson's?

The idea came to her that she could simply throw herself down the stairs. Surely the creature inside her couldn't survive that. But then *she* might not survive it either. And even if she did, she could break both her legs, or her neck, or crack her skull.

The thought of broken bones triggered something inside her, some fleeting thought, like the remnant of a dream, or a buried memory. She saw herself actually standing there, swaying at the top of the stairs, searching for the courage to do it. Then she felt the crunch of bone, the gurgling of blood in her throat.

The taste of blood made her insides heave and she fell to her knees again, clutching the toilet. There was nothing left in her stomach, but that didn't stop her body trying to purge itself again.

When the wave passed, she pressed her forehead against the cold porcelain, gasping for breath. *That's it*, she thought. She couldn't take it anymore and she *wouldn't*. Other women might be willing to endure this, might even perversely enjoy the experience and say it was all worth it once they held their perfect little angel in their arms. But Liz wasn't a masochist, and she did not want to be a mother. She loved Nick desperately and she wanted him all to herself. Once she was rid of this thing that had driven a wedge between them, they could go back to the way they'd always been. Liz and Nick against the world.

She struggled to her feet and rinsed her mouth again. Even the water tasted vile. She wanted her body back. She couldn't believe she'd let it go on this long.

What were her options, then? She rolled the possibilities round and round in her mind and returned every time to the same conclusion. Abortion. But how could she do it without Nick finding out?

She sat down with her laptop and opened an incognito window in her browser. Then she typed the word. Seeing it in black and white was chilling. She had no moral or ethical issue with termination, but it still wasn't an easy thing to contemplate, even if she suspected that her own situation was abnormal.

But there was the matter of cost, and it was no trivial amount. She found the website of a private clinic who listed their prices for various types of termination, some of which were upwards of a thousand pounds, depending on whether or not you wanted anaesthetic. Liz didn't have that kind of money lying around and she couldn't take it from their savings without Nick noticing. She tried to access the NHS website but only got an error message saying they were experiencing technical difficulties.

A half-hearted search for natural alternatives turned up a fascinating page on the history of unwanted pregnancy and its often dubious solutions. The Victorians had their own tonics – remedies designed to "restore female regularity" or "remove impurities from the system". There was one cryptic advertisement for something called Beecham's Pills that Liz found strangely unsettling.

Two young women in bathing dresses stood on a beach, one with a seashell pressed to her ear. "What are the wild waves

318

saying?" read the elegant script above them. "Try Beecham's Pills." The text beneath the drawing proclaimed it "The World's Medicine", and listed among its curative powers was the coded message that it could "assist Nature in her wondrous functions".

Liz gazed at the picture for a long time, and in particular at the smaller of the two girls in the drawing, the one holding the seashell. The girl's eyes gazed right back at Liz. There was something of Vanora in the fey expression that made her feel uneasy.

She exited the browser and closed her laptop. For a long time she sat staring into space, her mind churning with thoughts and nightmare scenarios. She imagined telling Nick her decision, tried to see him taking her hands and telling her it was fine, that he would go with her and be with her all the way through it, that he wouldn't hate her for it. But the Nick in her mind refused to play along with her fantasy. He glared at her and gripped her arm tightly, telling her she would not kill his child. *His* child! In another scenario, he insisted that she at least let it be born. Then she could give it up for adoption so that someone else might love it. In his eyes was the smug assuredness that she would change her mind once she looked into their baby's eyes.

She shook her head, sickened by her mind's betrayal and even more sickened by Nick's transformation. All morning she wandered the empty house, weighing the options, debating the consequences.

There was no other way. She would have to do it herself.

PART THREE

TERMINATION

CHAPTER 35

Liz carefully washed the dragonfly hatpin with peroxide. Then she carried it into the bedroom as though it were a priceless item, the key that would save her life. She spread a towel over the bed and stepped out of her knickers, hitching her skirt up around her waist. Her head was pounding and so was her heart. Although she was afraid, her actions were mechanical, clinical. She wanted the foetus gone. There was no question of that. What was she afraid of, then? The pain? The possibility that she might do some damage? She knew it could be dangerous but it didn't have to be fatal, not in this day and age. If she made herself infertile in the process, well, that certainly wasn't a problem. And if there were complications afterwards, then she could tell Nick it had been a miscarriage.

She lay down on her back and pulled her knees up as high as they would go. Then she lowered the tip of the pin towards her sex. Her hand shook so much she had to stop and take several deep breaths to calm herself before she could continue. The room smelled foul, and she had to wait for the nausea to subside.

This time she brought the pin right to the edge of her labia, spreading herself open with her other hand. The sharp point grazed the delicate skin and she gasped, jerking it away. After a few breaths she made another attempt, only to shy away again once the point made the slightest contact. It was like trying to push two magnets together, fighting the powerful force of resistance.

She knew where the resistance was coming from and it made her shudder. The creature inside was trying to stop her. Liz gripped the hatpin more tightly and this time she managed to make some progress. With her eyes closed she circled it gently inside her, trying to find the point of entry to her cervix. Each time she pricked herself she cried out. How the hell had women in earlier times ever managed to do this?

Closing her eyes, she tried to visualise her insides, tried to sense where the foetus lay coiled and pulsing, a creature that must be slain. She found what she hoped was the right place and gritted her teeth as she angled the pin into position. Then she boldly slid it in. She bit back a scream at the pain as she forced the pin deeper, resisting the urge to yank it back out again. It was like trying to push a spike into frozen meat. She could feel the sharp end penetrating flesh, but was it her own or the baby's?

Gasping with pain, she withdrew the pin. There was only a tiny drop of blood on the tip. It couldn't possibly have gone deep enough. Tears sprang to her eyes. Throwing herself down the stairs was starting to look a lot more appealing now.

With a cry of frustration she lay back. And her heart nearly stopped.

The plaster face of Carson Menrath was glaring at her. In fact, it seemed to have moved, as though the head itself had turned so that its eyes could meet hers.

All the blood drained from her face. She felt pinned to the bed and a violent chill swept through her, as though she'd been touched by a corpse. As though a cold, dead finger had suddenly pressed itself up inside her, to stroke and reassure the foetus.

The scowling effigy seemed closer now, inches from her face. She opened her mouth to scream but the only sound she could manage was a pitiful gasp. There was the rumble of a deep male voice, like distant thunder in her mind. Her own voice was there as well, submerged but screaming.

A familiar smell reached her senses. Sweat and chalk. With it came flashes of memory, of the night she had blocked from her mind. She recalled with horrible lucidity the fear and confusion, the perverse union, the pain and the awful sense of violation.

Knowing she had shared that horror with Vanora only amplified the experience and the fact of her resulting condition was truly obscene.

Liz squeezed her eyes shut tight and gritted her teeth. She wanted to tell herself it wasn't real, but that was like saying the Earth didn't turn. There was no denying it. Not without cutting herself loose from reality and abandoning herself to the same madness that had eventually claimed poor Vanora.

Liz was convinced she could feel Carson's hot sour breath on her face as the huge bust pressed down closer and closer to hers. It was like being trapped in a coffin. There was an icy tingling in the back of her skull and she wondered if it was her sanity beginning to unravel. Because if *this* was real, surely anything else might be. The worst things she could imagine might be nothing beside what was possible in such a world. If she opened her eyes and confirmed it, that would be the end of everything.

It seemed like years before she became aware of a piercing ache in her right hand. The hatpin. She was clutching it so tightly her nails were digging into her palm. She loosened her trembling fist a little and felt the tingling of returning blood flow. The sensation swarmed up her arm like ants. The looming presence still had her body paralysed but, bit by bit, she was able to readjust her grip on the hatpin, rotating it outwards in her hand as she brought it up to her chest. She held it firmly, brandishing it like a tiny lance, quivering all over with terror as she steeled herself to strike.

When the moment came she didn't plan for it; she let her instincts guide her. Her arm jerked and the hatpin struck home with a chalky *thunk*. A tiny shower of dust tickled her face and there was a sudden updraught as something pulled away sharply. She felt rather than heard the roar of savage rage her action provoked. Her eyes flew open in time to see the plaster head drawing back against the cornice, its open mouth contorted in pain.

Liz didn't wait for its eyes to open. She leapt up from the bed and ran for the door, but it slammed shut just as she got there. The pounding of her heart was so loud that she almost missed the heavy creak of the floorboards. Someone was standing behind her.

She could feel the slow trickle of blood from within, like a tiny serpent making its way down her leg. Not enough, though. Not nearly enough. She knew she hadn't succeeded. She thought of wounded animals, attacking in furious retaliation. Then she dismissed the thought. It was just an embryo, surely one of the most helpless things in existence. It should be easy to kill. Even wounded, it couldn't possibly fight back.

Could it?

Her vision dimmed and blurred, and for a moment she thought she would faint. She tried to reach out for the door, to turn the handle, but the effort was simply too much. Helpless, she sank to her knees, fear and sickness swirling in her guts. She imagined a deep red channel, a tunnel of glistening muscle and blood. It led all the way inside her, to where the hated creature lay. Not sleeping. Never sleeping. Waiting. Watchful.

Her thoughts blurred, clouding her reason. From somewhere far away she thought she could hear Jane. Kind Jane, who had faced Carson boldly and tried to protect her mistress. Then the voice faded and Liz couldn't remember who Jane was. She could barely remember who she was herself, where she was, or when.

The veil had descended again and she felt herself falling. Her head thumped the floor and she gazed along the skewed sightline, unable to make sense of what she was seeing. A woman, clad in a long nightgown, her hair in disarray, was crawling away from her. *Vanora*. And yet at the same time she knew that the woman was Liz herself. She could feel the chill hardness of the floorboards beneath her bare hands and feet, smell the sour sweat that clung

327

to her thin body.

She crept towards the far wall, towards Vanora's ruined alabaster bust. Only it wasn't ruined, not entirely. The wallpaper was vibrant and new, the room full of unfamiliar furniture. A wave of nausea rolled in and Liz shut her eyes for a moment, wishing it away.

When she opened them again the view had changed. Now she was crouched beneath the head. The sculpture was lovely, a very good likeness of the sad-eyed woman, but there was something wrong with the chin. It looked as though it had eroded, like a cliff against the onslaught of the sea.

She tasted chalk, and bile rose in her throat. She swallowed it down, grimly determined not to be sick. Had she taken some pills? Crazily she thought of Beecham's Pills, the World's Medicine. Her head swam and after a moment she became aware of the unfamiliar weight in her hands. She looked down.

In one hand was a chisel, in the other, a hammer. She was standing on a chair atop a large mahogany desk, a fine layer of white dust settling over its expanse. Gouges in the floor showed that it had been dragged here, just beneath the bust. Was she dreaming? Sleepwalking? There was the soft *chink* of the hammer and a piece of alabaster the size of a billiard ball fell, striking the edge of the desk. It bounced off and rolled to a stop beneath the window.

Vanora clambered down and retrieved it. The material was soft and powdery and Liz allowed her own hands to be guided, pounding it into tiny crumbs. A glance up at the bust showed that the face was now shockingly disfigured.

The work was hard but Vanora was determined. Again and again she climbed back up onto the desk, chipping away at her likeness until she could reach no higher. One eye remained, staring across the room at Carson with what seemed an accusing gaze. She tasted dust. Not pills, then. Something worse.

Vanora smashed another chunk of the sculpture. Without hesitation she brought a piece to her mouth and ate it. It was like biting into a handful of crystals, cold and salty. Liz wanted to spit it out but Vanora made her swallow. Her tongue was coated with powder and her teeth and jaw ached horribly. The room swam in and out of focus and her head pounded with the noise of grinding, crunching, chewing.

When the first tooth broke, Vanora yelped with pain. Liz tasted blood and gagged but Vanora forced it down in one long painful swallow, broken tooth and all. Liz was certain she could feel the chunks of alabaster dredging flesh from her throat as they went down. They would tear her stomach to pieces.

No, Liz thought, chilled. *They weren't intended for her. They were for the baby.*

Vanora was mad but there was a sick logic to her madness. Whatever she ate, the creature within also had to eat. She had no access to the remedies of her time, so instead she fed them both on jagged shards of cold stone.

After breaking another tooth Vanora began to cry, and then her stomach finally rebelled. She coughed, choking on the unnatural diet. When she retched, the vomit was full of blood and fragments of stone, now stained a horrible red. She was sick again and again as her body tried to purge itself. With trembling hands she clutched at some of the larger pieces, but she couldn't bring herself to eat them again. She wrapped her arms around herself and lay there, cowering, until Jane found her and took her back to bed.

***

Liz came to, feeling ill. Her mouth was full of the taste of stone and blood but when she spat, there was only saliva. It took her a while to realise where she was. She had crawled across the bedroom and she now lay beneath Vanora's mutilated bust. Her fingers flew to her mouth but a quick examination reassured her.

Her teeth were all there still, unbroken. She shuddered to imagine the kind of desperate madness that had driven Vanora to do what she did, but worse was still to come. Helpless to resist its pull, she closed her eyes and fell through into the dead world once more.

CHAPTER 36

Endless hours passed. Centuries and centuries. Eternities. Still, through the silence, something pulsed. Something waited.

The first thing that came to her was pain. It began as a dull ache in her back and in her belly. Then it began to progress down her body, like a sheet being drawn back on a ghastly revelation. When the awareness reached her legs, the fog began to clear and Vanora remembered what she had done.

The stairs.

She saw herself standing at the top, tall and regal. Just as she had stood that night at the ball, gazing down on all the gaily costumed revellers, all of them waiting to see her. How she had adored that night! How she had adored Carson too. Tears burned her eyes at the thought of how much things had changed. He had soured after the first baby, and grown cold and cruel after the second. Vanora no longer recognised the kind gentleman she had met on the pier one day in the distant past. It seemed at times as though she were remembering someone else's life entirely.

But the stairs.

It wasn't such a long way down but she had still been very frightened. Jane had taken good care of her after finding her that time, filthy with blood and sick, caked with dust from her ruined sculpture. Jane had wept with pity for her. But she had also been horrified at the realisation of what her mistress had been trying to do.

"It's a sin, Miss Vanora," she had whispered, her eyes full of terror. "It's against God's will."

God's will. Was it God's will that had cursed her with "abominations"? Was it God's will that had turned her husband from a loving man into a monster? Was it God's will that made him do what he did to her night after night?

Far back in her mind was the fond memory of their wedding night, the fear and exhilaration that had come from their coupling. The tenderness and love. The joy and anticipation of their first child. But it had all crumbled to dust at the sight of that malformed infant. Carson had been less gentle with her the second time but still, the love was there. Or so she had thought. After that, his affections had blackened like scorched earth and his touch had turned to cruel persuasion.

The stairs.

She had stood as though at the top of a hill, gazing down into a valley far below. There were thirty-six steps. She had counted them twice. Twice then and many times since, as the idea had taken root and flowered in her mind. Jane had refused to go into town for her, refused to find a physician or an apothecary from whom to procure remedies that might accomplish the task without violence. The poor maid had burst into tears, pleading with her mistress to let her send for the vicar instead, urging her to pray for strength and understanding.

God's will. There was no other way, then.

Vanora had closed her eyes and indeed said a prayer, a tiny one. She had asked for help, for forgiveness. Then she had simply let herself go limp, as though fainting. Her stomach swooped as she began to overbalance and for a split second she nearly lost her nerve and grabbed for the banister. But a split second was all that was needed to invoke the image of the two-headed calf in her mind. She saw it as clearly as if it were before her now, drifting in its chemical prison.

Her ribs crunched against the hard angle of a step as she fell. Instinctively she tucked her head in, throwing her arms over her face to protect it. Her legs flailed wildly, one ankle striking the balusters with shocking force. She heard the splintering of wood as she came untangled and continued to fall, turning head over heels. There was the sense of plunging through a vast open space, a feather at the mercy of the wind. Except that feathers didn't break. There was the crack of more wood and a thought swam into her head like a tiny fish in a lake. No, not wood. It was *she* who was breaking.

It seemed an age before she finally came to rest, landing in a crumpled heap at the bottom. She lay dazed and insensible for a while, disorientated by the unfamiliar view, feeling as though she were lost in a dream from which she could not wake. The newel posts reared before her, the dragons eyeing her impassively.

And then the pain made itself known.

She came awake with a scream she could not suppress. Her lower body burned and the slightest movement was agony. There was the sharp, bright smell of blood as well, its spreading pool both a horror and a comfort. Surely the infant could not have survived the fall. But the pain made her question whether she herself had perished too. Was she dead? Was she in Hell? Was this punishment for going against God's will?

Her head swam with pain and sickness and the room around her swelled to monstrous proportions. She felt like an insect trapped in a huge cauldron, one hanging over a blazing fire. Each tiny movement awakened new areas of pain but still she tried to crawl away. The blood disturbed her. She feared it might come to life, rise up over her like a blanket and smother her, drown her in its wet fury.

But she couldn't crawl far. Darkness became brightness, became oblivion as she faded in and out of consciousness. Occasionally she woke to more pain but swiftly bit back her cries, as they only made it worse. She scarcely recognised her own voice. It sounded different. It sounded mad.

She imagined her body sinking beneath the floor, down into the earth beneath the house, food for worms, her bones all that would remain. Maybe in a thousand years' time someone would find her. She lay still, watching the stained-glass window wheel above her, diminishing into a pinprick of light as she fell. From somewhere in the house a clock chimed, counting off the years, tolling her life away.

But what felt like an eternity to Vanora was in actuality only minutes. Long, agonising minutes. It was Carson who discovered her. He stood for a time looking down at her, his eyes blazing with anger and disgust as he took in the sight of her crumpled body, her shattered ankles. Then his lips twisted in a cold smile and he leaned down to whisper to her.

"You're mine," he said. "Forever."

CHAPTER 37

Liz's eyes flew open and she cried out as she realised where she was. She clutched at the banister, dropping into a crouch and wrapping her arms around the topmost newel post as she stared down at the long expanse of steps. The staircase warped before her eyes like a suspension bridge twisting in a storm.

She didn't want to imagine how close she had come to stepping off into a fall, *Vanora's* fall, breaking every bone in her body as she tumbled down the hard, unyielding treads. Carpeted, yes, but no less like teeth for that. A dangerous animal could still bite you through your clothes.

She cowered at the top, clinging to the post just as Nick had once clung to her at the top of Glastonbury Tor. And as she eyed the steps that had almost killed her, she fancied she was looking down an equally ancient rise. She tasted chalk again. Chalk and dust and earth. She thought of a grave, could almost hear and feel the solid chop of a spade into thick, hard-packed dirt. But whose grave? What was inside?

The onionskin of the world was gradually peeling away, layer by layer. There was something terrible in this house. Something that had taken over Carson Menrath and turned him into a monster. Something that had driven his helpless wife insane. Something that had used them both for its own vile purposes but been ultimately thwarted by poor, mad Vanora. Something that was still here and was now using Liz.

The way in. The way through.

She succumbed to another wave of vertigo as she tried to puzzle it out. But the more she tried to fix on it, the more it eluded her, like a fading dream.

Carson had built the house on the site of an ancient gate. But who had built the gate? And for what purpose?

Her head was beginning to pound and she felt the foetus slithering inside her. In her mind it moved like an eel, swimming freely in and out of her womb, twining around her organs, giving each one a proprietary squeeze, just to let her know that her body was not her own. She had tried to kill the creature and failed. Vanora had also tried, but she had destroyed herself in the process.

Liz closed her eyes, and found herself seeing again through Vanora's. Her legs tingled with the memory of pain, the bright screaming agony of her injuries and the warm, numbing glow of laudanum that followed. She was not paralysed. That might have been a mercy. But she would never walk again.

"Wake up," Liz growled. "You're not Vanora."

Her voice echoed inside her head and the swarm of memories receded. She could still feel them, pushing against her mind, like bees searching for an opening in a wall. But she kept talking to herself, drowning out the buzzing insistence with the sound of her own voice.

She went to her desk and dug through her handbag until she found her phone. Her nervous fingers seemed determined to resist her efforts but eventually she pulled up Gwen's number and pressed the CALL button. She paced along the corridor as she listened to the digital buzz on the other end. After six rings, it went to voicemail. Liz didn't know what to say. It was all too crazy to leave in a message and it seemed even crazier the more she thought about it. It would only make Gwen worry, and make her come rushing out to see her, only to be told there was nothing she could do. Because there *was* nothing anyone could do. With a deep sense of misery and shame, Liz disconnected the call.

Who else was there? She saw her mother's entry as she scrolled through her contacts and a little tremor of uneasiness made her swipe past it quickly, going back up through the alphabet.

Jack. She relaxed a little at the sight of his name and the smiling avatar beside it. She stabbed at the button and listened as the phone rang and rang.

"Oh come on," she muttered, "where are you? Pick up."

Then she remembered. Her brother was in Hawaii. Lord only knew what time it was there. He could be on top of a mountain or forty metres beneath the Pacific for all she knew. Wherever he was, he was out of reach. Far, far out of reach.

Blinking away tears of frustration, she threw her head back and her eyes were drawn to the trapdoor. She had been standing just beneath it. A chill went through her at the sight of the little rope hanging down. It reminded her of a noose. She remembered the morning Nick had woken her, claiming to have heard something scream up there. They hadn't found anything. She had a vague memory of being up there on her own some other time, of hearing noises herself. But no, that had been in the bedroom, behind the wall. Where the bones had been hidden.

The trapdoor worried her, though. She stared up at it for a long time, unsettled. She thought of holes and crawling things, of weak mewling cries and the smell of decay. Her insides quivered. Startled, she pressed her hands against her belly, trying to suppress the little fish-flick of the embryo. She tore herself away from the corridor and returned to her desk.

As she replaced the phone in her bag she noticed a scrap of paper. An address. And a name that made her dizzy with relief. Will Pritchard. If anyone would understand, it was him.

A glance towards the window showed her a bleached sky and snow-laden trees. Weak and sickly light shone on the pale hills beyond. It wasn't yet noon but the sun was already low in the winter sky and it would be completely dark by four. There was no time to lose.

Ten minutes later she was bundled up in thermal layers, boots and a heavy coat. The air outside attacked her face and the wind turned her bones to ice in seconds. The Moon and Sixpence was only a mile away. She could walk there in twenty minutes, but it was far too cold to go on foot. She hesitated beside her car and glanced back at the house. It seemed to beckon her with seductive warmth, a siren song of comfort. For several long minutes she stood debating whether to go back inside, to just abandon the silly endeavour and take herself to bed. Forget all about trying to go anywhere.

"No," she said, pushing aside the temptation. "Go and find Will."

The little Peugeot coughed and wheezed before the engine finally sputtered into life. Liz's breath steamed inside the car and she waited for what felt like an eternity for the heater to take effect. When the windows were finally clear of ice, she reversed out from beneath the archway and was reassured by the solid crunch of tyres on gravel. The snow wasn't that deep, then. Even so, she took it slowly, edging the car gradually down the sloping drive.

Her insides burned as she made her way through the thicket of trees and shrubs, all blanketed with snow. The glaring whiteness felt alive, watchful. She could almost see the trees quivering, ready to shake their burden down onto her and bury her. She didn't like the idea that she was bound to the house, that something didn't want her to leave.

Two enormous buddleia flanked the drive halfway down and she recalled with a pang the vibrant purple sprays of flowers they had sported in the summer, the countless butterflies that had flocked around them. How beautiful all this had seemed then! She tried to hold the happy memory in her mind as she drove past them, using it like a talisman to give her courage. But the seductive image betrayed her. She only closed her eyes for a moment, but a moment was all that was needed.

The House of Frozen Screams

The car slewed wildly on a patch of ice and her foot went instinctively to the brake. The wheels spun as they tried to grip the surface but it was no use. The car slid sideways and even when Liz realised what was happening and pumped the brake to stop the skid, it was too late.

The shrubs and brambles were no match for the little Peugeot as she left the drive and swerved into the woods. The right bumper struck a glancing blow off a tree and slid to the left, thumping down an even steeper slope that led into a small grove of trees. Liz screamed as the trees grew larger and larger in the windscreen. Then everything happened at once. She heard the crack of glass and the grinding of metal. Something seemed to explode. Lights flared, then dimmed, then brightened again. The airbag was in her face, and the car lurched to a stop with a heavy crunch.

For a long time she didn't feel anything. She sat still, frozen with fear as a creeping ache made itself known in her neck. Pain pulsed behind her eyes and she began wiggling her fingers and toes. She didn't think anything was broken. Which was more than could be said for the car. It was canted at a forty-five degree angle, nose down in a ditch. The driver's-side window was smashed. Liz battled her way out from behind the deflating airbag and wrenched open the door. The angle of the car made it swing away from her as though it had been yanked from her hand and she nearly fell out into the snow. She gasped and clung to the dashboard as the car rocked with the force of the door's violent movement.

When the vehicle seemed stable again she tried moving her limbs one by one to check for injuries. Everything was fine. Everything, that was, except for her necklace. Her good luck charm was smashed. It felt like an omen. She brushed the pieces from her lap and stepped gingerly out into the snow. She was unable to restrain a cry of dismay at the sight of the buckled front end of the car.

A sense of disquiet made her scalp prickle. It hadn't been an accident. It was a warning and a threat. Something hadn't wanted her to leave. She could easily have been killed, but that wasn't the point. The parasite wanted her whole and unharmed. How else could she give it life?

She had no choice but to walk now. At least the rush of adrenalin was helping to warm her from within. Now even more determined, Liz wound her scarf tighter, pulled her woollen hat down over her ears and used the trees as handholds to clamber down the hill to Old Church Road. Brambles tore at her gloves and scarf, snagging and unravelling them, but she pressed ahead stubbornly, her legs crying out at the exertion. Once upon a time she had been a keen hiker, but Wintergate had turned her into a shut-in. It felt as though she hadn't been walking for years and she had to force her body to keep moving.

The sound of snow crunching beneath her boots made her shudder and she tried to drown it out by singing to herself. And when her lips became too numb to sing, she hummed. She followed the road past St Andrews' church and made her way through Poets' Walk. The trees were hung with icicles. They looked like crystals in the dying light of the day. It should have been magnificent, a true winter wonderland. But she was alone in the icy woods with only the mournful cry of seagulls to disrupt the stillness. That, and the hiss of the waves.

What are the wild waves saying?

Liz pushed the image of the seashell-girl's face from her mind and carried on.

The marine lake came into view and for a moment she thought she saw the little boy trying to sail his boat across it. But there was no one there. The lake was frozen solid and the seafront was deserted.

Of course it is, she thought, trying to be sensible. *It's bloody freezing!*

The Moon and Sixpence was open, however, and she stumbled with relief into its cosy warmth, stamping snow from her boots. She turned immediately to the window where she'd sat with Will, eager to see his fatherly face. He wasn't there. She glanced around, hoping to spot Hyperion, but aside from one small family and the grumpy flat-capped man she'd seen before, the pub was as empty as the seafront. She clattered up the stairs but there was no one on the first floor at all. Dejected, she went back down and looked around again, although there was no way she could have missed Will, let alone the massive dog.

"Can I help you?"

She turned to the man behind the bar. "Yes, I'm looking for Will Pritchard."

The man shook his head. "Nah. He hasn't been in for a couple of days. Expect the weather's keeping him at home. Along with all my other customers. You want anything?"

She did. She desperately wanted to slug back an entire bottle of vodka, or whisky, or tequila. Whatever would obliterate the nightmare she was living in. But she shook her head. "Sorry. I'd love to, but I have to go."

He looked her over, frowning at what he saw. When he spoke

again, he sounded wary. "If you don't mind me saying so, you look like you could use something strong." He hesitated a moment, then grabbed a glass from the rack overhead. Before she could protest, he'd poured a shot of something caramel-coloured and passed the glass across to her. "Here. On the house."

"Thank you," she said, relenting. Whatever it was, it was warm and lovely and she wanted to weep with gratitude for it. And when she caught a glimpse of herself in the mirror behind the bar, she understood his act of charity. A line of blood had congealed on the right side of her face and her cheekbone was bright red.

The words "It's not what you think" were on her lips, but she knew how that would sound. And if she told him she'd crashed her car, he'd only want to call an ambulance. There was nothing she could say. Instead, she dabbed at the blood with a cocktail napkin as the man turned discreetly away.

After she'd tidied herself up, she pulled out the slip of paper with Will's address on it. "You don't know where this is, do you?"

"Seavale Road? Sure, that's just around the corner. Turn left out of here and follow the beach up towards the roundabout. It's the first street on your left. You can't miss it."

"Thank you."

Liz pulled a few strands of hair down from her hat to cover the

347

bruise and gave the man what she hoped was a pleasant smile as she turned to go.

"Take care of yourself, pet," he said, his voice both kind and firm.

"Don't worry. I intend to."

She had actually walked right past Seavale Road on her way to the pub so it was no trouble to backtrack and find Will's house. It was a cosy little cottage and, oddly enough, the front door was open. She didn't have a chance to knock before Hyperion appeared in the doorway, chuffing softly, his tail wagging as he recognised her. He was so tall Liz didn't have to bend down at all to pet him.

"Hello, boy," she said. "Is your friend in? I really need to see him."

It felt completely natural to talk to the dog, comforting even. But of course Hyperion couldn't answer her. He cocked his head, seeming puzzled by her anxiety.

Gradually a murmur of voices reached her from within and an elderly man made his way to the door, leaning heavily on a cane. Not Will, but someone who looked very much like him. A brother perhaps. He was dressed all in black and had obviously been crying. Liz's heart sank like a stone.

"Oh no. Please, no. Not Will."

The man nodded sadly and put a comforting hand on her shoulder. "It was peaceful," he said. Then, before she could ask, he added, "His heart."

Sorrow swelled her throat so much that she couldn't speak. If she tried, she would burst into tears. They were both silent for a while. Hyperion nuzzled her hand and she stroked him, wondering obliquely if he could carry her weight if she collapsed.

"Do you want to come in? The whole family's here."

She shook her head, gathering herself. "No, I can't. I didn't know him, really."

Will's brother looked down at her hand, still absently caressing the dog. "I'm sure Will would be happy for you to be here."

"I really can't. I only met him once, but he was a lovely man and he helped me a lot. I'm sure he'll be missed." Her emotion was starting to get the best of her and she felt compelled to get away. "I'm- I'm so sorry for your loss."

And before the man could say anything else, she hurried away.

It was a long, cold walk back to Wintergate. Her skull felt as if rusty nails were rattling around inside it, jabbing at the inside of her scalp and pricking the backs of her eyes. Several times she had to stop and wait for the waves of pain to subside. Tears froze into crystals on her face. She scrubbed them away, trying to steer her thoughts away from one terrible prospect. It hovered in her mind, teasing her, tormenting her.

She desperately hoped it had been peaceful. She hoped it was true about his heart. But in the back of her mind was a nagging thought she couldn't shake – that he had been *silenced*.

CHAPTER 38

The first thing Nick noticed when he pulled up to the house was the absence of Liz's car. That was odd, he thought. Where would she have gone, especially after dark?

He unlocked the front door and switched on the light. Then his eyes widened as he saw the mess in the hall. At first he thought it was littered with broken glass, but on closer inspection he realised the glinting shards were crystals. They were scattered all across the floor, along with countless beads and feathers and fiddly bits he didn't know the names for.

The tiny pieces crunched beneath his shoes as he made his way to the stairs. He thought back to the night he had found Liz standing at the top and he had a crazy image of her falling to the floor and shattering like a crystal chandelier, bleeding pixie dust and fairy tears.

He reached the landing and saw that her worktable was still there. It hadn't collapsed or toppled, spilling its contents into the room below. Had she just knocked some boxes over then? She'd been so testy lately; maybe she'd had a bit of a tantrum and flung stuff around. Whatever the case, he was more concerned with where she was now. She shouldn't be out in the cold after dark, not by herself. Not in her condition.

He pulled out his phone and called her. He jumped as he heard a burst of short vibrations only a few feet away. Her handbag was sitting on the edge of the worktable and her phone was inside it, buzzing.

He frowned in confusion and disconnected the call. Then he headed down the corridor. "Liz? Where are you?"

The bathroom door was closed. When he pressed his ear against it, he could hear the faint splash of water from within. He knocked softly.

"Nick? Is that you?" She sounded frightened.

He couldn't help but smile. "Of course. Who else would it be? Can I come in?"

After a slight hesitation, she said yes. He opened the door into a wall of steam. Liz was in the tub, buried up to her chin in a huge froth of bubbles. She looked awful. Her skin was bright red from the scalding water and her face looked bruised. He suddenly understood why her car was missing.

"Oh my god, Liz, what happened?"

She turned to him, her eyes puffy and bloodshot. "I wrecked

my car."

Panic surged through him. "When? Where? Are you hurt? Shouldn't we go to the hospital?"

"I'm fine." She sounded weary. "Nothing's broken and I don't want to go anywhere."

"But your face-"

"Is just bruised. I'll live. Leave it alone."

He knelt beside the tub and plunged a hand into the bubbles, seeking hers. "But what happened?"

She managed a weak smile as he squeezed her hand. "You'll ruin your jacket," she said.

"I don't care. Just tell me what's wrong."

Her eyes filled with tears and she gazed down at their entwined fingers. She traced the gleaming gold of his wedding band, then drew it to her lips and kissed it. "Everything," she said, her voice hoarse. She was silent for a long time before adding, "Will's dead."

Nick had to think for a moment before realising who she was talking about. "The bloke who wrote the Clevedon book? The one who told you about the bones?"

She nodded. "I went out to see him. It was so cold but I needed- I had to ask him something." Her expression clouded with confusion and she shook her head. "I can't remember what it was now but it was important. I was upset."

It was all he could do not to shake her to get the story out. Had she run the guy over? Was that what she was so upset about?

"The driveway was icy and the car slid. I couldn't stop. Didn't you see it? It's stuck in the trees."

"It's dark. I didn't see anything at all."

"Oh. Of course. The snow. They said it's supposed to thaw tonight, so maybe we can dig it out tomorrow." She pressed her fingers to her temples. "Sorry, I'm a bit woozy. I took some painkillers. A lot."

Anxiety leapt in his chest and he fought to restrain himself. He didn't want to fight. Instead he pursed his lips and nodded, urging her to continue.

"My head," she murmured. "It was killing me. I broke the window with it." She giggled at that but her mirth faded fast. "I just slipped off the road into the trees. Car's a write-off. So's my good luck charm. Not that it was bringing me much luck anyway–"

"What's this got to do with Will?" Nick asked, growing impatient.

"I went to his house to see him, and his brother told me he'd died." At that she began to cry, letting go of his hand so she could wipe her eyes.

Nick knew his feelings were unreasonable, but he resented her grief for this man he didn't know, this stranger whose house she had visited without him. Liz and the baby - they could have been killed, and Will was responsible, however indirectly. He kept his mouth shut though, and let her cry, stroking her back as she shook with quiet sobs.

"I'm sorry," she whimpered at last, sniffling and wiping her nose on a washcloth. "It was just a really bad day."

"I gathered that from the mess downstairs," he said coldly.

She flinched at his tone. "Yeah. Sorry. I lost it a bit."

He took a deep breath. "Well, I'm glad you're safe now." He stood up and slipped a towel off the rail. "Come on, it's time to get out. You look like a lobster in a pot." She stepped gingerly into the towel and let him wrap it around her, patting her gently, drying her like a child.

"Thank you," she said. A dazed expression came into her eyes and she smiled, murmuring something that sounded like "Jane".

Nick dismissed it. She was off her head on painkillers, that was all. There were ready meals in the fridge. Some food would probably help to bring her back to her senses. He would just have to look after her until then.

In the dining room she wrinkled her nose at the curry he'd heated in the microwave. "I'm not really hungry," she said.

"Look, you need to eat something. You hardly ate all weekend. Now please just humour me."

"So sleepy..."

"Eat."

She obeyed, slowly forking chicken into her mouth. It took ages for her to chew the first bite and when she finally swallowed it she made a face. "It tastes like chalk," she complained.

"It's probably all those pills you took."

She lowered her head, chastened, but she continued eating.

Afterwards Nick helped her up to the bedroom despite her protest that she wasn't an invalid. The room felt stuffy and stale. He supposed it was the wall Liz had smashed through. The dust had taken ages to settle and the room had smelled musty ever since.

He got her into a flannel nightgown and put her to bed. It felt good to take care of her, for her to *let* him do it. She smiled wanly but he didn't dare delude himself into thinking it was because she was charmed by his fatherly manner.

"I'll call in sick tomorrow," he said.

"Why?"

"I want to stay here, to make sure you're okay."

"I'm fine, really."

"Well, I want to make sure."

She sighed and closed her eyes without saying good night. He watched her for a while before turning off the light. When she fell asleep he heard her murmur something, something that sounded like "home".

CHAPTER 39

"Am I home? Are we there?"

"Oh, Miss Vanora. Your poor legs."

"Mother? Is that you?"

"No, miss, it's me. It's Jane."

Vanora moaned. She had been dreaming of New York, of friendly faces and familiar comforts. But now that she was awake, she saw that she was still here, still trapped. For a while she kept her eyes shut, wishing the world away. She knew that once she opened them again, she would have to face whatever she had done. And she had done something terrible, hadn't she? Something desperate and pitiable. Something *against God's will*.

"Jane?"

She felt as though she were pinned beneath wet blankets. The room was icy but her clothes were soaked with perspiration.

"I'm here."

There was a sudden pressure against her hand, as though someone had taken it in order to lead her away.

"When are we going?" Vanora asked.

Jane made a sound like a little sob and squeezed her hand tightly. "No, Miss Vanora, you can't go nowhere. You had- you had an accident."

Vanora frowned. "But I want to go home. Back to America. I don't think I can ride, though. I think I twisted my ankle on the stairs."

"Miss, please open your eyes."

Vanora did as she was asked. For a moment all she could see was the fire flickering in the hearth, its orange glow making a monstrous show of the shadows around her. Then a face swam into focus. A kind, round face, flushed and full of concern.

"Do I know you?"

The woman's eyes shone with tears. "You do, miss. It's me, Jane. Don't you remember me?"

Vanora blinked. It took a long time to make the connection, as though something were stopping her thoughts from working properly. "Jane," she said with a sigh. "Of course I remember you." Her head felt light, her thoughts fuzzy. There was the taste of brandy on her lips and something bitter and medicinal underneath that. "Would you get my travelling coat for me?" She made to sit up.

Jane opened her mouth to protest but she didn't get as far as finding the words before Vanora cried out. Jane pushed her down on the bed.

"Please, miss – you mustn't try to move."

"What's happened?" Vanora gasped. She could feel the bones in her legs move, in ways they shouldn't.

"You had a fall. On the stairs. Your legs are..."

The memory settled on her through the fog, blurring everything into a white haze and dampening all her hopes of fleeing to New York. She saw the entire adventure as though in a dream, in drunken slowed-down time. She heard the crack of bones meeting wood and felt her head connect with the hard tile of the floor. She smelled blood, the thick, awful blood that at least meant that the thing inside her was dead. Then she heard Carson's voice, low and menacing.

You're mine now. Forever.

"No," she whispered. "Have to go, have to leave." She tried to move again and her body howled with anguish.

"Oh miss, please don't try to move." Jane held her down, her hands gentle but firm. "The master sent me for the bonesetter. He's coming soon."

The words chilled her. "Bonesetter?" she repeated in a trembling voice. The shadows leapt like horses across the walls.

Jane pressed her lips together and gave her hand another squeeze. "You be brave, miss. He'll have you right as rain."

Right as rain. Hadn't the girl said that before? Yes, and then they had made plans to escape. But it had never happened. Carson hadn't let them.

Jane turned away then, unable to meet Vanora's eyes. She began whispering a little prayer.

"It's all right," Vanora said, trying to find the courage she'd had before. "I had to do it."

Jane flinched, but didn't speak.

Vanora's eyes fell on the brandy bottle beside the bed. Beside it was a little phial she had seen before. Laudanum. She knew it wouldn't have been Carson ministering to her.

"Thank you, Jane," she said. "You're an angel."

She hurt everywhere. It was impossible to know how many bones she had broken but she knew with crystal certainty that her ankles were among them. It felt as though an animal had chewed off her feet. If it weren't for the icy chill against her toes, she might believe it had actually happened.

"Could you make up the fire? I'm ever so cold."

The maid's eyes widened and she pressed a hand to Vanora's cheek. "I daren't, miss; you're burning up."

It made no sense. How could she be burning up when she was shivering so? But she didn't have the strength to argue so she glanced pleadingly at the brandy instead. Jane followed her gaze and poured a small measure into a glass for her, holding it to her lips so she could drink. The act of swallowing sent a jolt of blinding pain through her chest and she cried out again. Every breath felt as though someone had slid a knife into her ribs, and the clicking she heard meant that something was likely broken in there too.

The brandy helped a little, warming her throat as it slid through her body, down to her belly, where there was even more pain to obliterate. The sticky blood drying between her thighs gave her some small comfort. At least she had succeeded there. Her eyes grew heavy and she shut them, bringing a veil down over the misery.

It seemed only a moment but when she opened her eyes again she heard a strange voice. A man. She also heard Carson.

The air in the room felt thick and heavy. Clotted. Virulent colours spun before her eyes like diseased stars in a dying sky. The strange man addressed her as "Mrs Menrath". She tried to answer but her tongue was pasted to the roof of her mouth.

Then the stranger's face was right up in front of hers. It was curiously gaunt, with a black, bristly beard. The man peered deeply into her eyes, prising them open one at a time. He mumbled something to Carson, who mumbled back. It sounded like a made-up language between them. It was very curious and Vanora wanted to laugh at the funny sounds, but she was frozen still.

After a while the words began to have meaning, as her mind finally began translating through the narcotic haze.

"She should be in a hospital, sir."

"No. No hospital. She mustn't be moved."

"But sir-"

"No arguments, man! You'll be paid. Now just do your job."

The stranger moved away, down to where her legs lay outstretched on top of the bed, pulsing with a dull, distant ache. They seemed far too long, like bolts of cloth unrolling away from her. He spoke again and this time she heard what he said.

"Hold her still."

Jane was immediately beside her, bending down over her. Vanora wanted to protest. She didn't need help getting up. But that wasn't Jane's instruction at all. She realised it just as the maid took hold of her slender arms, gripping firmly.

"Jane, what are you-"

Her tongue had finally come unstuck but it was all she had time to get out before her whole murky world came apart. Stars splashed across her vision with such a blinding fury that at first she could only fear for her eyes. But that wasn't where the pain was. At last she realised what was happening. The stranger had hold of one of her feet and was wrenching it with savage, indifferent violence. Agony fled like a swarm of rats up her leg as she screamed and screamed, thrashing wildly in Jane's strong embrace.

All around her the light flickered and dimmed, but it didn't fade entirely. Now Jane was looking deeply into Vanora's eyes, her own wide with horror and shining with tears. How could the girl let them do this to her? How could she... But there was no time to question anything. Before she could begin to plead with her tormentors, the stranger had grasped her other foot and Vanora was screaming again before he'd even begun to force the bones back into place. Darkness enfolded her in its liquid embrace at last and she lost consciousness, blissfully disconnected from the excruciating pain.

When the voices began to reach her again through the fog, her eyes fluttered open and she stared vacantly at the ceiling. She fancied she could see it dissolving, opening like some strange window into heaven. Her body felt weightless, as though she might float right up into the clouds if she weren't held down. The only sounds were the crackle of the fire in the hearth, the murmur of male voices, the visceral throbbing through every inch of her skin.

"Miss Vanora, please say something."

Jane's frantic voice brought her back down and she moved her lips experimentally, trying to form words. All that came out was gibberish, she was sure, but the stranger seemed satisfied.

"Keep her warm," he said gruffly. "Don't let her try to move. I doubt she'll ever walk again."

Jane wiped her eyes at that and Vanora heard Carson promise him that his wife wasn't going anywhere. She detected a hint of satisfaction in his tone and knew better than to hope it was just her imagination.

That night he stood over her, a cruel smile on his lips. "You will never leave this house," he said. "Not while you're alive." He pressed his hand against the side of her face, a mockery of the tenderness he had once felt for her. "You will give me what I want or you will die trying." His eyes blazed with fearsome zeal and she shuddered at the realisation that he was far more mad than she.

It was only the laudanum and brandy Jane plied her with that made the passing days bearable. The girl was utterly devoted to her, staying by her side night and day, tending her, feeding her, washing her, dosing her. Vanora soon lost any sense of shame or embarrassment, accepting her helpless situation and the loss of her dignity without complaint. She'd destroyed the monster inside her, but Carson would have his revenge. Now she was truly a prisoner. Now he would destroy *her*.

From time to time he would stop by her room. If Vanora heard him coming she would feign sleep. Other times she feigned disorientation. Many times she didn't have to feign either.

For days upon days she lay in bed, growing weaker with the passage of time. No one from the outside world came to visit her and she had to wonder whether people believed her to be dead. Carson might have told them that to keep them away. She'd heard stories about unscrupulous husbands committing their wives to ghastly institutions for the insane. No one would question the word of a man like Carson Menrath. And they certainly wouldn't listen to the ravings of a madwoman.

She was getting better slowly, but she was still unable to move her legs without enduring terrible pain. At least her arms were fine. She was rarely hungry, but Jane doggedly brought her food and insisted that she eat. Her tongue probed the chipped teeth in her upper jaw and she listened to the curious rhythmic clicking inside her chest whenever she breathed. She didn't know how much time she had before Carson deemed her well enough to perform her marital duties again. All she knew was that this time she would not let him. He had killed two of their progeny and she had done away with the third; there would not be a fourth.

When he came to see her, she refused to speak to him, refused even to look at him. But her fierce resolve would crumble once he thrust his face into hers and forced her to meet his eyes under threat of further pain. All he need do, he said, was to take hold of an ankle and twist. Time and again he reduced her to a whimpering wretch, pleading with him not to hurt her.

She didn't know when she first began to see the creatures. At first she took them for opium-induced visions. They crawled like spiders over her skin, tickling her with their many legs, revolting her with their fat, worm-like bodies. But as they appeared more and more frequently, she became convinced that they had come to devour her.

"They're all over me," she cried, brushing frantically at herself. "Get rid of them!"

"But there's nothing there, miss. I promise."

"There must be hundreds – don't tell me you can't see them!"

But Jane could only shake her head in dismay. "I give you my word, it's only a phantom. See? My hand must be passing right through them."

"They want to crawl inside me. I can feel them. I can hear their teeth – listen!"

"It's only your ribs, miss. It's the bones knitting together."

Vanora covered her eyes, sobbing. She desperately wished she could believe Jane, believe that the creatures were only a fever dream. But she knew the sound of her broken ribs. She'd been living with it for weeks. She knew the way the bones clicked and pulled inside. And the creatures sounded nothing like that. She could feel them.

Jane gave her more laudanum and she slept. But even in her dreams the creatures persisted.

***

The days wasted away, and Vanora along with them. She grew so thin and frail that Jane at last appealed to Carson to take her away to a sanatorium in the countryside, where she might regain her strength, and her wits. Vanora heard their voices from beneath the deep warm sea of brandy and laudanum. Both bottles sat on her bedside table within easy reach and she used them liberally to blot out the pain and fear. To escape.

She couldn't quite discern what Carson was saying, but she knew the tone well enough. Jane had really provoked him this time. Vanora tried to speak, to warn the maid to keep silent, not to test him. But it was too late. Jane would not be stopped. The girl was simply too good, too loyal.

Both voices were raised now and Vanora could just make out their shapes beyond the open doorway, warped and distorted through the glass of the brandy bottles. They might be tiny figures trapped within those bottles, illuminated by the flickering candle. It was such a curious sight. She wondered if the world had shrunk. She herself might be only the size of a doll. Or smaller. An ant, perhaps. Then she might scuttle away unseen. But the thought of scuttling made her think of the creatures with their many legs, and she recoiled from the fantasy.

Now she could see Jane clearly, hands on hips, face red with outrage as she confronted her master, like someone facing down a bull. Then there was silence, a deep, expectant silence. Like a well into which anything might fall.

Vanora held her breath, picturing the cold fury in Carson's eyes, imagining how terrible it would be to see. But it wasn't just fury, she knew. His wildness was more than anger. It was madness. Unchecked, dangerous madness.

Her heart fluttered with fear then for Jane, her only friend in the world.

"Jane," she whispered, "no..."

But the murky cloud descended on her, blanketing her fear. Her eyes grew heavy and then she was lost to her dreams once more.

When she opened her eyes again it was Carson, not Jane, who stood over her. His hands were dripping with blood.

It seemed an eternity that he stood there, panting with exertion, but when he finally spoke, his words chilled her to the core.

"It's time, my dear. I've been patient long enough."

Vanora lay trembling as he peeled back the blankets and clambered on top of her. The room reeked of sickness, of blood and fear and hate. Her heart twisted. At first all she could think of was Jane. Poor, dear Jane who had loved her and cared for her, who had only wanted to protect her. Grief churned within her like a foul brew and she longed for oblivion. But Carson was bearing down on her, reaching down to lift the hem of her night-dress. A scream froze in her throat and she prayed for the wriggling creatures to appear, to gnaw their way through his flesh, to feast on his wild, blazing eyes.

But nothing came to her aid. And with Jane gone, nothing ever would.

With barely another second's thought she flung out her arm and grabbed the neck of the nearest bottle, swinging it round to smash into the left side of Carson's head. The little brandy it had held splashed into his eyes and he sat back with a roar, rubbing frantically at his bleeding face.

The neck and half the bottle were still in her hand, the remnant now a jagged weapon. And when Carson dropped his hands, she struck, plunging the broken glass into his face and twisting it hard, twisting as he had threatened to twist her ankles. She drove the glass shards deep, barely noting his screams of agony as he clawed frantically at the bottle. There was the satisfying crack and snap as several of the larger pieces broke away, embedding themselves in his face. She couldn't restrain a cry of elation as she saw that she had blinded him.

He cursed her, flailing wildly at the air, not realising that her weapon was now useless. In his panic, he fell to the side, unable to prevent himself from toppling. He hit the floor with a thud and then crawled away like a helpless infant, like the *abominations* he had brought forth from her poisoned womb. Howling in pain and fury, he squirmed towards where he must believe the door to be.

371

How fitting if he were to plummet down the stairs to his death in his sightless state! But then he turned towards the bed and began groping his way back to her.

Vanora no longer had anything to fear from him, though. She calmly drew her legs up, ignoring the flares of pain as she bent her knees and manoeuvred herself into a sitting position. There was another bottle of brandy on the bedside table, this one filled to the top. She raised it high over her head, waiting for the moment to strike.

When he was just below her, she brought the bottle crashing down on his skull. This one shattered completely, spraying amber liquid in a glittering fountain across the room. Carson reached out a quivering arm for a moment before slumping to the floor in a heap. Somewhere someone was laughing and it was a little while before Vanora realised the voice was her own.

It was over. The nightmare was over!

But her triumph was short-lived.

You will never leave this house. Not while you're alive.

She sank back onto the pillows with a sob. Jane was dead. And she herself was ruined. She had nowhere to go and no means to get there in any case. Even if she could somehow find her way into town and book passage on a steamer, she would never survive the journey to America.

"You witch..."

She gasped. Carson had woken from his stupor. He was still clawing the air, searching for her. In the candlelight his shadow was a vengeful spectre.

"Kill... you..."

The walls began to move then, to warp and buckle, like writhing things beneath tissue. The creatures were there, waving their legs, mocking her. She knew they weren't real. They couldn't be. If they were, Jane would have seen them. But that didn't matter. What mattered was that Vanora saw them. She would *always* see them. They would be there to torment her. Forever.

The candle flickered, its sinuous flame like a beckoning finger.

Miss, you're burning up.

Vanora closed her eyes and took a deep breath, pushing all thoughts from her mind. All but one. She took hold of the candle. For a moment she simply held it, admiring the simple magnificence of the tiny flame. Then she let it fall.

The brandy caught fire instantly, and the lumbering body of Carson Menrath with it. His voice went from hissing contempt to unrestrained screams of agony. Vanora felt nothing. Even when the flames began to engulf the room, she was not afraid. All the pain would soon be over.

After a while the screaming ceased and she lay back, listening to the crackling of the fire and watching the flames lick at the ceiling and the walls around her. She quickly grew dizzy from the smoke but there was nothing left to fear. The creatures were retreating. They would never find the way through now.

The last thing she saw was Carson's face as it bubbled in the heat of the flames, melting like wax.

CHAPTER 40

And then the wax was dripping, pooling all around her, seeping through the bedclothes.

Liz found herself struggling, gasping for air and coughing, choking. Her arms flailed as she fought her way out of the dream. She resisted the hands she felt pressing against her, battling them furiously until she realised that it was only Nick shaking her awake.

"What? What is it?" she mumbled.

"Liz, come on, you have to wake up!"

She felt dazed, drugged. It took her a few seconds to realise she was neither. That was when she smelled it.

Nick switched on his bedside light. He angled it towards the centre of the bed to reveal a wet stain. Something dark and putrid was pooling between them, seeping down through the duvet. The smell was appalling and Liz felt her throat hitch. She covered her mouth with both hands and then wriggled towards the edge of the bed, away from the foetid puddle.

Slowly they both turned their gaze towards the ceiling. At the spreading patch over their heads.

"There's something up there," Nick said softly.

Liz felt as though someone had doused her in ice-water. Her insides writhed. It was a feeling she had come to know well, that very special kind of dread. It was the kind familiar to criminals or anyone who had something to hide. She didn't know why, but she knew she must not let Nick go upstairs. There was something he mustn't see.

"Christ, it smells," Nick said. "I can't believe we didn't notice it before. Especially you. You're the one who's here all day."

All day sent another stab of panic through her. Yes, she realised, she *had* noticed it. He must have too. But something had hidden it from them, just as she had hidden things from him. If he only knew what she'd been trying to do the day before, right here on their bed...

The mattress bounced as Nick threw the duvet back and swung his legs off the edge of the bed.

Liz's heart began to pound. "Where are you going?"

He nodded up at the ceiling. "To get rid of whatever the hell that is."

There was something in the attic. Something he mustn't find.

"No!"

He jumped, startled by her cry, but he quickly collected himself. "Liz, we can't just leave it. It's dripping through the ceiling!"

"But you can't-"

"It's probably just a dead rat."

"Nick, please don't!"

He paid no attention.

"I'm sorry!" she cried, flinging the words out in sheer desperation.

Now he turned to her, looking baffled. "For what?"

"For - not noticing. And for crashing my car." For a split second this seemed like a brilliant idea. She would claim she felt faint. She must have hit her head harder than she thought. Maybe she ought to go to hospital after all...

But Nick only shook his head in frustration. "What are you talking about? None of that was your fault."

There was a sickening splash as another droplet fell into the puddle. Liz imagined a poisonous sea, a churning maelstrom of waves crashing down upon their whole world, pounding it to sodden dust.

What are the wild waves saying?

All the tears she had held back came spilling from her eyes

now. She clambered out of the ruined bed and ran to Nick. She flung her arms around his neck and sobbed into his chest, babbling a broken plea for him to stay with her. He shook her off. "Liz, what the hell's wrong with you? I have to go sort it out."

He peeled her arms away and she crumpled to the floor, begging him not to leave. He stared at her for a moment, his expression a mixture of confusion and horror.

"I'll come right back, I promise."

She crouched there motionless, listening as he moved from the bedroom into the corridor. His footsteps grew fainter as he padded down the back stairs to the kitchen. Then she heard him rummaging in drawers and cupboards, presumably looking for bin bags and rubber gloves.

Another globule dripped into the congealing mass on the bed. Liz stared at it, unaccountably afraid. After a few moments she heard Nick coming back up the stairs. He stopped in the corridor and the wooden trapdoor creaked as he pulled it down. She felt pinned to the floor, helpless to stop him as he climbed the steps to the attic.

A powerful sense of déjà vu surfaced in her mind. Something like this had happened before. Only that time it was a scream that had lured Nick up there. A scream they had never learned the source of.

Something terrible was waiting up there for him.

She was shaking with fear and drenched in icy sweat. It ran into her eye, salty, burning, and she reached up to wipe it away. But when she lifted her hand to her face she was surprised to find it clutching something. Her eyes widened as she stared at the object, not comprehending. It was a dragonfly. No, it was a dragonfly perched on an antique hatpin. *The* hatpin.

She clearly remembered cleaning it up and putting it back on her desk after her failed efforts. How had it got here? The idea that she'd slept with it under her pillow sent another wave of sickness through her, as well as an unexpected sense of purpose. Of resolve.

Deep inside her womb, the foetus squirmed.

CHAPTER 41

The smell grew steadily worse as Nick reached the top of the ladder and he had to pull his pyjama top up to cover his nose. It was ripe and pungent, the smell of decay. For a moment he hesitated, feeling not just sick but afraid. Surely no single dead rat could be responsible for such a smell. Had there been a colony of them up here?

He hesitated before switching on the torch, dreading whatever he would see but knowing he had to do something about it. He also couldn't shake the primal fear of darkness. He was worried that the torch might not come on, that the trapdoor might slam shut, that he might be locked in here with whatever had died. And whatever had been left alive.

Frustrated with himself, he thumbed the switch and a cone of light sprang into the shadows, forcing the darkness back. The support posts wavered as he swept the light through the room, pausing at each dark patch he found. Nothing. No rats. Yet the stench was almost overwhelming.

He could hear buzzing from somewhere. The empty space

played tricks with the acoustics and it seemed like the sound was all around him, even though he could see nothing. Once he overcame his initial disorientation, he realised that he was facing the wrong way. The ceiling of their bedroom would be to his left. As soon as he turned, he knew something was there. A heavy dark shape was crouching behind a post, half-obscured by a sheet of torn plastic that hung down from a beam. His heart fluttered in his chest as he steeled himself to go nearer.

He stepped carefully from one joist to the next, worried about putting a foot through the ceiling. Something scuttled as he aimed the torch beam at the shadows, and his breath caught in his throat when the hulking form came into sight.

It was Liz's sculpture. The monstrous woman and her monstrous offspring. They were clambering over the corpulent body like hellish cherubs, and their bright black eyes tracked him as he made his way closer. His stomach gave a lurch at the sudden notion that Liz might have filled the hideous woman's swollen belly with dead rats. It was all he could think of to explain the evil stench. He almost turned and fled. But then a shimmering cloud of flies lifted from the crumpled shape behind the sculpture. And he understood that the reality was even worse.

What lay there was a real body, a real corpse. He recognised her at once.

***

Liz's hand ached, so tight was her grip on the hatpin. The fire opal flashed in the moonlight and she was convinced she could hear the dragonfly's tiny gold wings flutter. The pin seemed to vibrate in her hand as she crept up the ladder and into the attic. Shadows danced a few feet away and she could hear the heavy, ragged breathing of someone gulping at the rank air. Liz barely noticed the smell.

She trod the joists like a gymnast on a balance beam, not looking down, not thinking, just focusing on the shapes in front of her, the living and the dead.

The pin gleamed in the reflected beam of the torch as she raised it high above her head. And then she brought it down.

***

The pain was bright and cold, like an icicle, and at first Nick thought water must have dripped on him from above. But then the shock of it wore off and he dropped to his knees with a gasp, clutching at the back of his neck. It was a deep, penetrating hurt, like the sting of a hornet. All around him the flies buzzed in an angry swarm, and he flailed at them with the torch, thinking he had disturbed a nest of vicious insects. Light and shadow leapt wildly in the space as he scrambled to his feet.

He almost didn't recognise Liz. Her face was contorted in what he took to be fear. Had she been stung too? He opened his mouth to tell her to run, to get out, that something was after them. He never got the chance.

She thrust her arm towards him. He was too bewildered to deflect the blow and something sharp sank into his left cheek. It stabbed through the soft flesh, straight into his tongue, and he recoiled in pain and horror as his mouth filled with blood. He lost his balance, stumbling over a paint pot. His foot punched through the flimsy ceiling and he fell sideways, landing hard across two joists. He felt something snap in his back. For a few seconds he could do nothing but lie there, dazed and blinded by pain.

When he was able to focus again he looked up to see Liz raising her arm. This time he saw what she was holding. It was some kind of decorative pin, long and sharp and dripping with blood. He tried to cry out, to scream her name, but the only sound he could make was a liquid croak.

He dropped the torch. It rolled from side to side on the floor, flinging garish light against the wall to his right and turning Liz into a terrifying apparition. Shadows leapt and retreated until the torch finally came to rest. Liz was advancing, her mouth twisted into an unnatural snarl.

Nick stared at her for what felt like an eternity, not knowing her. He tried to speak, to say her name, to plead with her and break the spell of this madness, but he knew it wouldn't make any difference. His leg kicked helplessly in the room below as she stabbed him again, driving the thin spike deep into his neck and twisting it hard, wrenching it around in a stirring motion. He screamed, coughing up dark clots. Gouts of brighter blood leapt from his neck as the pin was yanked free. The deep pulsing sensation grew fainter with each spurt. Blood screamed across the plastic sheeting all around him and he knew with sick certainty that he was going to die.

To his horror, Liz smiled then, an ugly, perverse expression that mirrored the face of the awful sculpture. Radiant. That's what she had called it. *Radiant*.

He reached out to her but she jabbed the pin through his palm, scorpion-quick. When he pulled away, it slid free and she raised it immediately, poised to strike again, poised to keep striking forever.

"Please," he managed to choke, "Hedgehog."

But if there was anything left of Liz in the creature hunched over him now, she didn't respond. Or couldn't. Her eyes were as cold and empty as a doll's, her face unrecognisable to him. Tears blurred his vision and he just had time to think that was a mercy before she brought the pin down again. Into his legs, his chest, his neck, his face. And finally his eyes.

He still kicked and struggled but he was helpless and growing weaker by the second. His hands flapped ineffectually against his attacker. He was only dimly aware of the floor shifting beneath him. His movements were widening the hole into the bedroom below.

The pain was fading along with his awareness. He could barely even remember what had brought him up here. Oh yes, the smell. That had faded too, along with the noise of the flies, and he knew with a faint dim fear that they would soon be swarming all over him. All that was left was a heaviness in his chest, a numbing of all his senses.

Liz. Her name was the only thing that made sense but he found he could not evoke her image in his mind, could not remember her as she had been. It was as though he had been blind all his life.

He thought suddenly of Glastonbury Tor, of the frightening climb to the top of the hill and the dizzying view from the top. He had fallen into the terrible maze after all, and he was lost. If he could only find his way out again...

But there was something in his way, some kind of vicious bird that swooped down on him, jabbing and pecking in fury. The eagle hadn't flown back to its nest after all. It had been waiting for him all these years. He felt its beak penetrate his skin but there was no longer any pain. There was only a profound feeling of sadness, of loss. Something precious had been taken away. He couldn't even put a name to what it was.

Both legs were now dangling into the bedroom. He was slipping, inch by inch, unable to stop himself. Where once such a predicament would have filled him with terror, now it only seemed a sad inevitability. His hands were slick with blood. He couldn't hold on to the joists and he felt himself sliding away. He let go.

The bird gave a squawk of fright as the plaster crumbled away beneath them both. Then he and his attacker were falling. It seemed as though he hung in the air like a bird himself, drifting slowly towards the earth. He couldn't see but he imagined a green quilted landscape below, a cushion of soft grass and flowers in which he would land. He came to rest with a warm and gentle thump.

From somewhere, not very far away, he thought he could hear a baby crying.

CHAPTER 42

When Liz opened her eyes, all she could see was red. Deep, velvet red. It filled the world. She smelled and tasted blood. Her hands were covered in long scarlet gloves of it. Even her eyes were filmed with red.

Her head was swimming. It was as though a dreamscape had exploded all around her, spraying her with the shrapnel of a thousand nightmares.

There was a gaping hole high above her, ringed with splintered boards that resembled a mouth full of jagged, broken teeth. Flies buzzed lazily around the opening. The teeth dripped with blood, and dust drifted down like a monster's foetid breath.

The next thing she noticed was the pain. Her right leg sang with bright, clear agony. She cried out, a strangled yelp that didn't sound human. The pain raced along her nerves like an electric current, sending shockwaves all the way up her spine. Her head throbbed and her vision flared white. Gasping, she collapsed back onto the floor in a heap, falling heavily onto something soft and wet and warm. She looked around in confusion. The bed was some distance away, so what was she...

Oh.

Oh God.

Through the red haze she saw Nick's face, the terrible ruin of it.

There was no slow dawning of comprehension, no gradual realisation. Not even blissful denial. What she saw was the awful, immediate reality, unquestionable and unalterable. Nick was dead.

Her husband, her lover, her best friend. The man she had loved from the day they met and vowed to be with for the rest of her life. A thousand memories flashed through her mind's eye, a lifetime of experiences crammed into a handful of years. It wasn't enough time.

Grief coiled inside her like a snake, winding her insides tight, knotting her guts. With one trembling hand she reached out to him. In a hoarse voice she croaked his name, even though she knew there would be no answer. Jutting from his chest was a long, slender spike. A golden dragonfly was perched on top, its opal body streaked with gore.

Liz pushed away, ignoring the pain in her leg. Nick was probably all that had saved her from breaking her back or being killed outright in the fall, but in that moment she only wished she could have joined him. In some dim, distant part of her mind, she was aware that she was responsible, that she was the one who had done this. There was a fragment of memory associated with the dragonfly, with the *pin*. Yes. There was something inside of her she had been trying to get out. Something she had tried to kill. Had Nick simply got in the way?

She didn't know. All she knew was that he was dead. Blood streamed from his eyes like scarlet tears, but her own eyes felt as dry as the dust that drifted around them. Worse than his mutilated body was his *absence*. The cold and utter certainty that all that had made him unique and alive and beautiful was gone now, gone forever. This poor, desecrated shell was all that remained.

Her heart wrenched inside her breast and she lost herself to the anguish. Deep, hitching sobs racked her body until she thought the agony would turn her inside-out. Her memories were hazy, fading like a dream.

She looked around her, blinded by tears. What was this place? What was she doing here? What were *they* doing here? She recalled a faint sensation of home, of belonging. Had they lived here?

Yes, they had. She knew they had. But so had someone else. Some*thing* else.

As she fought her way through the confusion, a cramp seized her and she doubled over, clutching her abdomen. The reminder was cruel and unequivocal. There was something inside her, something unspeakable. She had tried to kill it, but it was stronger. It was the one in control. Of her. Of everything.

She had to get out of the house.

It took all her willpower simply to wipe the tears from her eyes so she could see. Her dressing chair was just within reach. It was a plush blue velvet affair with a high, curving back. It had been a Christmas present from Nick the previous year, because she needed somewhere to sit to do her makeup. The thought sent another stab of pain into her heart and she pushed away the memory of sitting there, gazing at Nick in the mirror, his hands on her shoulders, his lips against her neck...

She had to stop torturing herself, had to stop the thousands of memories that would assault her and beat her down.

She swept away the jumper and sweatpants she'd dumped on the chair the night before and, using the seat for balance, she levered herself up onto her good leg. Even without putting weight on it, her injured right leg protested with every movement. The bone shards ground against one another, crunching like footsteps in the snow. At times the pain was so great it threatened to overwhelm her. Helplessly, she thought of her mother, wishing she could cry and be held and be the vulnerable little girl Rachel had always wanted.

Rachel. Something stirred in her mind at the thought of her. But before Liz could find the memory that would tear everything open, the house began to groan.

At first she thought she must be imagining it. She looked up at the gaping mouth in the ceiling. More dust filtered down and the cloud of flies renewed their frantic buzzing, disturbed by the noise.

There was another low rumbling groan, almost a growl, and Liz felt something stirring beneath her, shifting uneasily. Her heart leapt and for one wild moment she thought it might be Nick, not lost to her after all. But another look at his bent and broken form confirmed that he was quite dead.

Her skin prickled with the sense of danger, and added to the smell of death was the smell of fear. Her own, hot and ripe.

A violent tremor shook the house and she almost lost her balance. If she fell, she might never be able to get back up again. She clung to the chair, listening in astonishment to the sound of glass ornaments clinking together on shivering shelves, of objects rolling in the attic above. Something fell and smashed to the floor at her feet. A misshapen baby figurine. Liz looked at the broken pieces in horror. The face had remained intact. It was staring at her with icy, evil eyes.

Liz knew then what was in the attic. She remembered what she had done. She heard the wet *thunk* of the hammer striking flesh, heard Rachel scream, heard the thud as her body fell heavily across the joists. Then the soft mewling sounds as Liz brought the hammer down again and again. They were almost words, those sounds. And it was a while before they stopped.

Trembling, Liz listened to the ghost of Rachel's voice, still pleading in her mind. Her heart curdled. Something hot and vile rose in her throat and the room grew blurry again as she swayed against the chair. She forced herself to breathe deeply, willing the nausea away. She couldn't afford to exhaust herself being sick, nor could she afford the luxury of facing the things she had done. The things she had been *made* to do. There would be time later to assimilate the full horror of it, once she was out of this house.

"Go," she whispered hoarsely. "Get out now. Have to. Move."

It was impossible to shut out the memories completely but she had to think of something else – *anything* else. She cast about for a random image to distract her, something comforting. The first thing that came to mind was the little painted fairy that sat on the edge of her desk. She urged herself to focus on it, to remember every detail: the delicately carved porcelain face, the wide green eyes, the shimmering gossamer wings. She tried to imagine her flying, lifting up from the desk and fluttering in the air. *Escaping*. Liz would escape with her.

But her imagination was too good. No sooner had she fixed the image of wings in her mind, she heard the buzzing of the flies. Then the buzzing morphed into the vibrating hum of a different set of wings, a dragonfly's. For a moment she was sure the golden insect had come to life to taunt her.

Once again pain flashed through her body. Her good leg threatened to give out but she held on to the chair grimly as another tremor rocked the house. She thought of earthquakes just as a long crack scurried across the ceiling, forking like lightning in every direction. But deep down she knew there was more to it than a simple shifting of the ground. The remains of Vanora's bust crashed to the floor, sending up a great choking cloud of alabaster dust.

Liz screamed and turned helplessly towards the door. It seemed miles away. But she had to get there. She had to get out.

Clutching the back of the chair with clammy hands, she began to limp towards the door, using the chair as a crutch. It made a horrible sound as it scraped across the parquet floor and she was unsettled by the idea that she was gouging open the skin of the house. Even worse was the movement of the broken bones in her leg, shifting together and apart like two ends of a bridge that didn't meet.

All the things that might have given her strength or positive distraction were now torments. She heard Nick's last word over and over in her mind. *Hedgehog.* Even the thought of the animal filled her with revulsion. She could still taste that rotting cake of spiny flesh. Instead she focused on words.

"One step," she said through gritted teeth, "at a time."

Her progress was slow and laborious. She pushed the chair ahead of her, wincing as it stuttered and shrieked across a scant few inches of floor. Then she braced herself and hopped, hissing with pain as the movement sent fresh hell through her bad leg.

She allowed herself a moment to catch her breath, a moment for her head to swim and her vision to blur, until she was sure she could continue without losing consciousness.

Drag, brace, hop, rest. Drag, brace, hop, rest.

And all the while she progressed on her snail-like journey, the house continued to tremble and the floor threatened to topple her at every step. More than once she pushed aside the sense that something was opening beneath her. Opening like a gate to admit her.

It seemed like hours before she reached the bedroom door and made it into the corridor. Sometimes she wasn't even sure where she was going. But when she stopped for a while, ready to sink to the floor and give in to sleep, she felt a strange urging to continue. There was a voice, a dim shadowy whisper. Her insides tingled, a sensation that was almost pleasant.

The baby. It was still with her, still a part of her. For a moment hatred flared wild and sharp in her mind. Why Nick and not the creature? But an answering flare of pain silenced her blasphemy. She remembered the dragonfly pin and what she had tried to do with it. What she had *failed* to do.

Another violent tremor rocked the house and the corridor seemed to writhe. Liz gritted her teeth, determined. If she fell, she would crawl. Wintergate would not claim her. It had kept her prisoner for months and robbed her of everything, but it would not possess her.

Moonlight streamed in through the stained-glass window as she reached the top of the stairs. Her strength was waning and she wondered if perhaps the monster inside her was directing her movements. Did it intend to make her suffer for trying to kill it? Would it throw her down the stairs like Vanora, as punishment?

Of course not, she told herself. *It wants me alive. It* needs *me*.

She made it to the banister and stared forlornly down the length of the stairs. Thirty-six steps, she reminded herself. On one leg. Tears filled her eyes. It was impossible. Gingerly she lowered her right foot to the floor and tested some weight on it. It was like dipping her toes into a mincer. Pain exploded through her body, blinding her. She screamed, stumbling as she tried to regain her balance. Sweat poured down her arms and the chair became slippery beneath her fingers. Her shoulders burned, the muscles quivering with overexertion.

It took her a while to convince herself she wasn't going to black out. The pain receded slightly, still brutal, but at least no longer incapacitating her. Spots flashed before her eyes like fireworks. When she could see again, she wiped her hands one by one on her nightgown to dry them, and took a deep breath.

Another series of tremors rumbled through the house and the foundation groaned again as the floorboards buckled. Liz could hear windows breaking and stonework crumbling in other rooms. A chunk of masonry came loose from the façade and she watched it fall past outside, breaking apart on the snowy forecourt. She leaned on the railing, gasping and panting, growing frantic. She couldn't afford to wait for the house to be still. Time was running out and she had to try to make it down.

She steeled herself. Then, with a little hop, she got herself down the first riser. Her broken leg screamed at her, and she screamed back at it. Above her the chandelier danced on its chain, the crystals jingling together, tinkling like laughter. It flickered on and off, throwing wild, garish shadows back and forth.

Thirty-five more steps, she told herself, while another voice told her it was impossible. Even if she could hop down one agonising step at a time, the pain was bound to overcome her before she reached the bottom. She would black out. Or lose her grip. Or simply give up.

"I'm not giving up," she told herself, barely aware that she was speaking aloud. She shook her head and willed herself to focus, to ignore the pain or at least to fight through it. With her gaze fixed firmly on the front door, she readied herself for another hop.

And then the chandelier fell. It came loose at the end of its arc, crashing onto the stairs and punching through several of the middle treads. She was stranded.

There was no other way down. Liz gave a cry of dismay at the unfairness of it. She was going to die here after all, buried beneath piles of rubble as the house folded in on itself and finally collapsed.

But something moved inside her. The baby had other plans.

The wall at the end of the minstrels' gallery began to shudder and the door swung open with a creak. A small hole appeared as bricks began to fall, punched out by something on the other side. Stars were visible through the widening hole and Liz clung to the railing in an agony of indecision. Was it another way out? Could she survive the fall from there to the ground? She looked down the length of the ruined staircase and for one wild moment she imagined herself straddling the banister and sliding down like a child.

And then what? Dance across the floor and waltz right through the front door? What then? You can't drive. You can't walk. You might crawl down the hill and start screaming. Someone might hear you.

Tears filled her eyes again and she wasted several valuable moments crying. She thought of Nick, lying dead in the bedroom by her own possessed hand. She thought of Rachel, slumped in the attic, a feast for the flies. All their hopes and dreams and plans, all destroyed. All because of something an evil man had done a hundred years ago.

Another tremor drew her gaze upwards, to her worktable, to the trinkets that were symbols of a happier, simpler life. Beads bounced and rolled and fell, raining down onto the foyer. The fairy she had tried to focus on earlier was still sitting on the edge of the table, wings glittering, tiny legs dangling. The eyes that had always seemed so friendly were now cold and lifeless.

Liz looked beyond her desk to the crumbling wall at the end of the gallery. The billowing dust played tricks with her, forming shapes that seemed to have meaning. She thought she saw a woman through the doorway, standing with her hands on her hips. Before her was the shape of a towering man. She gasped. Carson Menrath. He had something in his hand, something that glinted. There was a scream and then the phantoms fell to dust again before her eyes.

There was a world beyond this one and Liz didn't waste any time wondering how she would find it. Instinct got her moving again. She was able to manoeuvre her broken leg back up onto the landing. The banister was now impossibly high above her but that didn't matter. It was only a few feet to the doorway. She didn't need her legs to get there. Hand over hand, she pulled herself along, using the balusters like a horizontal ladder. Her leg protested all the way but she was learning how to ignore the searing pain. Dimly she thought she could taste brandy.

When she reached the doorway she gasped. Beyond it was the rest of the house. It was charred and blackened and open to the sky. Wisps of smoke rose from parts that were still smouldering, as though the fire had happened only yesterday. A few walls of the top floor remained upright, the burnt timber rising as high as ten feet in places. Floorboards extended far enough to mark out where the rooms had been.

At the far end of the wing and across a chasm of swirling shadows was the wreckage of a bedchamber, the bed itself a scorched ruin. The centre of the room had caved in, with bent, blackened timbers bowing down into the room below. This was where the fire had started. On the ground floor were other rooms, all opened and exposed by the blaze.

Liz looked behind her. The rest of the house was still coming apart, the floorboards shrieking as they buckled and twisted. The stained-glass window smashed under the pressure, showering the gallery and the main hall with shards of coloured glass. Liz pulled herself across the threshold and onto the charred landing, reaching out for the banister to help her along.

Looking down, she was not surprised to see another staircase rising from the darkness. It was the mirror image of the one behind her. It too was scorched and blackened, but it looked solid enough to hold her weight. It had to be; she had no other choice.

She manoeuvred herself into a sitting position and began to shift herself down, one step at a time. The steps were warm against her body and the crispy sound of ash giving way beneath her was almost pleasant. All around her rose the remnants of the burnt house, like some strange spectral forest, its jagged remains clawing at the night sky. It reeked of smoke and burnt timber but at least it didn't smell of death. The desiccated branches of the trees whispered around her like conspiratorial voices.

Gradually she made her way down, stopping occasionally to catch her breath and wait for the stabbing pain to fade to a manageable level. But it was growing less intense the further she went. Each step brought her more and more relief.

When she reached the bottom, she remained sitting for a few moments, wondering what to do next. Without giving it any conscious thought, she reached for the banister and began pulling herself to her feet. The charred wood crumbled beneath her grasp, but it offered just enough support for her to clamber up. Bone fragments crunched inside her leg but the pain was entirely gone. She was astonished to find that she could actually put

401

weight on it. Had she simply damaged it to the point of paralysis?

Even as she had the thought, she knew it wasn't true. The pain was still there, hiding beneath the numbness. All she needed to do to feel it again was resist the creature's influence. Because it was the one guiding her now. Vanora had lost.

For a few moments she stood, catching her breath. Then she looked around, feeling as though someone had called her name to draw her attention. Beneath the staircase was a cellar door. Liz was drawn towards it without being aware of moving. Paint flaked off it as she clasped the warped handle. It sizzled, searing her skin and bringing with it the smell of singed meat. But Liz felt no pain, only a vague warmth.

She peeled her hand away and stared with dismay at the raw flesh of her palm. The handle had burned away a layer of skin. Dimly she sensed something like alarm, but the feeling was so far back in her mind that she couldn't connect to it. The meaningful thing was that the door was open now. She was *meant* to go inside.

From somewhere high above came the piercing screech of an owl and then the near-silent flutter of its wings as it passed overhead. She saw its pale form swoop through the ruins. And then the dark, clawing spires of timber seemed to waver, rippling like a far-off city seen through a heat haze. The ruins held their shape for a few seconds, then crumbled to dust. One moment it was as though she were standing in the aftermath of a forest fire, and the next, the skeletal trees collapsed into piles of ash around her, blackening the snow.

All that was left of the burnt house was the main body of the staircase, the open cellar door, and a flight of wooden steps leading down into more darkness. Clouds of dust billowed into the air, obliterating the moonlight. Liz stepped through the doorway into the shadows, limping only slightly.

She moved as though in a trance, her bare feet feeling for each step as she descended, her broken leg crunching with every movement. The real world seemed far away, like the hazy fragments of a dream she couldn't quite recall. Fear lurked far in the depths of her mind but the controlling presence had cut her off from it. It had also isolated her from her thoughts. She was only aware of what was around her. The steps, one after another, the darkness, and the chill of the damp stone wall she pressed her hand against for balance.

After a while, her surroundings changed. The steps became irregular and the surface felt very cold. The wooden staircase had come to an end, and she was continuing down a crude one of stone. The rocky steps were wet and slimy but she didn't slip once, not even when she began to encounter ice. The space around her glowed faintly, a pale, ghostly blue. She was permitted to wonder how old this place was, but she was still powerless to resist the will of whatever was drawing her deeper.

Water dripped, slow and steady, and the resultant echo bounced off the walls of her surroundings. There was a rich, mossy smell that became danker and more pervasive the deeper she went. The passage narrowed until she had to crawl to fit through it. Had she entered a cave system? The steps here were very crude, barely even ridges, and she used them like handholds, pulling herself along. The tunnel doubled back and then circled around again, giving the impression that she was following a ragged spiral down to the core of the earth. Panic flickered at the distant edges of awareness, but was suppressed by the compulsion to keep going. She could only move forward, and if the passage should suddenly end, she would be trapped. Lost forever in an unknown world.

Liz didn't know when she first became aware of the voices. Perhaps they had been whispering the whole time, calling to her, urging her on. She couldn't make out individual words, just a low, resonant hum, like the noise of a murmuring crowd. It was seductive, that chorus, and suffused with an unmistakable air of ceremony.

At last the tunnel began to widen again, opening into a short corridor. The floor was damp and crusted with ice but warm yellow light flickered from a passage off to her left. She wondered how far down she was. Instinct told her that she was directly underneath the house.

Underneath the gate.

Her breath ghosted in front of her. Although her body shivered, she didn't feel the cold, any more than she felt the pain of her bad leg or burned hand. All she was aware of was the urge to keep moving. The passage widened as she continued and the murmuring grew steadily louder. Her insides clenched and for a moment she *did* feel something – in her abdomen. Something writhing. Something excited.

She had reached the entrance to an immense chamber, vast enough to dwarf the tallest cathedral. Stalactites the length of temple columns hung from the ceiling, which itself was hidden in darkness. It took some time for her eyes to adjust and even longer for her to realise that she was not alone.

In the centre of the chamber stood a crowd of people. They were unlike any she had ever seen. Short and stocky, their thick bodies were clothed in roughspun tunics. Although they were human, there was something distinctly ape-like about them. Even their vocalisations were primitive. Not a language as such, just sounds that presumably had meaning for them.

This was no delusion, no hallucination. Everything was far too vivid. Her mind was spinning at the possibilities, unable to grasp even a single one. The sense of disorientation was devastating and she wanted more than anything to believe she was only mad, that what she was seeing was just the product of an overwrought mind. But then, she knew her dreams had been more than just dreams. She had found "the way through". This was the place she had unknowingly been searching for, the gate Carson had tried to open.

Some people even walled up living *things.*

She shook her head to clear it, closed her eyes, then opened them again. The scene had not changed. Whoever – or whatever – these people were, they had discovered fire. Several of them held torches, illuminating the ancient cavern. Shadows danced in the twilight glow like spectral animals. Mesmerised, Liz watched the leaping patterns, searching for meaning and finding none. She felt for Vanora in her mind, but she was gone. This was something the poor woman had only seen in dreams.

Impatient with her hesitance, the group beckoned to her, grunting and gesturing. Liz felt a jolt of fear, which was instantly quelled by a pulsing warmth from inside her belly. She wasn't meant to be afraid; she was meant to go to them. To join them. If they were at all frightened or intimidated by her, they gave no indication of it. In fact, they stared boldly at her, their eyes keen and bright, their expressions full of primal eagerness.

The huge space amplified the voices, which grew louder at her approach. Now they seemed to be chanting, although Liz couldn't make out anything that sounded like words. The group was arranged in a rough circle but they broke apart as she drew nearer. Was *drawn* nearer. She glided into their midst and they closed around her like a fence.

Now that she was here, her domination by what clung to her womb began to lessen, and she felt her sense of self returning. Her heart wrenched as she thought of Nick, and she was suddenly and deeply afraid. She was alone. She couldn't run, couldn't get away. Along with her returning fear came the pain, and within moments she felt herself on the verge of fainting from the intensity. The faces blurred around her, taking on a predatory aspect. A wave of agony flashed through her leg, making her dizzy. She cried out as she felt herself about to fall. Immediately there was the pressure of several pairs of coarse hands, holding her up. Panicking, she batted at her captors, but they only grew more excited and gripped her tighter.

When they lifted her off her feet, she screamed. The firelight wavered all around her as the crowd brandished their torches and renewed their chanting. They carried her a little way and then deposited her on a large limestone slab. It appeared to be a stalagmite that had broken off at its wide base, but to Liz it looked uncomfortably like a plinth. Or worse – an altar.

One of the men grabbed her wrists and yanked her onto her back while the others shrieked and waved their arms. There was something horribly celebratory in their movements and Liz screamed again, this time in renewed agony, as someone else grabbed her ankles, wrenching her broken leg. The world turned white-hot around her. When she next opened her eyes, several ape-like faces were peering closely at her as the creatures poked and prodded her with short, stubby fingers.

"Please let me go," she gasped, knowing that they couldn't understand her but unable to help herself. "Please..."

Her words only seemed to indicate to them that she was unharmed, and that therefore they could proceed. They plucked at her nightgown, appearing puzzled by her strange clothing. With a few brutal tugs they yanked it up to expose her below the waist. The act triggered a wave of shame and terror, but there was nothing sexual in their actions. They seemed unconcerned with stripping her completely but that gave Liz little comfort as they took hold of her legs and prised them apart.

The pressure on her bad leg made her scream again, and the hands adjusted their grip. But her leg was no longer the source of the worst pain. She barely had time to process the humiliation of her position, spread and splayed, when a searing cramp tore through her insides, flooding her nerves with fresh agony. She screamed, again and again, arching and struggling on the cold, hard stone.

At her movements, the chanting became feverish, almost hysterical in its frenzy. Liz gasped, hissed, whimpered and howled at each new wrenching spasm. But the group held her fast, inflamed by every cry, thrilled by every tensing of her body.

Something was coming.

She knew enough about babies to know it was far too soon for this one to be born. But then, this wasn't really a baby, was it? She knew that now more clearly than ever. Whatever it was, it was ready, and these terrible people had brought her here to usher it into the world. Her, its mother. The thought made her shudder. Who – or what – was its father, then? For she knew now it wasn't actually Carson Menrath. It couldn't be. Something had possessed him just as surely as it had possessed her. And Nick as well. Vanora was the only one who had been spared. If you could call her madness that. She had destroyed herself and Carson too before the influence could fully take hold. And she had tried to spare Liz, tried to warn her. But the house – the *gate* – had been too powerful.

Another cramp seized her and she screamed, one long ragged primal wail that shredded her vocal cords. The chanting around her had grown strangely rhythmic. The tone had shifted. They seemed reverential.

Liz felt wetness trickling between her legs. She had no idea if she was bleeding or if she had simply wet herself in helpless terror. The sharp smell of blood soon answered her question and she renewed her struggles as something began to move deep down inside her. She raised her head, terrified of both seeing and not seeing it. She felt herself being opened, felt something pushing to get out.

It scrabbled inside her like a rat, tearing her with sharp claws in its frenzy to escape. She sensed its fury, its hunger, its terrible *eagerness* to be born. Liz screamed again, but this time there was no sound. Her voice was gone. Now she smelled blood, thick and pungent. It pooled between her legs and spilled onto the floor of the cavern.

The chanting rose in volume and tempo. The group was delirious with excitement. With sickening clarity she heard the wet slap of their bare feet as they danced in her blood.

And then, at last, the thing inside her tore free of the confines of her womb and clambered into the fleshy tunnel that would lead it into the world. Liz could feel every inch of its relentless progress. She thrashed in the arms of her captors, fighting the revulsion. She wanted it out of her, but now she was even more afraid of seeing it. Inside, it was a dreadful unknown but she could pretend it was merely abnormal. Once it was free, however, she would never again have the luxury of denial. If only she could keep it trapped inside, crush it somehow, starve it of oxygen, kill it. But the thing was shockingly strong and much more determined than she was.

Her head swam with nightmare flashbacks of its conception. It dug long furrows into the tender lining as it tunnelled through the birth canal, finally reaching the end. Liz clenched her pelvic muscles against the pressure but she had no hope of containing the monster. A chilling cry came from inside her and she froze in horror at the sound. The creature renewed its clawing and she could do nothing but let it tear its way out.

The searing pain weakened her further as a thick and rounded form began to push itself free. She imagined constricting herself around its neck, strangling it, but it was already clawing her further open. She threw back her head and surrendered herself to this inverse rape, rending her throat with soundless screams.

She knew the creature was all wrong. Its body was far too long to be human and she could feel more than four limbs digging into her. *Abomination.* Her mind formed an image too grotesque to contemplate and she wished the cave would collapse and kill them all. Anything to obliterate her senses, anything to keep her from seeing.

When at last it wriggled free, the primitive congregation fell silent. She heard the wet smack as the creature plopped to the surface of the altar. It made no sound and for a moment Liz dared to hope that it was dead. Then something grazed her inner thigh and she jerked away. The creature stayed where it was. She felt something thin and light, delicate as spider's silk, brushing against her skin, tasting her, but this time she could not move. The fine thread tickled her again. There was something expectant in its stillness. It was waiting for something.

She didn't want to look, didn't want to see it at all, but she couldn't help herself. She lifted her head and peered down the length of her body, dreading to see a malformed human baby, reaching for her with too-thin fingers.

It was worse than she ever could have imagined.

What sat between her bloodied thighs was not human. Nor had it even begun as one. It was sickeningly pale, almost white, with a fleshy, worm-like body about six inches long. A fist-sized bulbous head bobbed on a long neck and, as Liz stared in horror, it jerked towards her. Tiny close-set eyes gleamed dully in the firelight and the gash of a mouth hinged open below them. It emitted a raspy squeak that made Liz's skin crawl. Even worse than the sound were the long, thin appendages that ran along the sides of its corpulent body. They moved with a kind of hideous grace, flickering like multiple antennae.

The creature looked impossibly ancient, from a time before even dinosaurs were on the earth. This was what Carson had been trying to call forth. This was what Vanora had seen in her drug-induced visions, trying to use her body as a conduit into the world. She had produced her own abominations, but at least those had been human. And Carson had made offerings of them. Burying them inside the walls of the house must have strengthened

413

whatever was down here.

But although he had felt its insidious pull, Carson couldn't actually have known what was down here, could never have imagined this chamber deep beneath the hill. Nor, indeed, could he have had any real idea what he was unleashing. No, just like her, he had been guided each step of the way. The gate was the way in, but not for mankind. It merely marked the spot where something waited. How many millions of years must it have been here? It had been waiting for just the right vessel. And now she knew an ugly truth: it could only gestate inside an unwilling host.

Liz felt her stomach lurch and she fought the urge to be sick. There was a grunt from the ape-man nearest to her and then strong hands pushed her back down. She was grateful not to have to look at the vile thing any longer. Her *offspring*. For a while her hoarse panting was the only sound in the cave. Then the creature uttered another rusty shriek and pressed itself against her as it crawled to the edge of the altar. Liz tried to pull away but her captors didn't let her move. She heard the thing drop to the floor and there was the terrible scuttling of multiple tiny legs as it moved rapidly across the chamber.

Before she even had time to be relieved that it was gone, Liz was racked by another searing contraction. Her confusion only lasted a moment. The hands holding her tightened their grip and the chanting began again as she writhed and contorted against the pain of yet more scrabbling legs. And then she knew – there was more than one. The movements within were the movements of many creatures. This time there was no confusion; she only wanted them out.

These were smaller than the first one. She shuddered at the thought that she had been infested with them. She bore down hard, pushing with what remained of her strength to expel them, to purge herself. If she had known their true form weeks ago, she would have injected her womb with bleach.

Another rounded shape forced its way through. The passage had been opened by the first one, widened and bloodied. Liz threw her head from side to side as, one by one, the creatures wriggled free of her womb and crawled out into the dank chamber of the ancient cave. They were uncountable, emerging in a stream of quivering antennae, more than could ever have fit inside her. They flowed over her legs, a scurrying sea of parasites, and she tried to tune out the clicking of their tiny jaws and their awful alien shrieks.

Liz had no idea how many there were. All she knew was the vague relief when their numbers came to an end and she was left feeling empty, exhausted. Contaminated. Only then was she released. The chanting had stopped some time ago but she had barely noticed. The crowd was moving away, the circle widening as her primitive attendants backed into the shadows, vanishing like phantoms. Perhaps that was all they had ever been. The fires no longer burned but Liz could see perfectly well. Her eyes had adjusted to the greenish glow of the phosphorous and she knew that she was finally, truly alone.

Her head swam as she lay staring up into the black recesses of the cavernous ceiling. She might be miles beneath the surface for all she knew. As she peered into the shadows she sensed the unseen hilltop crumbling far above, opening to the world, although she could see only emptiness. For a while she was too weary to feel anything but relief that the ordeal was over. She closed her eyes, wishing that she might sleep, and wake, and find that it had all been a dream. A hideous, horrible dream.

She might have been alone in the cold stony chamber of the cave, but she was not alone in her mind. She heard a scream, and then another. The voices were female and filled, she knew, with precisely the same horror she had just known.

There were others out there like her, in other places like this. Her insides ached in concert with her sisters as she thought of all the ancient places in the world, all the strange monuments and formations, and all the speculation through the years about their purpose. They were all gateways. Whatever had lain dormant beneath them for uncountable millennia was ready to be reborn. All it needed was a host. Liz was merely the first.

The blackness above her stretched to encompass the world, seeping into the sides of the cave like ink into water. Her stomach tingled as though she were travelling upwards at great speed, but nothing moved past her to mark any sort of journey. There was only darkness. Emptiness.

How long it lasted, she couldn't tell. But she felt unable to move from where she lay, bloody and spent. There was nowhere for her to go anyway. She could never make the climb back through the tunnel and up those stone steps. Even if she did, what remained of the world she had known? Had it been changed forever? Or was the birth of the creatures only the beginning?

Her answer came soon enough. The unnatural night began to ebb and a familiar sight presented itself to her mind's eye. Glastonbury Tor. Snow bleached the landscape as far as she could see but the hill rose like an alabaster mountain from the flat surroundings. And Liz knew with a dread certainty what lay beneath its five hundred feet of chalky soil and clay.

She recalled her nightmare of searching for something buried deep beneath the snow. A dream she now understood she must have shared with others.

A distant rumble broke the silence and the ground began to tremble. The hill quivered, shaking snow from its summit like a dog shaking water from its coat. The tower crumbled and fell, a handful of insignificant pebbles. Liz saw it through twin perspectives, as both participant and helpless witness. She could do nothing but watch as the snowy peak erupted. It was as though someone had set off a bomb underneath a termite mound. Pale shapes swarmed down the sloping sides and across the snow, their wriggling forms barely discernible in the blinding white of the winter countryside.

Then there was the sensation of dizzying height, as though she were soaring just above the ruined hill. Thousands of waving antennae teased the air as she passed above them, a sea of prehistoric monsters. At the same time she was also miles away, looking down at the great stones at Avebury, and then Stonehenge. The ancient monuments rocked in the unstable frozen ground, levering themselves out of their centuries-old placement as the pale creatures scuttled over them like rats in the rubble of demolished buildings.

Further on, she watched as Silbury Hill disintegrated, bringing forth even more of the writhing things. A sob caught in her throat as she realised this hellish tour might go on forever. She closed both sets of eyes, inner and outer, unwilling to see any more.

There were other places in the world, places much larger and far more ancient. She couldn't bring herself to imagine what might be emerging from peaks the size of the Himalayas.

It had only just begun.

THANK YOU FOR READING

Thank you for taking the time to read this book. We sincerely hope that you enjoyed the story and appreciate your letting us try to entertain you. We realise that your time is valuable, and without the continuing support of people such as yourself, we would not be able to do what we do.

As a thank you, we would like to offer you a free ebook from our range, in return for you signing up to our mailing list. We will never share your details with anyone and will only contact you to let you know about new releases.

You can sign up on our website

Http://www.horrifictales.co.uk

If you enjoyed this book, then please consider leaving a short review on Amazon, Goodreads or anywhere else that you, as a reader, visit to learn about new books. One of the most important parts about how well a book sells is how many positive reviews it has, so if you can spare a little more of your valuable time to share the experience with others, even if its just a line or two, then we would really appreciate it.

Thanks, and see you next time!

THE HORRIFIC TALES PUBLISHING TEAM

ACKNOWLEDGEMENTS

I've taken a few liberties with the geography of the Clevedon coast, adding a second promontory below the hill fort on Wain's Hill. My apologies to the owners of the allotments there; I stole your land to build my haunted house on it. My apologies also to the Clevedon librarians, none of whom are anything like the clueless lady I have invented here. And I have no idea whether the Moon & Sixpence allows dogs inside, but I hope they didn't mind me sneaking Hyperion in.

A massive thank you to Graeme Reynolds, for letting me join the Horrific Tales family.

Special thanks to:

Adam Nevill, for poring over an early draft and offering many dark, wise words over the years.

Katherine Easton-Campbell of Miss Kitty's Monsters, for telling me all about the world of handcrafted jewellery.

Mark Howard Jones, for the gift of a Victorian-era guide to Clevedon. The runes inside were successfully passed to someone else.

But most of all, thank you to John, my husband, best friend and fellow dark voyager. We will always live in the castle.

ABOUT THE AUTHOR

Thana Niveau was born to the wail of the Wendigo and the whisper of warp engines. So it's no surprise that her literary aspirations have combined both the mythic and the speculative, gaining her publication in *Black Static*, *Interzone*, and numerous anthologies.

Her fiction has been reprinted in *Best New Horror* and she has garnered British Fantasy Award nominations for best story and best collection along the way.

America wasn't scary enough for her and so she moved to England's West Country, where her new surroundings inspired this novel, her first.

She is a Halloween bride, sharing her life with fellow writer John Llewellyn Probert, in a crumbling gothic tower filled with arcane books and curiosities. And toy dinosaurs.

ALSO FROM HORRIFIC TALES PUBLISHING

High Moor by Graeme Reynolds

High Moor 2: Moonstruck by Graeme Reynolds

High Moor 3: Blood Moon by Graeme Reynolds

Of A Feather by Ken Goldman

Whisper by Michael Bray

Echoes by Michael Bray

Voices by Michael Bray

Angel Manor by Chantal Noordeloos

Bottled Abyss by Benjamin Kane Ethridge

Lucky's Girl by William Holloway

The Immortal Body by William Holloway

Wasteland Gods by Jonathan Woodrow

Dead Shift by John Llewellyn Probert

The Grieving Stones by Gary McMahon

The Rot by Paul Kane

The Last Veil (Testaments I and II) by Joseph D'Lacey

The Rage of Cthulhu by Gary Fry

Song of the Death God by William Holloway

The House of Frozen Screams by Thana Niveau

COMING SOON

House of Dolls by Chantal Noordeloos

The Cold by Rich Hawkins

The Black Church by William Holloway

http://www.horrifictales.co.uk

CPSIA information can be obtained
at www.ICGtesting.com
Printed in the USA
LVHW111702230119
604976LV00001B/3/P